THROW DOWN YOUR SHADOWS

DEBORAH HEMMING

Vagrant
PRESS

Vagrant Press is an imprint of
Nimbus Publishing Limited
3660 Strawberry Hill Street, Halifax, NS, B3K 5A9
(902) 455-4286 nimbus.ca

Printed and bound in Canada

NB1469
Editor: Sarah Faber
Editor for the press: Whitney Moran
Design: Jenn Embree

Library and Archives Canada Cataloguing in Publication

Title: Throw down your shadows / Deborah Hemming.
Names: Hemming, Deborah, 1989- author.
Identifiers: Canadiana (print) 20200159356
    Canadiana (ebook) 20200161512 | ISBN 9781771088381 (softcover)
    ISBN 9781771088640 (HTML)
Classification: LCC PS8615.E487 T57 2020 | DDC C813/.6—dc23

Nimbus Publishing acknowledges the financial support for its publishing activities from the Government of Canada, the Canada Council for the Arts, and from the Province of Nova Scotia. We are pleased to work in partnership with the Province of Nova Scotia to develop and promote our creative industries for the benefit of all Nova Scotians.

This one is for little Deborah.

Though we had never met, he waved at us like he knew us. An open palm raised above his head. Bewitching grey eyes under dark, curly hair.

What is a wave, really? It is recognition. It is *I see you*. But it's not always a gesture of welcome. Sometimes a wave means caution. *I see you* (stay back). *I see you* (I'm busy). *I see you* (please, not now). His palm was raised, demanding our attention, letting us know we had appeared in his world. But his hand stayed frozen, inert. He didn't move it from side to side, like you do with those you're happy to see.

His hand was a stop sign but we mistook it for a green light.

AFTER

⁂

Th_ere is a moment when I first open my eyes. Not even a moment. It's gone before it begins. The night before, all its destruction, the fire, a dream. Something imagined. Confusing and irrational. I blink hard, but my eyes can't unsee. All that smoke, the heat. Don't fool yourself, Winnie. It happened.

I contemplate never leaving my room. Staying in bed with my hands clamped between my knees, turned towards the wall forever. What does the morning after look like? Not knowing makes me squirm.

I wonder if Ruth will do the regular things. Make coffee, serve it up hot. Did she bother to put on pajamas last night? I slept in a T-shirt, no underwear. I felt the need to let my whole body breathe.

Toast. She always makes toast. But who will eat it? And what about Mac? I don't think he came home last night. I didn't hear him. He tends to stomp up the stairs and across the hall. I would have heard the stomping and the opening and closing of doors. I would have heard them talking. Or maybe there was nothing to say.

I slide out of bed and into sweatpants. I listen before I open the door. Nothing. My hand hovers above the doorknob and I wait for a sign of what comes next. There's a strong chance everything will be different today, the old ways of doing and being no longer suitable. This is not a place that changes much but even those who are stuck and stubborn can't ignore such a profound disruption.

I finally turn the knob. I tiptoe downstairs, past the closed door of Ruth's bedroom. The house is unusually quiet. Dark corners and the echo of a clock hand. It's the end of October and the cold haunts my bare feet. I continue past the living room, the dining room. Everything quiet and empty and cold.

I nearly jump out of my skin when I find Ruth at the kitchen table. She's wearing pajamas.

"You scared me," I whisper. "Your door was closed."

She points upwards and I understand. Mac is sleeping.

She made coffee but no toast. She pours me a cup and we sink into silence. We wait.

BEFORE

〜✿〜

Mona warned me. It was the only future she ever accurately predicted, our local psychic who couldn't see rain rolling in from the other end of the valley. I didn't believe in fortune-telling or astrology or anything like that, but Mona was my mother's best friend and my best friend Jake's mother. If she wanted to read my future, I wouldn't stop her.

"Hi, Mone," I said, opening the door of her tiny office.

"Winnie, come in." Her voice was low and hushed.

I sat down on the empty chair, the only clear space in the small room. Her office was tucked into the east corner of their farmhouse. A room with an unusually low ceiling, jam-packed with junk. There were crystal balls and heavy curtains and charts of the night sky, dirty teacups everywhere. But there were also used batteries and too many stray pens, milk crates full of old electronics. Radios and VCRs, a broken toaster.

"I'll need a moment," she said, gathering herself, eyes closed. A big bowl of water sat between us on her desk.

Mona was not a small woman. She was tall and broad, like her son Jake. They both had the same blonde hair, the colour of wheat, though Mona's was long and stringy, reaching down past her sagging breasts. She didn't dress like a psychic. No glittering scarves or gaudy jewelry. That wouldn't be practical on the farm. Mona dressed like every other farmer. Jeans with plaid, roomy shirts she didn't mind tearing on the pasture fence. The only difference between farm Mona and psychic Mona was her hair. When she was working on the farm, she wore it tied back in a long braid. During readings, it hung long and free.

I breathed in deeply. The room, like Mona, smelled of sweet beeswax and hay. They kept hives on the farm and she used the wax to make candles. She sold them out of her kitchen. The hay was just something that followed you around where we lived.

She opened her eyes. It seemed she was ready.

"I asked you to come in for a reading, Winnie, because I had a dream about you two nights ago. I don't usually dream about people I know. My dreams are full of strangers, faces I don't recognize." She tilted her head to the side, considering. "The dead, perhaps. I've always thought I might also be a medium."

I nodded. I was used to this. Mona and my mother, Ruth, had been close friends for as long as I could remember. On the surface, they seemed like very different people but they shared an unconventional sensibility, an eccentric way of moving and being in the world. Mona as a psychic, Ruth as an artist.

"But the other night, I dreamt of *you*, Winnie. You as a grown woman. You looked different, more like your mother. But it was you, undeniably. Red hair. Same dark brown eyes. You were living somewhere far away. A foreign place that looked a bit like home. Rolling fields, a river. You were happy there. I thought we could try to conjure it, that place. You, there. I thought if I could see it more clearly, we could locate it. See where you're headed in this life."

I wondered how she knew the place was necessarily elsewhere. *Looked a bit like home.* Sounded like home to me.

"It's been a while since you've done a reading. I'll remind you that I ask you to remain silent throughout the process. When I am done, you are free to ask one question. I will let you know when you can speak. Until that time, please try to sit still to ensure the reading is as accurate as possible."

I suppressed a small laugh as she waved her hands over the bowl of water. This was how she did her readings, how she mined the invented futures of our most gullible neighbours: the recently divorced, the grieving. She claimed to interpret energy as it bounced off the surface of the liquid. As a child, I'd sat for many readings. When I was eleven, Mona told me I would attend eight funerals in the next five years, that I would need a passport by the time I turned fourteen, and that I had been a Salem witch in a past life. The predictions didn't come true and the third claim just seemed absurd. I stopped doing the readings when I realized it was all a hoax. It had been a while and I'd forgotten how seriously she took it.

After several minutes of hand-waving, Mona stopped, stared at the bowl, and frowned. "I'm not seeing that place today," she said. "I'm just seeing home. The valley. *You* in the valley."

I wanted to say, *maybe it was always the valley.* Maybe your dream was just like any other dream, a messy pastiche of memory and imagination, snapshots of life cut through with nonsensical intrusions and nothing more.

She continued to wave her hands once again and I realized I needed to pee. Gazing at the bowl of water, unable to move.

"Ah, here's something." Mona brought her hands to her chest and looked at me, suddenly intent. "I'm getting change from you, Winnie. Dramatic change. Everything is going to change for you this summer. You will become a woman. The woman you're meant to be."

She let the words sink in for a few long moments and then continued. "Also, you should avoid anything hot. Definitely don't take up smoking. No bonfires or fireworks, Winnie. I smell smoke in your future."

When the reading was finished, she told me I could ask my question.

I yawned, looking around. "What do you keep in that locked cabinet in the corner?"

Mona turned to face the cabinet behind her and then back at me. Her green eyes were large and blinking. I wasn't doing this right.

"That's all you want to know?"

I shrugged. "I've always wondered."

I'd forgotten about the cabinet, which I had tried to break into as a child. We didn't have locked cabinets or drawers in my house and so it fascinated me, this mysterious space, off limits to anyone who didn't have a key. Mona's son Jake and I took turns guessing what might be inside. I imagined important documents or shiny, expensive jewelry. Maybe even stacks of money. It was fun to think Mona might have another life, exotic and confidential, the evidence hidden behind the cupboard doors. Could she be a spy? A criminal? Nothing about her life or personality suggested this was the case but it was fun to indulge in the fantasy. I liked reading books about people with secret lives—double agents, assassins— and it was thrilling to pretend I might know someone living a life in disguise.

I became obsessed with the locked cabinet. I wanted to open it. I felt entitled to know the truth. On many occasions, Jake looked on, quiet and nervous, while I unsuccessfully stuck a bobby pin in the lock, jiggling and listening for a click, like I had seen people do on TV. Eventually, unsuccessful, I let it go. Of course Mona wasn't a spy. I didn't think she was even a real psychic.

"Winnie, come on. You have nothing else to ask? You only get one question, remember."

I crossed my arms. "Nope."

"I keep my money in there," she sighed after hesitating for a moment. "Payment for my readings. You know I usually charge for these right? Fifty dollars for an hour of my time. You're lucky I do yours for free."

So I had been right, partially.

"Satisfied?"

"Sure," I said, though now that I knew the answer, I was already bored with my question.

⁐

It was the summer of 2005 and I was newly sixteen, but flat-chested and narrow-hipped. I had gotten my period a few years earlier, but none of the good stuff that was supposed to come with it. My mother, Ruth, told me that would come in time. She had been the same.

I looked forward to these physical changes without quite knowing why, a vague desire for the next stage of my physical development to begin. I envied the slope of Ruth's hips and the curve of her breasts, visible through clothing. When would I look like that? Would I ever?

But just like Mona said I would, I changed. I had my future read in the spring and by the end of the first week of summer vacation, I needed a new bra and I slipped into my mother's jeans as if they were my own. It seemed to happen overnight. I was a carbon copy of her. Same height, same red hair; just younger. Ruth was delighted. "Now we can *really* share clothes!" she said, grinning.

I sat on her bed while she held up shirts I might like to try on from her closet, a mild discomfort taking me by surprise. I had wanted to look womanly—like Ruth, but not *exactly* like her. Now that I was faced with our new similarity, an irrational fear blossomed inside me. I started to worry I might adopt her other traits as well.

Despite being beautiful, Ruth was deeply insecure. Women were told beauty was a goal, an answer—to be beautiful was to be complete—but I had grown up around a gorgeous woman who wasted far too much time seeking reassurance of her beauty. I saw it in the way she smiled, twinkling and bright, craving flattery. It was there too in the way she maintained a careful looseness in her body, limbs relaxed, posture inviting. She was an expert at throwing back her hair when she laughed, making it dance down her back. These were strategies to solicit both men's attention and women's envy. Her beauty wasn't an answer. It was a question she never stopped posing. She sought affirmation to feel whole.

I didn't want to rely on others' approval. I never had before. But watching her flit around the room, grabbing clothes, I saw how it could happen, how that need could develop.

"What about this?" she asked, holding up a striped shirt in a pale mint green.

Ruth had a uniform. She wore tight, faded jeans that sat high on her waist and oversized button-up shirts in every shade of pastel: robin's egg, buttercup, petal pink, lavender. She tied them in a knot under her ribs, showing just a sliver of skin.

"I need something different." I nodded in the direction of her shirts, hanging neatly in her closet like a sun-bleached rainbow. "I need my own thing."

She nodded wisely. "Then we will find you your own thing."

She took me to Frenchy's. That's where we bought most of our clothes, second-hand and picked-through, but she always knew how to sort through the large bins of used clothing to find the best items. We found jeans that weren't quite as tight as Ruth's and I fell in love with a T-shirt, yellow and faded, the words Hello Sunshine looping across the front. It had a tiny hole on one sleeve.

I loved that hole. I wondered how it got there and who had owned the shirt before me.

"I want more like this," I said, holding up the T-shirt.

Again, Ruth nodded. She could really be very focused when she wasn't distracted by other people's attention.

We settled on vintage T-shirts as the foundation of what Ruth called "my look." Some with funny sayings and others with the names of bands or sports teams. I liked the baseball tees best, the ones with contrasting sleeves: red and white, navy and heather grey. Ruth even found me a few worn sweatshirts in the same style for colder days.

⊱⊰

The day Caleb arrived, I awoke to the sound of the tractor next door. I splashed water on my face in the bathroom and pulled on one of my new tops. I packed a backpack with the necessities: two books and a pair of sunglasses, a water bottle and my bathing suit.

Ruth was already downstairs making breakfast. I could smell buttered toast. When I came down, she had coffee waiting.

"Morning," she mumbled, not looking up from the paper.

I yawned. "Morning."

We lived in the white house with the blue door on the Gaspereau River Road, and always had, as far I was concerned. Ruth sometimes spoke about a time before, just after I was born, when we lived in a friend's basement in Halifax. She recalled a mildewy smell and a chilling dampness that took hold of your bones and didn't let go. She described holding me close at night, a tiny baby, fearing I would grow up to mind the slightest draft, given my cold first months in the world. But I preferred to ignore that period of our history. It didn't fit with who we were now.

The window above the kitchen sink framed a perfect summer day. Blue sky and lush green fields in every direction. I sipped my coffee and leaned against the counter. Ruth was reading "The Cruiser," a weekly roundup of police reports, published in our local paper, the *Gaspereau Gazette*.

"Cruiser highlights, please," I said.

The familiar smell of manure drifted in with the breeze through the open window.

She cleared her throat dramatically. "*There were 12 reports made to police regarding the Gaspereau Valley area between June 20th and 26th*," she read. "*On June 21st, a 42-year-old man was pulled over by police for speeding down Greenfield Road at 1:24 A.M.*" She paused for effect. "*He explained to police he was trying to convince his wife to invest in new tires and 'burning rubber' was the quickest way to wear out his old set.*"

I grinned into my mug. "Well, of course. What other way is there?"

"Right? Oh, this is good. *On June 24th at 11:13 P.M., police received a call about a group of rowdy teenagers walking down High Street. When police arrived to the scene, the teenagers were no longer present; however, the High Street road sign was missing and appeared to be stolen.*"

"Classic. Happens once a year, at least."

"Totally." Ruth took a bite of toast and chewed quietly, scanning the paper. "Oh, and last but not least. *On June 26th at 10:09 A.M., there was a report of a loud dispute between two neighbours in the Gaspereau area. Police determined the dispute to be regarding property lines. A large tree needed to be cut down and neither neighbour was willing to pay for the tree's removal. Police consulted an official municipal map to resolve the dispute.*"

We laughed the same laugh, the same red hair falling into our faces.

"It's too good. People are ridiculous. Why do we live here again?"

"Sometimes I wonder. But then…." Ruth gestured to the window. The sun seeped in like warm honey.

⚜

Ruth's love for the Annapolis Valley had been immediate. She was pregnant with me when she first came here, living in Halifax and finishing her last year of art school, only just turned twenty-two. She and the man neither of us referred to as my father took a weekend trip to the valley to see fall's changing leaves and go apple picking. They stayed at a nice bed and breakfast and wore thick sweaters as they wandered through orchards, happy and pink-cheeked, high on the crisp autumn air, two artists marvelling at the landscape.

He was thirty years her senior. She was his former student. Two artists who flung their passion at each other for a brief time. He was gone before I was born. Some howling fight she didn't like to talk about.

But that weekend trip must have been good, because during those two short days she decided the Annapolis Valley would be the place where she would raise her daughter. This valley that forms a great gorge and carves out the western edge of Nova Scotia. Between two mountains, incorrectly named the North and the South, lies ceaseless farmland studded with towns and villages—communities that vary in character. Some are wealthy, some are not. One has a university. One has a tire factory. They all have a church, though many of those churches are now up for sale. Too few people, changing times.

She picked Gaspereau, a smaller valley within the greater Annapolis Valley, because it was close to Wolfville, the major town in the area. Wolfville is a university town, cultured and wealthy by Nova Scotian standards. There's an independent cinema and farmers' market, a fair-trade coffee shop, and a nice art gallery. Ruth knew she could access these places and sell her paintings while still living a slow, rural life in quieter Gaspereau. Wolfville acts as an anchor for many small communities like ours. It's where you go to run errands, maybe see a concert.

Ruth also liked that Gaspereau was near the ocean. Most valley towns are landlocked, distant from the crack and heave of the Bay of Fundy, home of the highest tides in the world. Every day, the Bay of Fundy fills in and empties out at least twice, the water levels sinking and rising to dramatic effect as the tides move a billion tonnes of water with each cycle.

Folks from down the valley live separate from this natural wonder. Most of them witness the tides only in the summer, taking an annual day trip up and over the North Mountain to spend a chilly day on a rocky beach. No swimming, of course. The tidal currents are too strong. But in Gaspereau, you're close enough to the ocean you can smell the tide changing, feel the shift in the way the wind blows. The Minas Basin, like a mutant limb of the Bay of Fundy, bends and curls inland. The Gaspereau River feeds right into it.

It took some time to save up the money, but Ruth had a vision: a quiet life with her daughter on a country road. In that first year or so of my life, she painted whenever she could while I was sleeping or when a friend agreed to babysit. She was completely exhausted, delirious most of the time, but buoyed by her vision. She ended up selling out two shows of her work in a row. It was enough for a down payment on a small white house with a blue door, perched on the Gaspereau River. We had lived there ever since.

After breakfast, I biked to work. In the summers, I kept watch over Gaspereau's only strawberry U-pick with my friend Tom. The sun was out but it wasn't too hot, almost as if the weather was holding back, treading carefully for our benefit. The sky appeared dreamed up by a child. Deep blue with cotton-ball clouds, the sky of a diorama. I gazed up while I biked along the river. I had never seen so many small, singular clouds in my whole life. They dotted our valley with little shadows, blind spots on paradise.

When I got to the berry patch, I unpacked my bag, setting up for the day in our open hut. A roof for shade, two chairs and a table. I counted the money in the till, made sure we had enough change. The farmer who owned the place always left the money waiting for us in the morning without fear of anyone taking it. Gaspereau wasn't that kind of place—at least not yet.

I pulled out my book, put my feet up on the table. It was an easy summer gig.

Every few pages I was interrupted. Eager berry pickers, slicked with sunscreen. "How many boxes?" I asked each time, in exchange for cash. Some of the pickers dressed for the job, wearing sneakers and work clothes. Others were less prepared. I rolled my eyes when they showed up in miniskirts or flip-flops.

After thirteen pages and three groups of pickers, Tom finally appeared on his bike.

"You're late," I said, glancing up.

"For good reason."

"Yeah?"

"Meteor shower," he said happily. "I was just reading about it."

"When?"

"Should be visible in a week or so. We'll have to wait for the moon to wane a bit."

Tom's bedroom walls were covered with vivid, celestial scatterings: posters of the night sky and the solar system. He was endlessly fascinated with the world above, shaking his head and blurting out, "The universe, Winnie! *The universe!*" whenever he learned something new.

For this, I was lucky. All through childhood, there wasn't a meteor shower or lunar eclipse I missed. He made sure we witnessed every spectacle the universe produced. We headed to God's Palm, the largest vineyard in the valley, just the two of us, the best place to look up. We would lay down on the grass, hidden by vines, far from any lights, quiet and still. We stayed warm under a blanket, sharing a bag of potato chips. The night passed through surges of laughter and hushes of thoughtful silence.

"Cool. I'll get Ruth to bake cookies."

"How many out there picking?" he asked, taking a seat.

"Ten or so. Not bad. This weather will keep them coming."

Tom pulled out his own book and we soon fell silent, pages open on our laps. We had been close for so long, speaking was often unnecessary. There was no need to fill the gaps in between conversations with small talk or meaningless chatter. When we spoke, it was real. How many people have that at sixteen?

✵❦✵

I met Tom on a swing set about a month into first grade. I was a loner, unsure about the world of "big school" and unaccustomed to spending my days with other kids. Ruth had always worked from her home studio, able to keep a close eye on me, and so I had never gone to daycare or nursery school. But then kindergarten started. To my horror, I was forced to sit next to others at cartoon-coloured tables while we learned the alphabet and how to count to twenty, boring lessons I had learned long ago.

About a month in, Tom appeared. I was planning my playground escape, wondering where I would be if I climbed through the hole in the fence, when a boy with bright blue eyes walked up. His hair was the ruddy colour of river mud. We were holding on to the tall poles that anchored the swing set, watching the other kids glide through the air, then push off from the gravel and let go every few moments.

"What's your name?" he asked.

I looked him up and down. "Winifred," I said, though no one called me that.

He gaped at me. "What?"

"Win-*a*-fred." I spoke clear and loud, like I was talking to a baby.

"Oh."

We watched the other kids fly and fall. After a while, I asked him his name.

"Tom."

I nodded. "Some people call me Winnie."

He looked at me again. "What?"

"Winn-*ie*."

"Winn-*ie*," he repeated. "Like the bear."

I told Tom I wanted to run away.

"Where are you going?"

"I don't know." I paused, considering. "What's on the other side of that fence?"

He looked where I pointed. "I don't know." His voice was hushed.

"I can see the woods. I think I was in those woods once. We got our Christmas tree there."

"I think I was in those woods once, too."

I nodded sagely.

"Do you want to be my friend?" he asked, looking at his feet.

"Okay," I answered, nodding some more. "We can leave together if you want."

Tom thought about that. "Or we could go on the swings."

"Okay," I said again, and we did that instead.

༺✦༻

I looked up from my book. A van-load of berry pickers had arrived, a group of ladies with grey hair, all sun hats and toothy smiles. I noticed Angela Lawson leading the pack, her tanned thighs jiggling under unflattering khaki shorts as she walked towards us.

If Gaspereau had been a real town, Angela would have been our mayor. She was from away, a never-married retiree with Ontario money and a horsey face. She moved to Gaspereau a few years back, buying a small, renovated bungalow with a sprawling garden and a nice view. More and more older folks were moving to the valley. Wolfville had a lot to offer to the newly retired, small enough to be walkable but bustling enough to host interesting arts and culture events, which they flocked to in droves.

But Angela chose to live outside of Wolfville—what we called "town"—in Gaspereau. To the dismay of some, she tried to insert herself into every facet of the community as soon as she arrived. She wanted to be involved in planning everything—dances, fundraisers, community meetings—and when she learned there wasn't actually much to plan (not a lot happened), she started hosting new events. She also founded the *Gaspereau Gazette* and was its only employee. Some people found her enthusiasm overwhelming. To me, she was just old and boring, unconnected to my life.

"Morning, kids!" she said to Tom and I, leaving her companions to survey the field.

"Hi, Angela," we murmured.

"Beautiful day."

"Gorgeous," Tom replied.

"I met these ladies in Wolfville," she said. "They're in town for a seventieth birthday trip. They seemed a little lost, wandering around looking in shop windows, not sure what to do next. I told them I'd take them under my wing, play tour guide for the day. First up, the best strawberries in the Maritimes."

"Cool," Tom said.

I busied myself with a hangnail on my thumb, returning my gaze to my book. Angela began counting out berry boxes. "Did you two hear the news? New folks moving in. Big moving truck up on Slayter Road. Looks like a family."

"Oh yeah?" Tom asked.

"Saw a boy around your age, maybe a bit older. Helping unload the truck."

I looked up, interest piqued. "The Taylor house?"

It was a property I had long admired. A grand, gothic Victorian complete with a turret, hidden in the trees on a winding gravel road, in the middle of nowhere. It had been empty for at least ten years. I barely remembered a time when it had been occupied. The Taylors were descendants of one of Nova Scotia's oldest breweries, rich and drunk. The home was passed down through the generations until the last family member finally moved away. It had stood dark ever since, caretakers and real estate agents its only visitors.

I liked to ride my bike up there and often wondered what the house looked like inside. Occasionally I even fantasized about breaking in. I had tried peering in the windows a few times but most of the curtains were drawn and those that weren't provided little view. The house was dark, everything inside laced with dust.

"That's the one," said Angela. "Not sure who they are. Thought you two might have heard something?"

Tom shook his head. It was surprising we hadn't learned about this new family sooner. Gaspereau was small, prone to gossip, and it had been years since someone else our age had moved to the area. That kind of news usually circulated quickly.

"I only saw the boy," Angela continued, "but it's such a big house, it has to be a big family, right? Anyway, just thought I'd mention it. After I'm done with this group, I'm heading up there to welcome them, whoever they are. Maybe you two can go up and make friends with the boy."

She handed over the money for the berry boxes and wandered off. The wind picked up and animated the fields, strawberry leaves and grass shimmering in the sun. I felt goosebumps bloom on the backs of my arms.

"I wonder who the new kid is," Tom said, watching the women arrange themselves in the field.

I shrugged. "Probably no one worth knowing."

⚜

It was a good day for the U-pick. We had nearly two hundred customers, most of them tourists. Other farms in the valley were larger operations and had numbers like that every day, maybe more. They had shuttle buses that took people out into the fields and brought them back after an hour or so, and sold T-shirts with their names and logos too. But they were also pesticide-soaked and who knew what the berries tasted like. We weren't that. We were walkable and no-spray. We were just a field of particularly good strawberries with a view of the river, owned by a family farm.

Tom and I were allowed to pick our own boxes for free at the end of every shift and we did just that, eating as we went. The berries were ripe, tart-sweet, and juicy. I picked a box and Tom picked two, then we counted the money. More than normal, but no matter the amount, we stole a single ten-dollar bill from the till. We dropped the rest of the money off at the farmhouse on our way out. Sid Lewis, the farmer, never said much and wouldn't make eye contact with me but he liked us, I think. We did good work and we were dependable, the stolen tens aside.

We stuffed the boxes of berries into my bike basket and took off, the day warmer than it began. It was a quick ride to Jake's house. He was waiting for us, sitting on the front step in a bathing suit, long finished his own day of work on his family's farm, which started before the sun rose. Jake and Sam formed the other half of our quartet.

"Hey ho!" Tom called.

Jake watched us glide in, leaning our bikes against the chicken coop.

Inside, we changed quickly. Me in the downstairs bathroom, Tom up in Jake's room. The darkness of the house was stale and I craved fresh air and space to move. I slipped into my bathing suit, still wet from the day before. A chill crept down my back and the navy one-piece pulled, uncomfortable at my crotch and sharp across the new fullness of my chest. I snapped the sides of the suit against my bum, yanking it down, then pulling my clothes back on overtop.

We squeezed onto the bench seat of Jake's family truck, squashed together with me in the middle. We drove towards the river, windows wide open. The day was perfect.

Jake drove fast on the familiar valley roads. We sailed by sloping vineyards, all neat lines, golden in the afternoon light. The metal rooftops of the wineries were ablaze and groups of tourists stood around with bicycles at their sides, sipping wine, looking relaxed. Tom waved at them as we passed, his arm hanging out the window and flopping up whenever we drove by a new group. They waved back, confused, uncertain. At the main bridge, we slowed. Sam was already there, leaning against his parents' minivan, trying to look cool in dark sunglasses, but his shirt betrayed him:

neon-green with *Day Camp* written across the front. That summer, he was working as a counsellor, leading activities for little kids at the community hall.

Sam hopped in the flatbed and we kept going. Jake drove even faster now. We pulled over where the road bent sharply, parking on the gravel shoulder and stripping down to our bathing suits, abandoning our shoes. I noticed both Tom and Jake turned away from me, which I was grateful for. My suit fit differently than last summer and they had noticed. A few days before, I had caught them watching me undress for a swim, staring a beat too long.

We rented tubes from Lord of the River Tube Rentals, situated in the one house on the river that just happened to be built where it was easy to catch the current. When we arrived, the lady in charge of renting out the tubes was lighting up her next cigarette.

"Been here before?" she barked.

We nodded. We came here at least twice a week in the summer but she never seemed to remember us.

"Four tubes, little lady," Sam said, winking.

"Eight bucks." She was automatic, unfazed.

Two bucks each for a tube. A bargain, especially since you could float down the river as many times as you wanted in a given day. We usually got two runs in if we were going after work. Tom handed over our stolen ten.

"Grab a tube," she said mechanically. "Now, a couple things to keep in mind. You're gonna wanna stick to the left side of the river. Whenever you come to a fork, stick to the left. Go right and you'll pop your tube on the rocks. It's too shallow. Use your hands as paddles to keep yourself to the left," she demonstrated, waving her hands behind her. "Oh, and there are three telephone pole-lookin' things hanging horizontal over the river. Don't try and go around them—"

"Go under them!" Sam said. We had heard all of this many times before.

"Right. Otherwise you'll pop your tube. And carry your tube like this, with the air nozzle pointing up. Okay? Any questions?"

We shook our heads.

"Have fun."

We walked along the wooded path, carrying our tubes over our shoulders, and came out where it cleared. The water was high that day. We had no trouble falling bottom-first into our tubes. The boys all yelped when they hit the river.

At first, the current was calm, lazily pulling us downriver. Tom grinned at me and I beamed back. We were both thinking the same thing: *this* was what summer was all about.

When we hit the point where the river picked up speed, our tubes rushed forward, slipping and crashing against the rapids. It made me laugh, the thrill of being carried away, no control over the course my tube would take. Water splashed against my body, a cold shock on my stomach, as the current threw my tube left and then right.

I reached out as we sailed past, trying to grab the low hanging branches that drooped over the water. The Gaspereau River was narrow, allowing us to see both sides of the grassy riverbank from our tubes. Lined with trees and a mess of wildflowers, the occasional farmer's fence. I loved how the birch branches leaned over us, their leaves waving in the breeze like tiny, excited hands.

I'm not sure who decided the river was fit for tubing but we often heard about a time before the Lord of the River as if it were legend. Back in the seventies, Gaspereau hosted tubing festivals in the summer. Young people on flimsy tubes. Drinking, smoking, and filling the valley with the echoes of folk music. They camped in a farmer's field right by the river, the stars above them, until the farmer called it all off because of the garbage left behind. Now tubing was a business. But still, we loved it.

The river slowed again and the sun fell on us through the trees, warming our faces and the tops of our legs. Up ahead, we could see the cow crossing that went right through the river. From the barn on one side of the water to the pasture on the other. It always freaked the tourists out to see a line of cows sloshing through the water, a farmhand pushing them along. That was when you really had to reach out and grab a branch to stop yourself from smacking into a cow.

"No cows today," Jake said, glum.

"No cows," Tom yawned, lazy.

I leaned back and my hair dipped into the water. I had fallen behind the others slightly but I could hear Sam asking if we had heard the news.

"New family moving in," he said. "People were talking about it at work."

"We heard," Tom called. He was at the front.

"I didn't," said Jake.

"They've got a boy in our grade," Sam said. "Moved here from some big city."

"You don't know where?" Tom asked.

"Maybe Toronto," Sam suggested.

"Maybe Montreal," Jake said. He had always wanted to go to Montreal, to the Jazz Festival.

"Not sure what they do. Someone said something about technology."

"Like computers?" Tom asked.

"Yeah, something like that."

"Let's drive up there and take a look," Tom suggested.

I tore my gaze from the sky above. All those little clouds, self-contained and perfectly content. Jake and Sam nodded and then they all looked at me.

"Fine." I shrugged.

⟡

Jake came into our lives shortly after that day by the swing set. Like most of our classmates, Tom and I had paired off, deeming each other best friends, forever and always. But there was one boy in our first-grade class who remained alone. Taller than the rest of us, straw-haired Jake tended to sit hunched over, his hands folded together and his eyes on his knees. He reminded me of a scarecrow.

I wouldn't have noticed Jake in all the excitement of my first friendship with Tom if it hadn't been for his timid smile, like a secret. One day the teacher said something funny and the flash of his teeth caught my eye. I felt warm at the sight of him, smiling like that. And sorry for him too. Why didn't *he* have a Tom?

"Do you want to be our friend?" I asked Jake shortly after, Tom by my side.

He nodded shyly.

It was a good fit. Tom and I needed someone subdued to balance us out, rather than add to our noise. Jake was timid but he was also funny. He had a special sense of humour, quietly clever, different from the other kids' who simply repeated jokes they'd heard on television in loud, obnoxious voices. When he laughed, it was silent laughter that shook his whole body, and despite his large size he was uncoordinated, bad at the games we played in gym class. Best of all, he was gentle with animals. I liked these things about him.

Sam came much later, and with resistance on my part. Most valley people never leave but some go away and then return years later, nostalgic and homesick. Sam's parents fell into the latter category. They returned to the valley with two kids, eager to give their family the childhood experiences they remembered. Sam's mother, Lorraine, was the police chief for the area.

On the first day of fifth grade, Sam was there, the new kid. He was small and skinny, with a mischievous grin and short hair so pale it appeared white.

"Who's that?" I asked Jake, who only shrugged.

Our teacher introduced him as Sam and we'd soon discover that Sam's parents knew Tom's father. They had all grown up together.

"Dad wants us to hang out with him," Tom told me one day.

"Fine. Whatever."

I didn't like the idea because I thought the three of us were doing just fine on our own. Adding a new member to our group might change the dynamic, the routines and inside jokes that formed the foundation of our friendship. And I didn't like Sam at first. He seemed obnoxious in the beginning, motivated by an unfounded confidence I couldn't understand. Tom and I were by far the smartest in our grade. We always raised our hands and answered the hard questions. But Sam would raise his hand even if he didn't have the answer. He just liked to talk, to be heard. And he tried to charm everyone with corny winks and obvious compliments. It seemed fake and showy.

I found myself growing quiet around him. I didn't want to compete for attention and Sam had plenty to say.

"Do we have to invite Sam?" I asked Tom occasionally, weary and annoyed.

"We don't *have* to," Tom would say, "but it would be weird not to, right?"

I conceded in those moments because Sam made Tom laugh and I liked seeing him happy. It took months but eventually Sam grew on me. Though Sam could be annoying, I realized, he was also unabashedly himself. He didn't apologize for being loud or alter his behaviour to please our classmates and I respected that about him. I was always telling Tom and Jake they shouldn't care what other people thought, and back then, Sam truly didn't.

That's how we became four. We had been friends for years and I didn't think we wanted for anything. We had fun together, spending our days as a group, separate from the other kids in our grade. Four felt like a perfect, balanced number.

꿈꾼

When the water got shallow and we could see the main bridge up ahead, we had to ease off our tubes and walk to shore. It would take too long to walk back to the tube rental lady, so Sam had left his family minivan waiting for us at this end.

I was the first one up and off my tube. I hurried up the bank, unease about driving to Slayter Road sitting low and heavy in my gut. I didn't like that the boys were so intrigued by this new figure, this boy. Weren't they happy with what we already had, the four of us? They followed behind me slowly, meandering.

We drove back, dropped off our tubes, and picked up Jake's truck. I said I would ride with Jake. I was especially annoyed at Tom who usually helped me keep Sam and Jake in line. We had an unspoken pact, the four of us. We didn't socialize with the others, the kids in our grade. They were vain and uninteresting, concerned with play-acting adulthood. They all wanted to seem older than they actually were. The girls coated in makeup they didn't need, the boys driving their family cars too fast and treating the girls as poorly as I imagined their fathers treated their mothers. They slept together and broke up and stole each other's girlfriends or boyfriends, all the while pretending that it mattered, when it was all just silly high school drama. Self-imposed exile was the only way to make it through these years intact.

Jake and I drove in silence, leading the way. Sam and Tom were behind us in the van. When we got to Slayter Road, we slowed, scanning for the Taylor house among all those trees.

"There," I said.

Once it came into view, it was unmistakable. Three towering storeys painted a dark, moody blue, an impressive stained-glass window above the bright red doorway. I noticed with a jolt the front door was open. I had never seen it open before. What was inside? Just as I wondered this, someone came out. A man. No, a boy. A boy who looked like a man. He was headed for the moving truck but he looked up at us and stopped. Had we stopped too? I watched as he raised a hand. Just held it there, above his head. My heart was huge and beating fast, and I felt he was staring right into me. I blinked, checking to make sure I still could.

"Keep going," I urged Jake, suddenly alert.

Ever obedient, Jake kept driving. Tom and Sam followed behind us.

AFTER

⸎

We are on our second pot of coffee when Mac emerges. He looks deflated and sleepy. He wears a rumpled shirt, unusual for him, and creases like dark scars line one side of his face. I find it hard to look at him but it's also impossible not to. Mac is usually a steady hand but today he radiates anger and sadness and I'm curious what that looks like coming from Mac, even if it's difficult to witness.

In a low, hoarse voice, he asks if there's coffee and Ruth pours what's left into his favourite mug, the one made by the potter who lives up on the North Mountain. Moody colours, indigo and a deep blue-green, and a smooth handle that seems to mold to the shape of your hand.

We used to have a matching set of two but Ruth broke the other mug out in her studio years ago, long before Mac. She was lifting up a canvas to show a potential customer and knocked the mug to the floor with the corner of the wooden frame.

"Shattered," she said, the pieces cupped in two hands. "Can't be fixed." The pieces went into a plastic bag, tied at the top, and then into the garbage. Until Mac, the other mug had looked lonely in the cupboard, mourning the loss of its partner. Neither Ruth nor I ever used it anymore, now that we couldn't drink from the matching mugs at the same time. But Mac adopted the lone mug like it was a stray dog, giving it a second life.

I peek over at him again, across from me at the table. His face is pale with unfamiliar stubble, flecks of grey in brown.

"Toast?" Ruth asks. We nod, but when the toast comes, we only pick away at it. It's brown bread, lightly toasted. She buttered it as soon as it popped up, making sure it had a chance to melt. She's good like that; she knows how to use food to make people feel taken care of.

What next? This is the question I am dying to ask. My palms are slick and I rub them on my sweatpants.

"I'm heading back to the police station this morning," Mac says, reading my mind; knowing, as always, what we need. "I wasn't in a right state last night. I barely remember what they told me. I need to get the details again and write them down this time." He pulls a small flip-top notebook with a worn, red cover from his pants pocket. "Do you have a pen?"

Ruth retrieves one from the kitchen drawer. He puts it behind his ear and it looks like it belongs there.

"Then," Mac continues, "I'll come back here and call the insurance company. See what can be done. If we're lucky, the money will come through for a rebuild in the next couple of months. We can at least get our main facility up and running, but we won't be able to plant again until the spring."

We nod blankly. A whole year lost. More than that. You can't just rebuild a vineyard. The winery, sure. The machines and the tasting room. But what good is all that if you've got no grapes to press, nothing to work with? Mac once told me the first three years of a vineyard produce unusable grapes. That time is about growing roots, developing complexity in the plants. It's only after ten years that the vines really mature. Mac's vineyard was planted twenty-two years ago. It will take decades to get back what he had.

"I feel sick," I say.

Mac looks at me. "It's okay, Winnie." He puts a hand on my mother's knee, moves his thumb back and forth. "We'll figure it out."

He leaves us to get ready and we remain downstairs. Ruth washes up the breakfast dishes and I start cleaning out the fridge, wiping down the shelves, discarding wilted produce and reorganizing the condiments by category. What else is there to do? We don't talk and I feel jumpy, my stomach tight and knotted. While we work, we listen to the sounds of his footsteps, the shower running, closet doors creaking, his steps back down the stairs. He calls "bye" halfway out the door.

When he slams it shut—something he's never done before, something he's scolded us for doing too often—I hate Caleb more than ever for what he's done.

BEFORE

❧

I saw Caleb again a few days later at the annual Canada Day fireworks. Gaspereau hosted the only fireworks show in the valley and it drew crowds from the surrounding communities. They shut down the main thoroughfare, the River Road, and everyone gathered near the bridge to watch the sky sparkle and fizz for a few short minutes. People brought lawn chairs and coolers stocked with snacks, arriving early to get a good spot on the bridge or the nearby riverbank.

We could have watched from my house. Our location on the river made for ideal viewing far from the crowds, which is what Ruth and Mona chose to do every year, huddled together under a blanket, drinking white wine, tipsy by the time we returned home. But the boys and I wanted to be at the centre of the excitement, or what we thought was excitement at the time. We took what we could get.

"Over here!" Tom called, waving at us from the bank. We had walked to the fireworks from my house, which took longer, but meant we didn't need to find a spot to stash our bikes amongst the throng. There were hundreds of people gathered near the bridge, the most Gaspereau would see all year. Tom had run ahead, worried we might not find a good place to sit. We joined him on a grassy patch sloping down to the muddy bank. The river twisted forward steadily below us while the crowd swelled with the arrival of more people. The sky was pink and the temperature was dropping. I could hear the peepers rising above the din of human noise, tiny frogs hidden in the trees and bush, chirring in chorus.

A young family I didn't recognize soon spread out a blanket next to us. Two young girls with their parents. The mother was nervous about everything: mosquitos, ticks, her children falling into the river or catching a chill, her husband drinking a beer and then driving them home. She expressed these worries in a frenzied stream of consciousness, one fear after the other bubbling up, hands flying while she spoke. I only half-listened to the boys, who were debating what movie to watch when we got home later. *Jurassic Park* or *Jaws*? They were in a nostalgic monster phase.

I was distracted by the mother but I soon realized the father, wearing a ball cap and silently drinking a beer, tuning out his wife with practiced ease, was staring at me. I blinked. His lips were parted, his gaze unfaltering. I had seen men look at Ruth this way before. I had thought it would make me feel powerful, attracting this attention, but it didn't. His scrutiny seemed to reduce me, making me feel like my very presence was dwindling. I kept looking away and then looking back, and still he stared. My face, my chest, my bare legs in shorts.

Strange, how his appreciation of me instilled a power in him. His lack of self-consciousness, his sense of entitlement, enjoying me from afar. He was taking without asking, without me consciously giving anything at all.

"Winnie, what do you think? Dinosaurs or sharks?" Tom tapped me on the shoulder to get my attention.

"Dinosaurs, obviously." I turned back to the boys.

"That's what I want to watch but these two idiots are voting for *Jaws*. It's times like these I think we need to make another friend."

I glanced back at the father who was now looking at the boys. He wore a peculiar look, like he couldn't make sense of the scene before him. A girl with three boys. None of these boys would have seemed to him to be my boyfriend (there were no obvious signs of affection or ownership; no arm slung over my shoulder, no kiss on my cheek) so what was I doing with them? Why was I so easy with them and them with me? Boys and girls at our age should have been charged with sexual tension. He gave me a last glance and then looked away, suddenly self-aware, the spell broken, watching his daughters carve shapes in the mud with sticks.

I was used to this, people thinking it was odd that I was friends with boys. In the early years, our teachers were always encouraging me to spend more time with the girls in my class, assigning me a desk next to another girl, never next to Tom or Jake, or later Sam. I often felt like I was segregated from the boys in class. They seemed to sit on one side of the classroom and I on the other. It can't have been that simple—I'm sure teachers weren't dividing their classrooms by gender—but I distinctly remember a feeling of forced separation, which caused me to become sullen and quiet. I had little to say to Becca, my desk mate, or Stephanie, my partner in reading exercises.

I also remember my grade three teacher fretting to Ruth that I spent "a lot of time with those boys." We were at the Thanksgiving social at school. It was one of those perfect fall days in the valley, the high sun keeping you warm despite the cool October breeze. We were on the soccer field, playing games to celebrate the harvest: apple bobbing, apple sack races, apple sorting and counting.

Jake and Tom and I were cracking into caramel apples, sitting in the grass, tired from all the excitement. Ruth stood with Mrs. Miller, close enough that I could hear them talking.

"Does she have any little girlfriends? It seems odd. I've never known an eight-year-old girl to spend all her time with two boys."

"I'm her friend," Ruth offered lamely. "She spends time with me."

"You might want to think about signing her up for an activity with the other girls. Gymnastics maybe, or ballet."

Ruth said she would think about it, which made me angry. I didn't want to do those things. I hoped she was lying.

I suspect Ruth's conversation with Mrs. Miller is the reason why I was forced to attend Emily Talbot's Spice Girls–themed birthday party a month later. Ruth was usually very lenient. As a child, I got away with almost everything. Or rather, I never knew when I was doing something wrong because she didn't seem to believe in punishing me. I could steal paint from her studio and cover the side of our white house with a rainbow splatter. She declared it beautiful, a work of art. I could drown in her favourite shirt, wear it for a romp in the woods with the boys, come back with it dirty and torn at the shoulder.

"I always wished my mother would let me wear her clothes," she laughed. "Looks good on you, Win."

This permissiveness was probably unwise of her but convenient for me. She let me run free.

Emily's birthday party seemed to be the one exception. In response to this unfamiliar rigidity, I screamed and cried, which was a new strategy for me. But she remained firm.

"You're going," she said, not looking me in the eye. "You don't have to dress up, but you're going."

All the other girls at the party were dressed like the Spice Girls in miniskirts and complicated hairstyles: pigtails, high ponytails, elaborate braids. The birthday girl wore a fake nose ring and black snap-on pants with white stripes down the sides.

I was the only one in regular clothes and I remember hating that a part of me felt bad about it. I didn't care about the Spice Girls. I had no interest in their music and I thought their girl power mantra was stupid. But standing there, watching the other girls dance in semi-synchronicity, a feeling of shame caught me off guard like a splinter. I felt left out of this particular group of girls, who seemed to have such an easy way with each other (singing loudly, faces close, holding hands), but also from the larger world of girls. Was there something wrong with me, that I didn't want to dress up like that and dance like them?

The party was unpleasant. The pizza was cold, the cheese congealed, and Emily took her time unwrapping presents, examining each gift in detail before moving on to the next. We all had to sit in a circle and watch her complete this tedious ritual.

Soon everyone was sharing their crushes. I recognized that these confessions served as a kind of offering, a sacrifice or tariff required for membership into girlhood. It was the responsibility of your girlfriends to hold your secrets and keep them safe from others. That was the pact upon which these friendships thrived.

When the party ended, I didn't feel closer to any of the girls. Instead, I felt burdened. I didn't care who they liked and I resented the obligation to now protect the truth of their crushes. It seemed to me this kind of intimacy was false and weighted. It would only slow me down.

I never had this problem with the boys, which was just one of the reasons I preferred their company. We didn't force each other to share or be vulnerable and we didn't have to prove our love for each other by bartering confidences. It was lighter and simpler this way.

"We watched _Jaws_ last month," I said, turning my back towards the family next to us. "How many times do we need to watch it before you two are satisfied?"

"Fine," Sam groaned. "Winnie always gets her way."

Tom gave me a victorious smile.

"I'm hungry," Sam said, sounding childish, sore about losing.

"Let's go to the store. Ruth gave me some money for snacks."

We left Jake and Tom to save our spot on the river and moved carefully, snaking through groups of people seated and waiting for the fireworks. I avoided looking at my admirer, though I could feel his eyes on me once again as I walked away.

The gas station on the corner was our version of a convenience store, a place to buy junky snacks and cold drinks. It was packed with people, other teenagers in shorts and flip-flops, sporting new tans. I recognized a number of kids from school, a few who lived down the road but most from other communities. There were only a handful of teenagers in Gaspereau.

I spotted Amber Foote and Jess Bigelow, two girls from school who were unrelated but looked like twins. Streaky blonde hair, short denim skirts. Amber was holding an open cellphone, hot pink and razor thin. She punched numbers furiously with her thumbs, texting someone, I presumed. She was one of a growing group of kids at school with cellphones. The boys and I didn't use them. For me, it was a matter of principle but I'm not sure about the boys. It may have just been their parents' refusal to pay for a phone that stopped them.

"Hey, Jess," Sam said as we squeezed by them in the aisle.

"Hey," Jess responded, her voice lax.

She was clearly stoned, wearing a lazy smile. A flush of sunburn pink on the tops of her cheeks and the ridge of her nose.

"Hey to you, too," Jess said to me. "Do you look different or am I just really high?"

Amber giggled and I rolled my eyes, ignoring them. I grabbed a bag of chips while Amber pulled Jess away, towards the cash.

"You didn't have to be rude," Sam said.

"I wasn't. I held my tongue."

"Yeah, exactly. You could have at least said hi back."

"Who cares?"

"I do!" said Sam.

We walked towards the cooler.

"She was stoned," I said. "And you were only talking to her because you think she's hot."

"She is! And I'll never have a chance with anyone if you keep scaring them away."

"Here," I thrust a bottle of water into his hands. "You're hungry now but you'll be thirsty later."

We stood in the long line to pay, not talking. Of the three boys, Sam was the most vocal about his adolescent lust, which didn't usually bother me. The chances of his crushes being reciprocated by the girls in our grade seemed slim. But that night his longing set me off. I couldn't quite locate the source of my resentment. I thought it was about Jess and Amber, whom I generally found loathsome, but I realize now it was actually that father back on the riverbank, how he made me feel. I didn't like thinking Sam could make someone feel that way too, even if it was only Jess.

When we finally paid, it was nearly dark. The fireworks would be starting soon. We moved through the crowd as quickly as possible, clutching our snacks. When we pushed past Angela Lawson, wrapped in a white sweater and reeking of bug spray, she told us to slow down and that made us laugh. I wasn't paying attention, giddy from the scolding and the cool night air. A few running steps and I smacked right into someone.

"Sorry," I said automatically, continuing past.

But something made me turn. When I looked back, he was grinning at me, amused. It was the boy from the driveway. He wore a solid black T-shirt and stood alone, as if the crowd had parted slightly in his presence. His tanned skin seemed to glow against the new darkness of night. I noticed his grey eyes again, hypnotic and bright, and I felt pulled to him. A new sensation for me.

"Come on!" said Sam.

I blinked and turned away.

Moments later, the fireworks began. Sam and I reached the others just as the first sparks whizzed and burst. While I watched the sky erupt above us, I wondered if I dreamt him up, this new boy whose name I didn't yet know. He didn't seem real, standing apart from the mass of people; he didn't look like he belonged here.

Like every year, the fireworks show seemed both unimpressive and too short. I guess our expectation and the ritual were the real fun. But that year, even the familiarity of it all—a summer tradition with my friends—felt interrupted.

⚜

The next day was a day off from the U-pick. Ruth and I had already planned to spend the day making jam, so I didn't see the boys. We carefully washed and dried pounds of wild blueberries, the hours falling away. There was a right way and a wrong way to do it. I can't remember when Ruth taught me how but I must have been young because it was second nature to me. We floated the berries in a sink full of cold water, scooped them out in small batches, and spread them on a dishtowel. We then grabbed the ends of the towel and rocked the berries back and forth until they were semi-dry. This method allowed you to clean the berries gently, without bruising or crushing, losing the juice too soon. We used the same process to get them ready for freezing.

It was odd, how particular Ruth was about food. She was so careless in other aspects of homemaking. It drove me crazy how often she forgot wet laundry in the washing machine. I'd open the top of the machine days later to start a new load and find the smell of mold clinging to the abandoned clothing, nearly impossible to get out. She also let the recycling pile up in the corner of the kitchen, bottles and boxes perched on top of each other, forming a haphazard installation of the recently consumed. I often ended up taking care of that kind of thing, eventually, when it bothered me enough.

But with food, Ruth was all about the rules, the proper technique. She made scrambled eggs over the slightest flame, insisting the eggs needed to be soft and creamy, no browning allowed. She sometimes grabbed a spatula right out of my hand, shaking her head, explaining all I was doing wrong.

I watched the berries collapse into each other over the heat. The air was sticky with sugar and our hands were stained purple. We jarred the inky sludge and then tried some on cornbread.

"Good," I said through a full mouth.

Ruth nodded in agreement, chewing.

Ruth's pantry was legendary. We had a true Nova Scotia kitchen with a door cut right into the floor, leading to the cellar. She stored all her preserves down there. Jams and jellies and pickles in jars of different shapes and sizes. She spent the summer conserving the valley's bounty. It made the colder months less bland, adding bursts of optimistic colour and unseasonal flavour—strawberry, peach, spicy radish, herbed tomato—to dark, frozen days.

"Time to shower," Ruth said, scrubbing the giant jam pot somewhat unsuccessfully. I usually did the dishes. "Mind taking over?"

I grabbed the sponge from her and plunged my hands into the soapy water. "You going out?"

"Dinner in the city."

I paused. "What's his name again?"

"John." She untied her apron, hung it on its hook. "He's nice."

"What about the market tomorrow?"

"No faith in me!" she shook her head. "You know I'll be back before you wake up."

"Right."

She walked over and curled an arm around my waist. "We never miss the market, do we?"

"Right." I shrugged her off. She was more physical than I was, all hugs and hand grabs and back rubs. I tolerated it, but only when I was in a good mood. "You go shower. I've got this."

I heard the water start upstairs, imagined steam escaping from under the bathroom door. It bothered me that she was heading off to the city to meet a man. She had done so ever since I was little, but I never got used to it. Back then, she'd drop me off at Jake's for the night. Mona always served a hearty meal (roast chicken and mashed potatoes; beef stew with turnip), and afterwards we would watch an old movie or play video games until we got too sleepy to hold the controllers.

It was different now. I had been allowed to spend the night by myself since I was thirteen, which was probably too young but Ruth was different than most mothers and I was different than most thirteen-year-olds. I could take care of myself.

I tried to remember if I had met John. The one with the gleaming black car and the moustache? Or maybe the one with the loud voice, the Rolex? They all seemed the same to me. Wealthy art collectors, older than Ruth. They tended to have a soapy smell and wore expensive, tailored shirts. They drove down from the city to visit her studio and see her work. They ended up finding something else they liked the look of even more.

It rarely lasted. A few dates, or often only one. I don't think she was looking for anything serious. She just wanted to be wined and dined, made to feel special.

"Come say bye," she called from the front hall. I was looking in the fridge, trying to dream up dinner.

"You look great," I told her, hugging her goodbye. She always dressed up. A nice dress and heels, red lipstick.

She did a little twirl. "Not bad, eh?"

I watched her pull out of the driveway from the front window. She looked like a movie star with those sunglasses. Now what? I had thought the day was ours. The day and night. I stared out the window, feeling empty, as though I was sinking. I didn't like it when plans changed at the last minute. When the course diverged.

I called Tom but his father told me he wasn't home.

"At Jake's?" I asked.

"Probably."

But they weren't at Jake's. Mona said he and Tom had taken off on their bikes earlier in the day and she hadn't seen them since. "Try Sam's," she suggested.

The boys weren't at Sam's either. His younger brother said he hadn't seen them all day. I thought about setting out on my own bike to look for them but figured it would be quicker to stay still, to wait. They would end up at one of their houses eventually and call me back. They always did. My stomach grumbled and I busied myself with fixing something to eat. I only ever made grilled cheese or eggs on toast. I wasn't a cook, not like Ruth.

By the time I finished my eggs, they still hadn't called. Where were they? I put my dishes in the sink and wandered outside. The day was fading. A blushing sky and the chirp of crickets hidden in the brush. Our backyard was in desperate need of mowing. Tom usually did it. I made a mental note to bring it up next time he was over. I crept barefoot along the worn path to Ruth's studio, a small, repurposed barn. The door was never locked.

The studio was a mess. Ruth wasn't a neat person but her art was born out of pure chaos: pencil sketches on every surface; used paint brushes scattered across her desk, the floor; a palette glistening with thick splotches of wet paint; an abandoned glass of red wine, half drunk. I could see she was working on a new piece, a view of the dykes that cut through the Minas Basin, with the cliff of Blomidon in the background. A familiar sight; the money shot. It was a view she and others had painted many times before but she had a knack for shedding new light on the familiar. She only painted landscapes but they were abstracts, created with broad gestures. Thick strokes of paint and muted colours.

I reached a finger up and held it there in front of the canvas. I wanted to touch; the texture begged for it. I told myself it must be dry—it looked finished—but as I pressed down the ridge of paint submitted to my finger, depressing and flattening. I snatched my hand back, my heart beating fast.

I moved on and looked at the other work she had in there, stuff I had already seen. I imagined her showing her art to her male fans. Laughing in that way she did. Tinkling, too generous. Sometimes I heard it from the house. I imagined her reaching a hand across the dinner table now, squeezing his, the man with the moustache, smiling at him. She would be back before I woke up but what would she do between now and then?

By the time I left the studio, the night was full and black. I could hear the river behind me. I expected there to be a phone message but there wasn't. The boys had found something else to distract them.

૬⚶⚶૨

Did I think about him then, the boy who looked like a man, waving at us from his driveway? The boy who made my pulse hammer just by standing there, smirking at me as I ran past him at the fireworks. I suppose he was only a figure at that point, an outline not yet filled in with detail. Perhaps I didn't know how to think about him quite yet, the first glint of new feeling too unfamiliar to identify.

I heard Ruth come in just after 6 A.M. The light was dim when she walked up the stairs and into her room. I imagined her hair was messy and her heels were off, hooked on two fingers, dangling at her side. Red lipstick long gone.

I had slept fitfully; I always did when she was away. I wasn't worried. I was more unsettled, like something was off. But when I heard her come in, I rolled over and tumbled back into sleep.

꠹ꕤꕥ꠺

Saturday was market day, warmer than the last few. We were in that stretch of early July when the good-weather days felt eternal, like the rain might never return. We didn't realize then that the following weeks would be so dry and parched. We would be begging for rain by the end.

Ruth and I dressed quickly, not stopping to make coffee. We would get it at the market. It was just too warm.

The drive to town was quiet. I could tell she was tired from her night out. I was tired from her night out, too.

Most Saturdays, Tom joined us. I would call him just before we left home. If he was even half awake he would throw on clothes and be waiting for us in his driveway, smiling and yawning at the same time, like his face couldn't decide how to be. But I didn't call him that morning. I was annoyed about the night before. Where had they been? Why hadn't they called me back?

It was still early and the streets of Wolfville were nearly empty. A couple worked in their garden. A woman sat on her front step, reading and drinking coffee.

We parked. The market was located inside an old warehouse, with a few stands spilling outside near the picnic tables and the music tent. The musicians were just setting up. Inside, we got our coffee first. Ruth flirted with the tattooed barista while I yawned loudly. He knew our order and served it up with an embarrassing wink for Ruth.

Next, we picked up vegetables from our favourite farmer. His table spilled over with an abundance of summer produce. Brilliant orange carrots with shaggy green tops and Romano beans like knobby fingers. Bunches of leafy kale and chard and spinach; baskets full of zucchini and summer squash. I spotted fresh-from-the-ground onions, dirt still clinging to the shining white bulbs, and the first raspberries of the season.

We bought sticky buns from the French baker and retreated outside to eat our breakfast. We found a picnic table to ourselves in the shade. The music was up and going now, a French-Canadian duo singing cheerful folk songs.

Ruth picked at her sticky bun and asked me what I did last night.

"Nothing," I said. "Read a little."

"You didn't see Tom?"

"Nope."

She wanted me to ask how her night was but I didn't want to hear about John and the crème brûlée they had shared at dinner. I stayed quiet, listening to the music instead.

We finished our breakfast, wiping our cinnamon-coated fingers on thin paper napkins, and watched them all arrive. We were early. The bulk of market-goers came around mid-morning. Some were tourists but most were locals. We waved at those we knew.

"Incoming," Ruth whispered, sliding her sunglasses off the top of her head and onto her face.

I looked up. Mac Elliott was walking towards us, smiling. He wore a denim shirt and carried a quart of lemonade in one hand.

He had light brown hair, balding a bit on the top, and a kind face with a broad nose. His skin was tanned and leathery.

"Beautiful day," Mac said, squinting at us.

"Perfect day. Why don't you join us?" I said. I had always liked Mac—he seemed down-to-earth—but Ruth found him annoying. Inviting him to sit down with us was a subtle form of punishment for her night in the city.

"It's a hot one," Mac said, leaning his elbows on our picnic table. "But I can't complain. My grapes love the heat."

I caught movement behind Ruth's sunglasses, the rolling of eyes. The main reason Ruth found Mac annoying was his tendency to circle conversations back to his business, the vineyard. Ruth said he was narcissistic, always wanting people to recognize the good work he was doing, but I didn't see it that way. Whenever Mac spoke about his work to me, he acknowledged the ways his business was dependent on an element of chance, of unpredictability. His grapes and wine were at the mercy of the weather, and from what I could tell, he believed he had limited control over the end product. I got the sense he thought of himself more as a cultivator, someone to oversee the process with a light hand and coax out what nature had intended.

"What about you, Ruth? Do you like the heat?" Mac asked.

"I like the coffee," she said, standing up. "I'm going to get some more. Winnie, you want some?"

I shook my head.

We watched her walk away and disappear inside the market. I noticed Angela standing by the market entrance, talking to someone unfamiliar.

"Who's that Angela's talking to?" Mac asked, reading my mind.

She was a tall woman, slim, with olive skin and long, dark, curly hair. She wore a short, grey linen dress and was nodding politely while Angela spoke. I knew who she was even before the boy walked up and joined her, heavy bags full of market groceries in his arms.

"They're the new people." I said it fast, catching up with my pulse. "Up on Slayter."

"Oh, right. I heard about them. They look like they're from away."

We were quiet as we watched them. The boy was looking around. Long, slow stares. He took in the musicians, the children playing nearby, the dog barking for its owner. He didn't set down the bags while he waited for his mother. He held them in his hands, his arms flexed.

Ruth emerged from the market with a new coffee and Angela waved her over. *Our resident artist,* I imagined her explaining. *Gorgeous abstracts!*

Ruth shook the woman's hand and nodded at the boy. Then she pointed at me.

My stomach fluttered. They were walking towards us. The boy was five steps behind them but soon he would be right next to me.

"Winnie," Ruth said. "This is Sylvia and her son, Caleb. They just moved to Gaspereau."

Sylvia stretched an elegant hand towards me. Long fingers with delicate gold rings. "Nice to meet you."

"And you." I felt a chill. Her hand was cold, even in this heat.

"Caleb," Sylvia said, looking behind her. The boy was still searching the crowd for something or someone of interest. I got the sense he was actively judging his surroundings, trying to make sense of this new place—the valley—and where he fit within it. When Sylvia called his name, his eyes found his mother and then me.

"Hi," he said, looking right into me.

I spent the rest of the day unsettled, unable to keep my spot on the page of a book, uncomfortable wherever I sat. I moved from the couch to my bed to the backyard, staying in one place for only short bursts of time. I was antsy, irritated by the close stuffiness of the house, the way the grass tickled my calves. I swatted at bugs with new vengeance, feeling their bites more acutely. I heard every sound as if it vibrated—harsh, shrill—inside my ear (the buzz of a wasp; black crows cawing across the river, the chorus of a murder). I was distracted, unable to focus.

Why couldn't I recall what I said to him? He said hi. What did I say back? Horrified, I thought maybe I'd said nothing. Had I told him my name? I remembered Mac shattering the moment. Caleb's intense stare, my consequent feeling of falling. Mac had said something about the lemonade in his hand. But what had I said to Caleb?

I didn't know what it meant: my confusion, the misremembering. I wasn't used to feeling spellbound by others.

Tom called after dinner. Ruth answered and gave me the look, the Tom look. I considered signalling to Ruth to pretend I wasn't home. I wasn't in the mood for anyone. But I was curious. What had kept them from me last night?

Tom sounded like he always did, cheerful: "Hey!"

"Hey."

"What's up?"

"Nothing," I answered, trying to sound distant.

"What are you doing?"

"Reading," I lied. I hadn't read a full page all day.

"Missed you," he said, a song.

"Yeah?"

"One night away and—"

"Away? Where did you go?"

He laughed. "Not me. You were the one who went away. Ruth time."

"Actually," I said, "Ruth went away. John time."

Tom knew I didn't like it when Ruth met men in the city. Usually, he would come over and keep me company. We'd rent a movie and order pizza or have a bonfire in the backyard. He'd fall asleep on the couch and I would sleep upstairs.

"Ugh," he groaned.

"Yeah. What did you do?"

"We were with the new guy, Caleb."

I paused a beat. "Oh yeah? What's he like?"

Tom laughed quietly, a hushed chuckle I hadn't heard before. Nervous? "He's...cool. A bit different, but you'll like him. We're meeting up with him tonight if you want to come."

If you want to come. I paused. "What are you doing with him?"

"I don't know. Meeting up at his place. Finding trouble."

⚜

The boys and I biked to Slayter Road together that night. Caleb was waiting for us. Sitting on the front step of that big house of his, looking up at the night sky.

"You can't see these where I come from," he said, pointing. "Not like this."

We glanced up at the stars, luminous that night, the sky speckled with more light than dark. I had never thought about our special, unfiltered view of the stars, about light pollution in other places. Caleb seemed impressed and I felt oddly proud.

"Where are you from?" I asked.

"West coast," he said. "Vancouver."

We nodded as if we knew Vancouver well, though none of us had travelled farther west than Ontario.

"Everything's different here," he said. "It's so quiet and empty. A house like this would cost millions where I come from."

He gestured behind him at the house, somber-looking, only one window illuminated on the third floor. Were we going to get to go inside? The thought was a flash, a shimmering possibility, but Caleb was already retrieving his bike, swinging a leg overtop and setting off down the driveway.

"Come on," he said. "Let's go."

The boys started to follow him but I stayed still. I asked where we were going, standing there alone while they pedalled away. I wasn't used to playing follow the leader.

"You'll see," was all Caleb said, words thrown over his shoulder.

We biked fast and quiet. I felt blind, the warm summer wind tangling my hair, chasing an unknown. We didn't have to go far. What Caleb had in mind was just down the road. He pulled over at the small winery on the very end of Slayter. It was owned by a European man who I had seen around but never spoken to. He sometimes offered samples of his wines at the market and other events.

"It's closed," I said. "And they wouldn't serve us anyway."

"Do you always need permission to do what you want, Winifred?" Caleb asked, his gaze settling on me for a moment.

"No one calls me that," I bristled, but he wasn't listening. He was looking around, finding a place to stash his bike in some leafy bushes by the road. He looked at us as if to say *What are you waiting for?* We hid our bikes next to his.

The vineyard was dark and quiet. A breeze rustled the grape leaves, the fields whispering all around us. I shivered as we followed Caleb towards the main building, pinching Tom on the back of the arm. He was nervous too but his eyes shone like full moons.

Caleb picked the lock of a back door with a bent safety pin from his pocket. I almost expected the winery door to be open. Gaspereau folk weren't great about locking their doors, not back then. I watched Caleb carefully, trying to figure out the trick. Where had he learned to do that?

While he fiddled with the lock, I noticed my body shaking slightly, my heart thumping at a new rate. The owner could return at any time. Maybe he forgot to do something before closing for the day or maybe he was a night owl who liked to work late. Maybe back at home he sensed our footsteps, crunching gravel in the driveway. The nerves I was feeling were intoxicating, an unfamiliar high. I looked over at the boys. They appeared shell-shocked, watching Caleb, not moving.

"There we go," Caleb said, satisfied. He opened the door and led us inside. The dark building was eerily alive. This was where they made the wine. The machines were asleep for the night but they seemed to emit energy into the air, sound you couldn't quite locate the source of, background noise that hummed. Caleb strode over to a stack of wine boxes. He pulled a few bottles out, looked them up and down and turned them around.

"What are you doing?" I asked, taking a step forward.

"What does it look like?"

It felt like an important moment. Resist or join him? I could choose to put a stop to the trouble or take part. In the past, I would have resisted—not because it was wrong to steal but simply because I hated being told what to do, especially by my peers. That was what most teenagers did, wasn't it? Follow along, collectively fixated on being cool. But this felt different and too exciting to refuse. My pulse continued to throb. What would it mean to take something from inside out? A token, a souvenir of our crime.

I strode over to Caleb. "I'm not drinking any red wine," I said, starting to root through the boxes. "Valley reds are crap."

I didn't know valley reds were crap from experience but I had heard Ruth say it more than once.

I could feel Caleb watching me and I liked it. It was different than the man at the fireworks. I wanted Caleb to notice the freckles on my cheeks, the thick softness of my hair.

"This looks good." I held up a bottle of sparkling wine. It wasn't very cold but it looked refreshing. Golden bubbles visible through the glass. A white label with silver writing.

"Looks great," he said. "Grab a few."

We stuck two bottles in the basket on my bike. Tom and Sam held the others against their handlebars. I was still shaking, teeth chattering a little. My whole body felt affected by the fact of our theft, awake and buzzing from within. I think the boys were excited too but I was so enchanted by my own high, I paid them little attention. Jake would have had the hardest time with it. He was the one with the solid moral compass.

We tore away, pedalling faster than I ever had before, laughing into the wind. I felt like I was flying, the night air tossing my hair behind me, my chest pounding even harder. We headed for Jake's house, which was Sam's idea. We needed a place to actually drink the stuff and Sam suggested the apple barn at the back of Jake's farm.

"No one will find us there," he said.

"Great idea, Samuel," said Caleb.

His insistence on saying our full names would take getting used to. I was Winifred and they were Thomas, Jacob, and Samuel. No one had introduced us that way, Caleb just started calling us that. I'm not even sure Jake's full name *is* Jacob. I can imagine Mona naming him Jake, putting it like that on the birth certificate. But accuracy wasn't what Caleb was going for. I would realize later how renaming us was a strategy, a way of subtly flexing control.

Making us feel like we were starting anew in his presence, which maybe we were.

Jake's apple barn had harsh fluorescent lights that made us all look pale and ghostly, even Caleb. We sat on work benches, pulled together in the middle of the room, and watched as Caleb popped the corks. Like the lock picking, it amazed me he knew how to do this.

Tom and I split a bottle. The others each had their own. It was our first real taste of alcohol. Not Caleb's, but mine and the boys'. We had all had sips of our parents' drinks, maybe a stolen beer or two at a family party shared between the four of us, but we had never been good and drunk before. That wasn't normal for kids our age, but it was a conscious choice on my part, one the boys followed dutifully. I knew the kids from school had parties where they drank until they puked or passed out but we weren't a part of any of that, and even in our little group, I hadn't wanted to edge too close to what was considered typical teenage behaviour. I feared teasing those boundaries might result in the crumbling of walls I had carefully built between us and the other kids. Sam, often tempted, was our weak link.

That night, though, Caleb made me forget my embargo on teenage drunkenness. It might have been the break-in and theft—the exhilaration of which still excites me, thinking back—or maybe it was just Caleb, his influence, my curious desire to please him. I didn't question opening the bottles and drinking them down and neither did the others. We didn't think; we just acted.

The wine was all bubbles. I expected it to be sweet, but it wasn't. It was something else that I didn't yet have language for. It made me feel light and happy, like my limbs were weightless, like the top of my head was drawn to the ceiling, an untethered balloon. All those bubbles bursting in my mouth as Tom and I passed the bottle back and forth between us.

Caleb got sillier as he drank. Jake's father kept a record player and a collection of old vinyl in the barn. Jake put on an album, sun-drenched music from sixties California. Caleb listened for a moment and then stood up and started dancing. Moving his hips from side to side, grinning with his eyes closed. He didn't look cool, dancing like that, but it was clear that looking cool wasn't the point. I loved that he didn't care how he looked or what we thought. Soon, Jake stood up and danced too. Jake appeared blissful. Eyes closed, hips twisting. That made me happier than the wine, my shy friend looking so free.

Sam became wild when he drank, like a little boy. I remember telling him, very seriously, to put something down, a dangerous tool of some sort. He ran around the barn like a toddler on a mission. Little pounding steps. We caught him eventually, and he put it down, whatever it was.

I remember getting sleepy near the end, limbs heavy and craving a soft pillow, an unwelcome contrast with the jittery thrill of breaking into the winery and the liberating power of being drunk for the first time. I tried to fight fatigue by standing up and stretching my arms, shaking my head yes and then no. Tom was dozing, laying horizontal on a workbench. Sam had wandered outside to pee. Suddenly, Caleb was beside me, grabbing one of my arms and pulling me toward him, the empty space of the barn he had turned into a dance floor. I glanced at Jake, who was seated on a bench in the corner, looking through the records his father stored in milk crates. He didn't look up.

Our bodies were turned towards each other, close enough that I could smell him. Sweat laced with a spiciness—his particular scent, which I loved right away. He held me by the crook of my elbow.

"Dance," he said.

For a moment, I resisted. I wasn't much of a dancer. But his fingers slipped past my palm and curled in between my own. "Dance with me," he repeated, holding my hand for real now. I swallowed. I kept my eyes on his, unable to look away, and started to sway my hips. The music was folksy, a woman's voice over delicate guitar. Not right for dancing. But once I started moving I didn't want to stop. If I stopped, I feared he would let go. That he would no longer look at me in a way that made me wonder what he was thinking.

AFTER

꧁꧂

There's a community meeting in the afternoon. A vigil of sorts, but also a chance to plan. How should we think about what happened last night? How do we move forward?

Ruth and I go to the hall together.

"Mac will meet us there," she tells me, and I nod.

We're quiet in the car, like we were at breakfast. The day is cruelly beautiful. Sunny and cool with blue skies, as though nothing has changed. Mocking us. We're driving away from all the blackness. A dark, gaping hole in our green valley. As if aliens landed or some unforgiving god took a branding iron and burnt her mark, oversized and devastating, on our home.

If I don't think about it, I can almost forget. The fields we pass on our way to the hall are just as alive as they were yesterday. Food growing, life thriving. Nothing visibly different at this end of Gaspereau. They say money doesn't grow on trees, but actually it does. On trees and in the ground and hanging from the vines.

I cough for something to do. "This is so...."

"Fucked up?" Ruth offers.

I laugh but it isn't funny. "Yeah, exactly."

"It is. Totally, completely fucked up."

"Will they be able to fix it?" I ask, voice quiet.

She frowns, considers. "Eventually, yes. But like Mac said, it will take a while. They'll rebuild and plant in the spring, but you can't speed up the clock. Wine is a slow business. Old vines, old wine. You know how it is."

I nod. "But what will people do while we wait? The people who work in the wineries?"

She tilts her head to the side. "Mac has insurance. They'll be able to rebuild. But there will be a loss. They'll lose time and money. Starting over is never easy." She shakes her head. "Things will be okay eventually, but it'll be hard for a while."

"But what about the employees?" I press, chewing my bottom lip. She doesn't seem to want to answer my question.

"There's no telling for sure when the wineries will be back in production. Most people will probably leave but there will be more people who come later on, once everything's back to the way it was."

"But do you think it will ever actually be like it was? Is it possible to recover from something like this?" My voice is more panicked than I would like.

Ruth kneads the steering wheel with her hands. I can tell I'm upsetting her with my questions.

"I don't know, Winnie," she says. "No one does. We just have to be supportive. Mac needs us to be strong right now."

I rest my forehead on the cool car window and close my eyes, breathing deeply. I wonder what I would be doing right now, if Caleb had never come here.

BEFORE

꽃꽃꽃

awoke the next morning without a hangover. I was expecting one. A thump of a headache, a churning stomach. That self-inflicted torment you hear about, the mark of a good night. Maybe I was too young to get one. I was disappointed when I sat up in bed, feeling perfectly normal. No wincing required.

The U-pick was dead that day. It must have been the heat. The sun was stark, no cloud cover. This, we would learn, was just the beginning. The heat would remain for the rest of the summer, making it one of the hottest and driest in a century. Over the course of a couple of months, the whole valley would turn into kindling, ready to catch.

At work, Tom and I moved as little as possible, thankful for the shade provided by our hut. We spoke even less, choosing instead to pass a water bottle between us in silence, each pretending to the other that we were suffering the effects of the night before.

"Quite a night," he said at one point.

I yawned in response, then gulped down more water. I kept reliving our night, especially how it had ended. Caleb and I had danced until the song was over. Then he abruptly let go of my hand and turned away. I watched him walk over to Jake to look at more records as if the moment, our dancing, meant nothing. I stood there, punctured and deflated. He had told me to dance and I had obeyed. What went wrong? There was music still playing; we could have kept dancing. Did my gaze not hold his, like his held mine?

After work, we went swimming with Sam and Jake at the Canal, a spot in the river where the water slowed down and formed a quiet pool. You could take a dip without being swept away. We were all unusually quiet while we waved our limbs in the water. I wanted to bring up Caleb—I'm sure we all did—but what was there to say? I couldn't locate the right words. We talked around him instead.

It was Jake who finally brought up the night before, how Sam had stood on a work table and recited the capital cities of every province and territory in Canada.

"I *did*?" Sam asked.

"Dude," Tom said, "I swear you did it in under a minute."

Sam shook his head. "I don't even *know* the capital cities of every province."

We all laughed and it felt familiar, comforting. For a moment, Caleb seemed like a dream, distant and half-remembered, and it was nice being alone with the boys again. Despite everything that had happened the night before, we were still us.

⌁⌁⌁

The boys were at my house the next time we saw Caleb, a few days later. We were in the backyard, eating slices of watermelon and sitting on the back step, spitting out the seeds. Ruth and Mona were walking around the garden, drinks in hand. Sweet vermouth with an ice cube and a slice of lemon, Ruth's favourite. It was a familiar scene.

"Hey!" I heard Jake say, surprised.

I turned and saw Caleb coming into the backyard.

"Hi," he said, like he came here all the time. He sat down next to us and started eating a piece of watermelon. Juice ran down his chin. He wiped it away with the back of his hand.

I wanted to ask what he had been doing the last few days but decided against it. I didn't want to appear too happy to see him. Instead, I became very aware of my T-shirt. Thick cotton, white and shapeless. I adjusted the fabric, pulling it down, smoothing the front.

Mona and Ruth walked towards us.

"You must be the new kid," Mona said, stretching out a hand.

Caleb stood up to take it. "Yes, I'm Caleb."

"Nice to meet you, Caleb. I'm Jake's mom, Mona. Did Jake tell you I saw you coming?"

"I'm sorry?" Caleb asked.

Ruth chuckled. "Mona's our resident psychic. She sees a lot of things coming."

Ruth fanned her face with her hand and I wondered what Caleb thought of her. Did he find her attractive? I was embarrassed by how young she dressed, cat-eye sunglasses and denim cut-offs, her long, thick hair in a bun on top of her head. She wore a paint-stained shirt, unbuttoned to reveal her tanned, freckled chest.

"Hot day," she said to Caleb. "Can I offer you something to drink?"

"Please, Ruth. Whatever you're having would be great."

I laughed and everyone looked at me. I expected Ruth to shake her head, to explain. But to my shock, she went in the house and poured him a vermouth. A generous pour, too.

"We'll have to try that some time," I whispered to Tom.

"Caleb, may I ask your birthdate?" Mona was peering at him intently.

Jake immediately turned pink. He looked like he wanted to push his mother into the river. He had long nursed a quiet embarrassment about Mona's side gig, blushing and growing quiet whenever someone mentioned his mother's "gift." I think he knew she was a hack.

"February first," Caleb answered, sipping neatly on his drink. "Why do you ask?"

"Ah, an Aquarius. I thought so. You have wise eyes. Intellectual, but aloof. Of course, I would love to do a full reading of your birth chart. Astrological signs," she laughed quietly, shaking her head, "are too broad. There's so much *more* going on." She looked up at the sky, as if it really was all written up there, just waiting for us to interpret it.

For the first time since we met him, Caleb looked like he didn't know what to say.

"Are you interested?" Mona asked. "In a reading of your natal chart?"

"*Mom*." Jake looked completely mortified.

"Only asking. He can always say no, my dear."

"Maybe," Caleb said.

"Wonderful! If you can give me the date, time, and location of your birth ahead of the reading, that would be most helpful."

I watched Caleb take another sip, his drink disappearing fast.

꒰֍֎꒱

Mona drifted back to the farm but Caleb and the boys stayed for dinner. Tom, Jake, and I played bocce while Sam and Caleb hung close to the barbecue, chatting with Ruth. The air smelled of smoke, and the heat of the day lingered into the early evening. Caleb had a lot of questions about Ruth's life as an artist.

I listened in as best I could, jealous that he was talking to her. I wondered again if he thought she was pretty (most men did), and if he did, what did that mean? Did he think the same of me? We looked very similar, but maybe that wasn't how attraction worked. Ruth had a vibe; I wondered if I had one too. I had never had to think about it before now. My jealousy made me annoyed at Ruth but also at Caleb. Why was he able to make me feel this way?

"Not to be blunt," I heard Caleb say, "but how do you make a go of it as an artist? You're kind of in the middle of nowhere out here. How do people even know you exist?"

Ruth considered, holding a metal spatula in one hand. "It took time. It wasn't immediate. When we lived in the city I had a lot more access to galleries, plus I was involved with the art school and there was an inherent visibility in being a student. They did a good job of showing us off." Ruth flipped the burgers, raw meat sizzling on the grill. "But moving here? Yeah, that was different. I got into the gallery in Wolfville pretty quickly, so I was fortunate there, and I actually held a show right here at home in the first few months. It was a good way to get to know the community, particularly the local business owners. The wineries were really supportive. Some of them bought paintings and some of them even sold my work for a small cut, putting it up in their tasting rooms. After that, it was just a lot of self-promotion. The wine industry provided a tourist boom and people from away are desperate to take a little piece of this place home with them. It doesn't hurt that my work is all focused on local valley landscapes. That's what they want. I give it to them."

"I'd love to see your studio some time, if you don't mind," Caleb said. I couldn't tell if his interest was genuine.

"Absolutely! Maybe after dinner."

I rolled my eyes and flung the bocce ball too hard. It flew in their direction. Sam had to sidestep to get out of the way.

We ate the burgers at our picnic table, overlooking the river. Caleb said how delicious they were, especially the aged cheddar cheese Ruth served as a topping with pickles and Dijon mustard, nothing else. He ate two burgers, chewing with his mouth closed, wearing his napkin on his lap. I wasn't used to seeing a boy with such good manners. Neither was Ruth. When he cleared the table without being asked, she raised her eyebrows at me, impressed.

"Did you want to see the studio now?" she asked when he came back.

"We actually have to get going," he answered, smiling. "These guys promised me a continuation of our tour. They've been showing me the sights."

We nodded like what he was saying was true.

"Oh well, next time. You guys have fun."

"Thank you so much for dinner," he said.

"It was my pleasure. You're welcome any time."

We left my house on our bikes and headed east along the river, the opposite direction of the main bridge and the gas station, Gaspereau's natural centre. It was fully evening now, daylight vanishing, turning the green fields a deep purple. I noticed Caleb becoming increasingly irritated by the mosquitoes, swatting at his bare legs and arms while he pedalled, cursing them as "bastards."

"They're not this bad out west," he said, smacking one at his temple. "These are monster mosquitoes."

It was odd to see him ruffled. So far, he had only shown us a cool steadiness.

"Where are we going anyway?" I asked.

Sam gave me a look as if to say, *Shut up.*

"Trust," Caleb said, and I decided to try. The other night had been worth it. Maybe tonight would be too.

We wandered down a quiet side road. Caleb turned into one of the driveways and we echoed his movements, biking up the empty drive. We dismounted in front of the darkened house. It was mid-sized and nice enough but nothing special. I wasn't sure who lived there.

Caleb led us around the back of the property and I started to feel like I had the night at the winery, alert and expectant. We leaned our bikes against the house and he swiftly opened the back door, which was unlocked. I had a feeling he had been here before, and that he already knew the best way inside.

"Come on," he said.

Tom looked at me for reassurance.

"It's fine," I whispered. "Let's go."

I followed Caleb in, the other boys coming behind me.

We were standing in a small mud room. I noticed a pair of child-sized rubber boots, pink with yellow ducks, tucked neatly off to the side. Jake bent down to take off his shoes.

"Don't," Tom said. "Just in case we have to leave quickly."

I nodded. Good thinking. Jake stood up, his face pale.

"It's okay." Caleb wore a serene smile. "You don't have to be nervous. They won't be coming back tonight. There's a calendar on their fridge. It says they're away on vacation for another week and a half. The house is ours."

Sam made a gleeful yelp. We all followed closely behind Caleb. I felt as though my senses were sharpened by my nervous energy, that I could hear and smell more acutely than usual. It was completely quiet inside, but still I listened for the fall and lift of a child's footstep, for the low rumble of voices in a distant room. The house smelled faintly of dirty laundry, like bedsheets that needed changing.

We entered a carpeted living room with big brown leather couches and bare white walls. The space struck me as under-decorated but also masculine, which was strange given the girly boots in the mud room. Where was the mother's touch?

"Whiskey, anyone?" Caleb asked.

He led us into the kitchen, glasses clinking on the counter, grabbing a bottle from the cupboard. We took the first pour as a shot, which burned all the way down. I much preferred the wine from a few nights before. He poured more whiskey and we sipped nervously. It was bizarre to be standing in a strange kitchen, the awareness that we were trespassing making me want to whisper, to tiptoe. But as the warmth of the drink spread within me, my head felt lighter and my body relaxed.

Caleb left us, busying himself with the sound system in the living room. Jake, Tom, and Sam looked at me, waiting for direction.

"Make yourself at home," I said, shrugging, then wandered down the hallway on my own. The boys suddenly felt like dead weight.

There was a dark office at the end of the hall and I turned on a desk lamp. Family photographs hung above the desk. A man and a woman with a baby. More photos of the same couple with a blonde toddler. But eventually, the family in the photos shrunk to two, just the father and daughter. I realized we were in the home of a widower whom I only vaguely knew of. The sense of a face. I wasn't sure we had ever spoken. Why would we have? I was a teenager with no connection to him or his daughter, or his dead wife.

His daughter had rosy cheeks and golden curls. She would be beautiful, like her mother. That would become difficult for him as she grew up.

There was music playing in the living room, but I wanted to stay in here alone a little longer. I sipped my whiskey and opened a few desk drawers, then rifled through them. He seemed to write a lot of notes to himself, to-do lists and reminders. I thought about what a struggle it must be for him, trying to hold everything together amidst the chaos of single parenting. One of the notes was a checklist (groceries, cupcake sale, laundry, book hair appointment, return library books) but only the first two items were checked off. I folded up the note and put it in my pocket.

I joined the boys back in the living room. They were sitting on one of the leather couches. Caleb sat on the couch arm, turned towards them.

"You should be listening to this kind of stuff," Caleb was saying. "This is the best music being made today. Someone in this house has excellent taste."

I didn't recognize the song. It was electronic-sounding, a male voice that went very high and then very low, stretching out the words so that the lyrics were hard to decipher. I found it strange but a part of me wanted to like it because Caleb did. Usually, I just listened to what the boys played, older stuff from the sixties and seventies.

I sat down on the floor, cross-legged.

"It's beautiful," Caleb continued. "But it's also intricate. There are references to literature and philosophy in the lyrics. It's not like that simplistic folk music we were listening to the other night. The music being made today is much more complex."

Jake looked down at his lap. I could tell he was uncomfortable.

"How do you know?" Sam asked. "About the philosophy references?"

"Well, you have to read the stuff," Caleb said. "You can't know it's there, buried in the songs, if you haven't exposed yourself to the original material."

Sam nodded pensively. None of us had read any philosophy.

"Did you study philosophy in school?" I asked.

"A bit," Caleb replied. "But I also read a lot on my own."

"School's pretty easy here," I said. "We don't really learn anything very difficult."

"That's a shame," Caleb said. "Challenge is what life is all about. We can't grow unless we're pushed. If you're not being challenged, you're not really living, are you?"

We answered the question with thoughtful silence. The truth of what he said felt profound. I realized I had been pushed very little in my life. Did that mean I wasn't really living?

"What are you reading now?" Tom asked.

"I'm a reading a book about climate change." Caleb splashed more whiskey into his glass. The bottle was nearly empty. I wondered if the widower would notice.

"What's that?" asked Sam.

"I know what it is," Tom said. "It's global warming."

"That's right," Caleb nodded, looking a bit like a teacher, patient and superior. "The average temperature of our climate is rising. Due to greenhouse gas emissions, the air and our oceans are getting warmer. That makes the ice caps melt and water levels rise. It's completely fucking with our weather systems. Haven't you noticed all the natural disasters recently? The tsunami, the crazy hurricanes? It's all connected to human activity."

It was 2005 and I had heard very little about this issue. I was impressed with how much he knew and the intensity with which he spoke. His whole face lit up while he talked. He gestured with his hands and I could see the boys were as impressed as me. Jake had looked up, gazing at Caleb with his mouth slightly open.

As the evening proceeded, Caleb continued to tell us about climate change, about the need to revolutionize our relationship with the natural world. How local measures mattered, and how we could still mitigate the problem, but we had to start now. He would later give us books on the topic, and other issues too. He scoffed at the spy novels I devoured, encouraging me to educate myself on the greater political and cultural realities of our world. He seemed to genuinely want to expose us to new ideas and change our understanding of ourselves.

That night, we mostly listened, asking questions only occasionally, allowing him to preach without interruption. I liked the sound of his voice and watching his hands move; I imagined them touching me. Holding my own hand again—the warm pressure of his grip, the startling intimacy of his fingers between mine—but also brushing my cheek, grazing my thigh.

⁊⚬⧉⚬⧉

There were more houses in the coming weeks. Caleb expanded our small world by opening up new spaces for us to explore, places that had always existed but that we had never considered. Now they were ours. We had crossed a psychic threshold, and soon felt entitled to the property of others.

We worked our summer jobs during the day and then we met up in the evening, hopping on our bikes and setting out on the near-empty roads with the sense of having a collective mission. Word of mouth in our little community helped us identify families on vacation and couples away for a long weekend, but Gaspereau was small. We soon had to branch out into neighbouring communities, where we looked for homes that were clearly second properties, modern structures owned by city people who came down to the valley only on weekends.

Some of the houses were unlocked, as if they wanted me to enter them; that's just the way it was back then. There had never been a real need to lock up because there was no real threat. The valley was a safe place full of trusting people. And if a house was locked, which the nicer, larger houses tended to be, we often found an open window and Sam's small size was ideal for squeezing through. Caleb could also pick locks in a pinch.

How the boys felt about our new evening activities wasn't something we spoke about. I could tell Jake had a hard time with it. He never looked fully comfortable—eyes flitting to the front door at the slightest sound, a glum reluctance to drink the alcohol we stole—and there were a few nights we had to convince him to join us. The four of us on his front step, awash in the light from the bare porch bulb, tempting him to come out and play, promising fun.

Tom, too, seemed hesitant in the beginning. Those first few nights I noticed him picking at the acne on his cheeks, opening scabs that had recently healed over, a sign he was feeling anxious. I grabbed his hand away more than once.

"It's okay," I said, squeezing his palm. "We'll be fine."

He nodded. He wouldn't have wanted to seem weak, and he soon stopped picking, distracted by the fun of it all. It was easy to trust Caleb. He was so confident, so at ease. He wouldn't let us get caught.

Sam didn't appear too bothered by what we were doing. He had always had a dark streak. I once caught him looking through Ruth's dresser drawers. I told him he was gross and he nodded but looked unashamed. Some part of him liked playing the deviant.

I didn't object to what we were doing either. I learned that breaking into homes was different from breaking into the winery. The transgression of a private space felt greater, and therefore more compelling. I took a deep, satisfied pleasure from invading the boundaries of personal spaces, uninvited.

I learned too that I preferred breaking into homes owned by people I didn't know very well. It allowed me to play detective, searching for clues about the inhabitants of a given property from what kind of clothing hung in their closets, what knick-knacks they chose to collect. I often took small souvenirs, like the widower's to-do list. It was never anything big or valuable. A fridge magnet, a single photograph. I liked keeping a record of where we had been, proof of our fun. I hid these souvenirs in the bottom drawer of my dresser and when I was alone at night, I spread the items out on my bed. Moths whirred at the screen on my window, attracted to my bedroom light. I examined each memento in detail, feeling strangely powerful.

෴

Our incursions were exciting but they were also how we got to know Caleb. Each night we spent with him, we seemed to discover another aspect of his unconventional world view. Caleb was intoxicating.

There was the house up on the South Mountain that belonged to an older couple who were away travelling. I could see they were hippies from their penchant for dream catchers and crocheted blankets, their yoga mats rolled up in the corner of the sunroom. They had very little furniture. They appeared to eat dinner sitting on the floor at a low, wooden table, which looked homemade and imperfect, roughly assembled.

In their fridge, I found Mason jars full of funky-smelling slaws and slimy noodle salads. They grew bean sprouts on the window-sill and seemed to drink copious amounts of green tea. I discovered half-drunk mugs all the over the house, the liquid cold and dark, developing an oily film on the surface.

I liked collecting these details, connecting snapshots of routines and proclivities to form stories about each home's inhabitants.

There was no booze at the hippie house. Caleb shrugged when Sam announced he had searched every cupboard and turned up nothing to drink.

"Let's do some yoga then," Caleb said.

"What?" asked Sam, confused.

"Yoga," Caleb said plainly. "It's a different high than alcohol, but it's just as good—maybe better."

We watched Caleb walk out to the sunroom, where he unrolled one of the yoga mats and slipped off his sneakers and socks.

"Coming?" he asked.

We stayed where we were, uncertain.

"You want to do yoga?" Sam asked. "Now?"

Caleb just laughed when we didn't move. He stood on the yoga mat and started reaching his arms over his head, bending at the waist, jumping back into a plank, and then gliding his chest forward.

Tom glanced at me, confused. Jake and Sam couldn't look away. It was the kind of thing you might laugh at, if someone else started doing it. But we were all silent, watching.

Caleb continued to move, pressing against the mat and floating his body into various elongated positions. He wore a T-shirt and shorts. The muscles in his arms and legs flexed with a strength that made me feel warm. The sun was low, flooding the windowed room with a rosy light. His skin glowed, luminous.

When he finished, he sighed deeply and turned towards us. None of us knew what to say. Jake was blushing. We had never seen a kid do yoga before, let alone a boy, but the confidence with which Caleb had pushed through the various positions was hard to sneer at. A part of me wanted to move like that too.

We would soon learn that Caleb not only practiced yoga every morning, he also went for hour-long runs every other day. He possessed a steadfast discipline that made us feel immature. He seemed grown-up and committed to self-improvement, both mental and physical. Caleb encouraged us to better ourselves in similar ways. He suggested Sam start lifting weights to bulk up his slender limbs. He instructed Tom to be religious about washing his face to prevent acne. He invited Jake on his morning runs and he gave me a reading list of literary fiction, more "nuanced" than what I usually read. The titles Caleb chose for me were lyrical and complex and as I read, I imagined the conversations we might have about them.

Since the night we'd danced in Jake's barn, Caleb had given no other sign that he might want me like I wanted him. Until one night a couple weeks later, when we were in a house owned by a local carpenter who was out of town. He'd built the house himself. The custom woodwork he'd done inside was beautiful and intricate. I was sitting next to Caleb at the kitchen table. We were all drinking and playing a card game. He rested his hand on my bare thigh, heavy and warm. I desperately wanted his fingers to move, to stroke my leg, to draw circles or a line upwards, and the anticipation was almost too much. But his hand stayed perfectly still until he removed it a few minutes later.

In response to this unfulfilled flirtation, I started having a new breed of dreams. The most vivid dreams I would ever have—Technicolor, pulsing—all featuring Caleb. Caleb standing in my room, watching me sleep. Caleb pulling my hair. Caleb kissing my eyelids. Caleb telling me I was smart, beautiful, perfect. Caleb telling me I was ugly, stupid, unworthy. Snapshots of possibility. In waking life, he gave me little sense of how he felt about me and my sleeping brain attempted to figure it out.

I awoke most mornings feeling agitated, unrested, and dissatisfied. Sleep and dreams, no matter how vivid, weren't enough.

"Do you think Caleb has a girlfriend?" I asked Tom the next day at work.

He looked at me. "Why?"

"Just wondering."

Tom considered. It was a hot, slow day, no one out picking berries. His feet were up on the table and he had crumbs in the corners of his mouth, remnants of lunch.

"Probably not," he said. "He moved across the country. Why would he keep a girlfriend back home?"

I nodded. That made sense.

"Do you think he ever had one?" I asked.

Tom frowned. "Do you like him or something?"

"I don't know. Why?"

"I don't think you're his type, Winnie."

"What's his type?"

"Dunno," Tom said. "But I don't think it's you."

We fell silent. There was no breeze, the air stifled by a fierce heat. You could hear the river in the distance. I was sweaty and wanted the workday to be over. Tom was being unnecessarily mean. I opened my book and ignored him.

"Since when are you boy crazy?" Tom asked, minutes later. His face was scrunched up, like he had smelled something foul. "I thought you weren't like that."

I kept my gaze on my book. "Don't be jealous, Tom. It's not a good look."

"I'm not jealous."

I laughed. "Sure."

"Whatever."

Tom stood up, then began wandering through the rows of plants. I watched him bend down and pick a few berries, popping them in his mouth. I shouldn't have been surprised by his reaction. There had been confusing moments in our friendship, and more of them lately, now that we were older. We'd kissed only once, when we were thirteen; I'd initiated it. We were up in his bedroom, reading after school. I leaned over and put my mouth on his out of pure curiosity: what did it feel like, to kiss someone?

I was surprised to discover his mouth had no taste. I noticed he closed his eyes as soon as our lips touched. Mine stayed open. His face was very close. It looked odd and lifeless in the dim light of his room, like a porcelain doll's or a ghost's.

I soon pulled away and returned to my book. Tom gazed at me for moment, then seemed to read the same page for a long time. I waited for him to say something, but was relieved when he didn't.

Since then, I would sometimes catch him looking at me in a particular way. Focused, his mouth closed, a slight frown. Like he was trying to figure out how I felt now that I had disrupted the boundaries of our friendship. Did I want to be more than friends? It would have been easy to try. Tom was good-looking and we obviously got along, but even before I met Caleb, I had a sense I was waiting for more.

⌘

In a bungalow not far from where I lived, Caleb started to reveal what he really thought of the valley. I knew the owners of the house, a local mechanic and a nurse, and their three young children. They were out of town for the weekend, camping in New Brunswick. They had asked Ruth to keep an eye on their property. A satisfying irony.

We sat at their kitchen table, drinking the mechanic's beer. It was pale and tasted pissy. I wished there was wine.

Caleb was drunk. He must have been drinking before we met up because he'd only had one beer with us, but his words blurred together and he wore a silly, sloppy grin.

"This is terrible," he said. "This is hillbilly beer, the cheapest you can get."

"Totally." Sam laughed. He was becoming a bit of a puppy, following Caleb around, and agreeing with everything he said.

"It's people like this who are the problem." Caleb gestured towards the walls of the kitchen, which were covered in outdated, flowery wallpaper. A picture of the kids on their dad's ride-on lawn mower was tucked under a magnet on the fridge. "They're the ones holding the valley back, keeping you all stuck. This could be a great place if people were willing to change."

"What would you change if you could?" I asked. I sometimes thought the valley was backwards too, but I was curious what Caleb would say.

"Everything! Take Jake's farm for instance." He pointed at Jake, who stared at his own hands. "No offense, but you don't seem to do anything particularly well there. You have sheep, you have chickens, you even have a fucking llama. You grow vegetables. But what is the focus? What is it that you're offering that's different from everywhere else? It seems to me every farm sells the same stuff, a random array of meat and vegetables, some grain, but no specialization. Again, I don't mean any offense, man. I know it's not *your* doing. It's just an observation. It seems to me it could be better."

Jake nodded with a grim smile, but why? Caleb was insulting Jake and his family. And what did Caleb know about farming anyway?

The boys and I remained quiet while Caleb took another large gulp of beer.

"That's just one example. There's also just a general laziness around here. No one seems willing to *do* anything. Why are the roads all crumbled to shit? Why isn't the wine world famous yet? Everyone's always talking about how good it is, but I get the sense no one's doing anything about it. No one's trying to grow the industry."

"I don't think that's true," Tom said. "Mac Elliott has always been an advocate for the valley. My dad told me he goes to international wine fairs in Europe, even."

"And why do we need to grow?" I asked, picking at the label on my beer, shredding it into little pieces. "Maybe the valley doesn't need to be big and famous. We have enough tourists as it is."

"That's another thing," Caleb said, laughing. "You all rely on the tourism industry but no one is willing to think like a tourist or cater to their needs. Take tubing, for instance. Why isn't there a shuttle for tubing on the river? This two-car nonsense is ridiculous. Tourists don't visit with two cars. There should be a bus or a van or something that takes people back and forth. It's a no-brainer, isn't it?"

"Dude," Sam said. "That's brilliant."

We all agreed. I didn't much like what Caleb was saying about the valley, and I felt especially protective of Jake and his parents, but he was right. There should be a shuttle. It made a lot of sense.

"You should suggest that at the community meeting," Tom said. "People would like it."

"Really?" Caleb smiled broadly. "When's the meeting?"

AFTER

꧁꧂

Before wine, it was apples. It was good for a while but then the market changed. That was before my time, but people here still talk about the shift, the downward spiral. I'm not sure when or how exactly, but big chain grocery stores were part of the problem, importing perfect, shiny apples from elsewhere, cheaper than those grown in our local orchards, but less fresh and not nearly as flavourful.

Because of that drop in demand, the apple growers couldn't earn enough to survive. That's when Mac stepped in with his vision. He saw potential, not in the trees but in the fields. *Look elsewhere*, he told them. *Grow something unexpected.*

Mac's grandfather was a fourth-generation farmer. Mac's father, a rebel, became a banker, so Mac inherited the land when he was just out of high school. He knew even then what he wanted to do. Grow grapes for wine.

People thought he was crazy. Wine in Nova Scotia? But Mac saw what others couldn't. Nova Scotia lies in one of the world's wine belts, on the same latitudinal line as Bordeaux. Plus, the climate of the Gaspereau Valley is similar to the Champagne district of France, making it perfect for sparkling wine.

They called Mac's land God's Palm and it was the envy of every farmer from here to New Brunswick. You could grow anything on that stretch of the valley, they said, and it would be the best crop you'd ever seen. Mac started growing grapes and to the surprise of everyone, they took. The magic of God's Palm persisted.

Mac was magic too. After he began production, he offered up sections of the land to others. He imagined a co-op of sorts, a main vineyard as a source of grapes for multiple wineries. Another local invested, deciding to put his lottery winnings to good use, and then they came from afar. Rich people from elsewhere in Canada and even some Europeans looking for a simpler life. We now have seven wineries in operation and some say we're making some of the best sparkling wine in the world.

That is, we *had*.

We *made*.

All of that is over now.

BEFORE

꧁꧂

aleb wanted us at the hall early. "We need to get good seats," he reasoned. "We need to be front and centre when we get our chance."

I noticed he did this a lot, referring to us collectively when discussing his own ideas. It was a way to share the mission, to make us feel that, together, we constituted a whole. It motivated us. We didn't usually attend community meetings—no kids did—but buoyed by the sense we were helping to carry out Caleb's plan, we went happily, thankful to be considered Caleb's collaborators. The alternative was perhaps the real motivating factor: exclusion from his orbit.

Inside the hall, Caleb groaned. "What the fuck?"

The room was almost full. Clearly, early wasn't early enough. Gaspereau folk looked forward to the next community meeting as soon as the last one was over. Highlighted on the calendar, circled, and underlined. There's just not much else going on. We grabbed four seats together near the back. Jake had to sit by himself, down the row a bit.

Caleb kept checking his watch. "Almost six thirty." He seemed eager for the meeting to begin.

"Don't count on anything in Gaspereau starting on time," I said. "It never happens."

Tom laughed. "Remember last year's Christmas breakfast? We didn't get our pancakes until mid-afternoon."

"Man," Sam said. "I was so hungry."

"Sam ate fifteen pancakes and puked in the snow," Tom explained.

"Where else was I gonna puke?"

"The toilet?" Caleb suggested.

We all laughed and Jake leaned forward down the row of seats. A long face, wishing he was in on the joke.

At 6:50 P.M., Angela took the stage. I had a theory the community worked together to stretch these events out as long as possible. Get there early, start late, let it take up your whole evening. A break from the television or yardwork.

"Evening, everyone," Angela began. "Thanks for coming out on a hot night. We've got a full agenda, so let's get started. First up, we've had some complaints about the new stop sign Rod Newton put up at the end of his driveway. I'd like to let Rod say a few words and then we'll open up the floor to discussion."

We heard all about Rod's new stop sign and then we had a report from Mac about wine tourism (our numbers were up from last summer by nearly twenty percent). We listened to Angela talk about the future direction of the *Gaspereau Gazette* (less local trivia, more 'Who's Your Neighbour?' profiles) and Sam dozed through a heated debate between Angela and Lawrence Buchanan, a rich local roofer with the largest house in Gaspereau, the beginning of which I can't recall. Something about ditch drainage and erosion.

"Now," Angela said. "A more serious item to discuss. There's been talk of a few break-ins this summer."

I elbowed Sam to wake him up, listening carefully.

"It seems folks are going away on vacation and coming back to find their homes messier than they left them. Dirt tracked in the house, books and CDs all over the place. Nothing reported stolen, from what I understand, but whoever is breaking in, they are drinking people's alcohol. My guess is teenagers."

I willed Caleb to glance at me, but his gaze stayed on Angela. Was he flustered by this? I hadn't thought anyone was on to us, but it suddenly made sense that they would be. We were usually tipsy when we left a house, and apparently not careful enough about covering our tracks.

"The police have been alerted but because nothing's been stolen or seriously damaged, they don't seem overly concerned. They wanted me to pass on a message that everyone should be extra vigilant about locking doors and windows, particularly if you're going away for an extended period. Please tell your neighbours who aren't here tonight."

Murmurs spread around the room. This news would be upsetting for many people, bursting the bubble of trust that had long encircled our community. Was our fun over? I hoped not. I liked that everyone was talking about what we'd done without knowing it was us. It made me want to do it again.

Next, Angela invited members of the community to ask general questions. Caleb's hand shot up immediately. Angela spied him at the back of the room.

"Yes? In the back?"

Caleb stood up. "Thanks, Angela. Some of you probably don't know who I am. My name is Caleb Graham. I recently moved to the area with my mother, Sylvia. We're in the Taylor house, up on Slayter Road."

A few heads in the room turned to get a better look. A teenager speaking at a community meeting was unheard of, but Caleb was a further curiosity because his family was somewhat mysterious. They had bought that huge house, they had come from away. No one understood what Sylvia did for a living. Caleb had told us his parents had founded a tech company that produced a device for reading electronic versions of books, but the locals didn't know that. They probably just noticed that she seemed to travel a lot. And where was the father? Who was this family, really?

"Yes, well. It's a beautiful area. We're still getting settled but we like it so far. I've made some friends." He gestured at us.

"Great," Angela said. "Glad to hear it. What's your question?"

"Well, the other day, I was tubing with my friends. We must have done four runs up and down the river that afternoon," Caleb said, smiling at the fabricated memory. We had taken him tubing once the week before and though he thought it was fun, he hadn't been interested in going for more than one trip down the river.

"After our forth run," he continued, "we debated whether we should go again. We were sitting near the bridge, you know, the end of the route, and a family was standing there holding their tubes. Two parents and two young kids, still wet from the river. Not locals, you could tell. They looked confused. They were looking around at the people piling into their cars, holding their tubes out the window. You know how it is. So Tom and I," Caleb said, putting his hand on top of Tom's head, who looked up, surprised, "we headed over. Asked them if they needed directions. *Directions?* No, what they needed was a *car.* They didn't know they'd need a ride back at the end of the run. They thought there must be a shuttle, some form of transportation to take them back to the start."

Caleb paused for effect. He was making up a story to sell his pitch. I watched Angela's smile sink into a small, perfect O. She was listening with full attention.

"We gave them a lift. Jake let them hop into his truck and we drove them back. It was fine, but it got me thinking. There *should* be a shuttle. A bus, or a van even. Something to take people back and forth. It would cut down on noise and traffic. You wouldn't have so many people parked on the side of the road down there by the bridge. I've heard folks say it's dangerous, and I agree. Someone could get hit if we're not careful."

Caleb paused again. I gazed up at him. His voice sounded different than it normally did; measured, almost pandering. No sign of the passion we were used to, that fire we all wanted to be near. He was adopting another approach. It struck me that Caleb knew how to read an audience, to adjust and perform accordingly. Clearly, there were many things I could learn from him.

"My friends and I," he said, "we think there should be a shuttle service. You could even charge a fee. Just something simple, so that you don't need two cars to go tubing. I'm sure lots of people here don't own two cars. Should they be denied the experience? I don't think so."

"Thank you for that, Mr. Graham. Thoughts?" Angela asked the group.

"It's a good idea," Mac spoke up. "I like it. It makes perfect sense to me and it'll be good for tourism."

"It *is* a good idea," Angela said, nodding. "But I'm not exactly sure how it would work. Who's gonna run this shuttle? Where will the van come from?"

"I could run it," Caleb said. "As a summer job."

"You have your license?"

"Of course."

"What about a van?"

Caleb blinked. "Isn't there money for that kind of thing? Or a community vehicle I could use?"

Angela laughed. It was hearty and patronizing, which surprised me. Angela had always seemed pretty mild, bland even. I noticed Caleb squeeze his hand into a fist.

"I wish, Mr. Graham. But no, not presently. No money for a van so you can make money for yourself."

I was impressed. Angela was being firm and a bit sassy.

"Making money isn't the point. Improving things around here is," Caleb shot back.

The crowd went dead silent. More heads turned, unsmiling faces. Caleb had taken the right approach in his speech, but his last comment was a mistake. The community was sensitive, allergic to critique. He had presented his idea as a good-for-all solution to an unacknowledged problem, which worked for this crowd, but he was now suggesting the community itself needed improvement. That was too harsh for them, too condescending. Jake may have accepted Caleb's criticism of his family farm that night in the bungalow, but this was a different crowd. They didn't need to impress Caleb.

Caleb flexed his hand and clenched it once more. His voice, however, stayed calm.

"It's just an idea," he said, softening, "but I think it's a good one."

Angela nodded. "It is a good idea but there are logistics involved. I'm not sure you've thought this through. Talk to us again if you can find a van. Any other questions tonight?"

Caleb sat down. His face was stony, his hand still closed in a fist.

§※§

After the meeting, there was coffee and dessert squares. I thought Caleb would want to leave the hall as soon as possible, his ego wounded, but he was firm: we should stay, at least for a few minutes. I guess he wanted to appear unruffled despite having just been shut down.

Tom and Jake and Sam and I stood off to the side, sipping weak coffee from Styrofoam cups. We watched Caleb speak to a few people and shake their hands. I wondered if he actually wanted to meet them. And if so, why? I might have been unlike most teen-agers but I still didn't care to socialize with anyone middle-aged. Perhaps, I thought, he was laying the groundwork to pitch his idea again later.

"I almost threw up when she said the police have been alerted," Tom said, voice low. "I thought we did a good job of cleaning up when we left."

"Has your mom said anything about it?" Tom asked Sam.

As police chief, Sam's mother, Lorraine, would know all about the break-ins.

"Nah. She doesn't tell me squat."

"Do you think they'll figure out it was us?" Jake asked. A deep worry line had emerged between his eyebrows.

I squeezed his arm. "No way. They have no reason to suspect us, and we'll be more careful from now on."

"From now on?" Jake asked.

"Well, yeah. I mean, next time. You don't want to stop now, do you?"

Jake looked pained but he said nothing. Sam raised his eye-brows, grinning maniacally.

I noticed Mac approach Caleb over by the cream and sugar. They spoke for a few minutes and then shook hands. Caleb looked pleased.

"Mac Elliott just offered me a job at his winery," Caleb said, joining us. "I start tomorrow morning. He said he liked that I think like an entrepreneur."

⟨≈⟩

I thought Caleb would let what happened at the meeting go. Mac's generous offer of a summer job was a win. He should have focused on that rather than his unrealized proposal for a shuttle. It shouldn't have been a big deal, but it became one.

We left the hall and biked towards Slayter Road under the clear night sky. A gentle breeze relieved the weight of the stifling nights that had come before. I felt an urge to go swimming, the tease of cool air making me crave the cold water. Being in the hall for hours had left me sweaty and restless.

But I swallowed my desire because Caleb was leading the way. I was having to do more and more of this lately, bending to his will instead of exerting my own to govern the boys, our daily routines. It was a difficult habit to break. I kept wanting to step out in front, to steer and manage. But I was okay with relinquishing my hold if it meant more adventures, more experiences. For now, at least.

I was thrilled when Caleb led us straight to his house instead. It felt like he was conferring on us a special privilege, finally inviting us into *his* home rather than a stranger's. We ditched our bikes in the driveway and climbed the front steps, silent. Caleb opened the red front door and led us inside. The house was even better than I had imagined. It had a grand entrance with a sweeping, carpeted staircase that led your eye upwards, made you wonder about the floors above you. All the rooms had tall ceilings and ornate crown moulding. The wood floors were warm and polished and there were several large fireplaces. The rooms themselves felt extravagantly Old World and smelled like a shop for rare books.

The only surprise was the decor. Modern furniture, all chrome and leather and harsh angles. It looked expensive and futuristic, clashing with the rest of the house. The artwork was also unexpected. Oversized pop art posters in bright shades of blue, red, and yellow like comic book illustrations. Standing in the living room, Tom and I exchanged a look. None of it fit. The sharp-cornered chairs, glass tables, and trendy posters seemed like awkward and temporary visitors in a foreign landscape.

"Mom," Caleb called. "My friends are here."

This was the third time he had referred to us as his friends, twice at the meeting and now. It flattered me to think he saw us this way. We weren't a mere convenience, neighbours to spend the summer with and then ditch once school started. He liked us enough to give us a name.

"In the kitchen," Sylvia called back, her voice low and velvety.

We followed Caleb through the house. The kitchen had a checkerboard floor and a large butcher's block island where his mother was standing, drinking from a mug with no handle. There was no book or magazine lying open before her, no radio on. I wondered what she'd been doing before we arrived. Her dark hair was tied back in a thick ponytail. She wore a linen dress like the last time I saw her, this one pale blue and semi-sheer, accentuating her tawny glow. I wished Ruth would dress this way. It was elegant and unassuming, seeking no attention from others.

"How was the meeting?" she asked.

"Pretty good, actually; I got a job."

Sylvia raised her eyebrows. "That's nice. Where?" Her voice was even, almost monotone.

Caleb told her about Mac's winery.

"Well, make sure you set an alarm so you're not late. I'm going to bed. There's iced tea in the fridge. Help yourself."

Sylvia drifted off, and I wondered how she felt about living here. Caleb had shared that his parents were newly separated. His father was still in Vancouver, at their old house. To move across the country, to leave a whole life behind—she must have needed a lot of distance.

Caleb poured us each a tall glass of iced tea. It was bitter and homemade, lacking the sweetness we were used to. Sam took a sip, made a face, and set it down.

"So," Caleb said. "What are we going to do about Angela?"

Tom and I had the next day off work. He came over after lunch and we lay on a blanket in the backyard to read, under the shade of a towering maple tree. I noticed he was reading one of the books Caleb had given him.

"'Phenomenology,'" I read from the cover. "What's that?"

"Still trying to figure that out." Tom frowned and we both laughed. "It's about consciousness, I guess. How we experience the world."

"Do you think we got the short end of the stick?" I asked. "Living here?"

Tom considered. "You mean, like, compared to Caleb?"

"Yeah."

"I dunno. He's much more informed about the world than we are, sure, but city life sounds toxic. All those people, the pollution. I would go crazy, I think."

Tom was already speaking like Caleb, whose influence had been swift and powerful. I wondered how much of an effect he'd had on me, if I was changing too.

A few hours later, we decided to bike to Mac's winery to check it out. We were bored and the day was nearly over. Maybe, we thought, Caleb would soon be finished his first day and we could all go for a swim.

I had only been to the winery once before, when Mac hosted an open house the previous summer. Tom and I had ridden our bikes over but ended up avoiding the celebratory crowd. Too much noise. Too many middle-aged bodies squeezed into jewel-toned capri pants. Instead, we'd hopped back on our bikes and cycled through the vineyard, stopping in the middle of God's Palm. It was one of our favourite places because it made us feel hidden and completely alone.

Today it wasn't nearly as busy. There were a handful of cars in the pebbled parking lot and I could see a few people inside the main building where Mac's team poured samples for visitors. The main building was actually a renovated barn. It had a modern look to it, minimalist and somewhat industrial. I wondered if Caleb would like it.

"Out there." Tom pointed.

We saw Mac, Caleb, and another worker out in the vineyard.

"Should we wait?" Tom asked.

"No. Let's go say hi."

We ditched our bikes and walked towards them. When Mac spotted us, he waved happily. They were standing with a girl named Tara. She had dark blonde hair tied back in a loose braid and wore colourful string bracelets on her bony wrists. Tara was a few years older than us, already out of high school. I knew her to say "hey," but I hadn't seen her much this summer. She nodded at me as we approached.

"Winnie, Tom, hi!" Mac said.

"How's your newest employee working out?" I asked.

Caleb gave me an irritated look.

"Pretty good. Today's been mostly about education, getting him familiar with what we do here. Tomorrow, the manual labour begins."

"Mac was just about to tell me about hand-picking the grapes at harvest," Caleb said.

"Mind if I continue?" Mac asked. "Don't want to bore you."

"Go ahead," I said.

"Hand-picking is incredibly important," Mac said. "Some wineries use machines to pick the grapes off the vine because it's much faster, but it's seriously detrimental to the quality of the wine. Our pickers are trained to leave behind the bad grapes, the moldy ones, or the ones the bugs got to. That means when you go to make the wine, you're starting with only the best fruit, the grapes you want. It's a form of quality control, really."

I thought about this. It made sense, and I loved knowing there were still places in the world where things were done in the traditional way, by hand, regardless of "efficiency."

"And with machine-picking, you risk getting other crap in your wine too," Tara added.

"Like what?" I asked.

"Basically, anything that hangs out in the vineyard," Tara said. "Mice, bugs, birds. All of that gets swept up with the grapes and it can actually end up in the tanks for the first grape pressing, stewing with the juice."

"That's disgusting," Caleb said.

"It's incredibly common," Mac said, scratching his head under his ball cap. "Especially at the large, corporate wineries. They're not careful because they don't have to be. Productivity is king. We're probably much slower by comparison but it's the only way, in my opinion."

"I'm vegetarian," Tara said. "It's important for me to know my wine isn't laced with dead animals."

Caleb laughed at that.

"It's all part of our low-intervention mission here," Mac said. "We don't use pesticides on our grapes and we don't add anything to our wine—no sulphites or extra sugar. Some places add that stuff to keep their wine consistent. They want every bottle of pinot to taste the same. We embrace inconsistency because we like to keep the process and the product as natural as possible. I think of wine as a living organism. As the winemaker, it's my job to nurture the life of a wine, not to corrupt or manipulate its expression."

Caleb nodded like he agreed.

"I think that's enough for today, Caleb. We'll pick this up again tomorrow. Winnie, do you have a minute?"

"Sure," I said, hanging back while Caleb, Tom, and Tara walked toward the winery.

"Do you know the Livingstons?" Mac asked me. "They're up on the South Mountain, near the lake."

"I don't think so. Maybe?" I was suddenly scared. Had we broken into their house? Is that what this was about?

"Well, their son is sick. Terrible thing. Only eight years old. Nothing they can do but make him comfortable. I'm organizing a charity auction for them. Gathering donations and such. All the money will go to them. They've had to take a lot of time off work, of course."

"That *is* terrible," I agreed, though I was relieved.

"Is Ruth home today? I've called her a couple times but no answer. I thought I'd drop by and see if she might be willing to donate a painting for the cause."

I smiled, seeing an opportunity. I liked Mac. He was a good man and he had a cool job. He could make Ruth happy, if she let him.

"Yes, she is home," I said. "All evening, I think. If she's not in the house, she'll be out in her studio. Don't hesitate. Just knock on the barn door. She'll be happy to help, I'm sure."

Mac smiled. "Fantastic!"

I knew I'd get in trouble with Ruth later, but I didn't care.

"You know what? She's been saying lately she wants to be better about helping others. Why don't you ask her to help you put the auction together? She throws a great party."

"You think she'd want to?"

"Sure. Why not?"

I imagined Mac knocking on her studio door. Her surprise, followed by annoyance. The two of them at the hall, arranging donations for auction. Ceramic mugs and Mona's beeswax candles and jars of preserves, gleaming like jewels. The two of them smiling at each other, Ruth really seeing him for the first time. Mac reading the paper at our kitchen table. Mac pouring Ruth his latest wine. Mac saying, "good morning" and "good night" and "you doing okay, Winnie?"

"That's just great!" Mac said, beaming. "Thanks!"

⁊⊗⁊⊗⁊

After we left the vineyard, Caleb didn't want to go for a swim. He shook his head at my suggestion, told us he needed to deal with Angela.

"Today?" I asked. We were still standing in the parking lot of the winery.

"What do you want to do exactly?" Tom asked, a quiver in his voice.

"I'm not sure yet. But I overheard her talking last night. She's away today, in the city. It's a good opportunity to get to know her better."

He was looking at me when he said it, as if he knew what I liked best about our forays into breaking and entering.

"Should we wait for Sam and Jake?" I asked.

"No," Caleb said. "I don't know when she'll be home. She's only gone for the day. Let's make the most of the time we have."

He asked if we knew where she lived and be both nodded. It wasn't far.

The day turned overcast, the air thick. The heat of the pavement made our tires sing. I could smell Caleb sweating next to me on his bike. The spice of a warm body like pepper or cumin.

I was feeling less excited than I had in the past about what we were about to do. Today felt more like work than fun, an obligation dictated by Caleb. The end goal was revenge, which seemed daunting and unnecessary because I didn't even really dislike Angela.

Tom also looked uncomfortable. He kept glancing over at me to get my attention. I tried to reassure him by looking straight ahead, pretending nothing was out of the ordinary, but I'm not sure it helped.

"Angela's retired?" Caleb asked us. "What did she do for a living?"

I tried to remember.

"Was she a teacher?" I asked Tom. She seemed like a teacher. I imagined her standing officiously at the front of a classroom, holding a piece of chalk in one hand.

"No, she was a lawyer," Tom said. "She worked for the government, I think. She lived in Ottawa before she moved here."

"Does she have any kids?" Caleb asked.

"Don't think so," Tom said. "I've never heard her talk about kids."

"No relationship either? Was she ever married?"

"Why do you want to know all of this?" Tom asked.

He shrugged. "It might be useful."

I wondered about Caleb's questions. He seemed almost obsessed, searching for a key piece of information. The night before in his kitchen he had wanted to know if Angela had any enemies in the community. We'd shrugged. We didn't think so. No one really had enemies around here. But Caleb made a point of collecting those kinds of details about people. He was always asking questions, looking people over and then finding a way into them. Maybe I was doing something similar when I looked through people's belongings in their homes.

Sweating, we biked up the hill on the other side of the river. A flashy red car with silver stripes sped by, squealing past us in a cloud of exhaust. I noticed a tanned arm resting out the open window.

"Fuck you!" Caleb yelled, coughing.

When we arrived at Angela's small green house, my legs were tired and heavy. I hated hills, especially when it was hot. I wouldn't have biked there for anyone else but Caleb. Realizing this made me uneasy. I wanted to be around him all the time, but I didn't always like the effect being around him had on me. The yellow flowers in Angela's window boxes hung their heads, depressed by the heat. Sweat bloomed on my chest and I craved a glass of water.

We walked our bikes to the back of the house, leaning them against the green siding. Caleb was already trying windows and the back door to see if they were open, but none were. Angela was from away. She'd probably locked her doors even before the recent news of our break-ins.

Caleb figured he'd be able to pick the lock on the sliding glass door that led to her deck. While he fiddled with the pin, I looked around. Angela's garden was lush but tidy and well maintained. Plenty of gorgeous flowers bursting out from neatly edged beds. She had worked hard on this. I didn't see a single stray weed.

"Got it!" Caleb said, unlocking the door. Immediately, I felt a tingling in my hands. We shuffled inside. We were in Angela's kitchen. It was small and clean, completely odourless. Nothing on the countertops and no magnets on the fridge. I had never seen a kitchen like this before: so carefully attended to, it appeared staged.

Caleb took off immediately down the hall. My instinct had been right: today wasn't about fun. He had a mission. I felt a strange urge to take off my sneakers, to set them on the mat. I took the time to unlace and remove.

"What are you doing?" Tom asked me urgently. He'd kept his own sneakers on.

"I don't know," I said. "It's just so nice and clean."

I usually found bare, clean kitchens depressing. Our kitchen at home was the opposite. It was lived-in, a focal point of the house that showed its wear. There were always a few flecks of food on the counter you couldn't catch with a sponge. An overflowing fridge, a crowded fruit bowl. The dishtowels used so often they never hung neatly from the oven door handle.

Overly clean kitchens often seemed sterile to me, suggestive of people dieting and counting calories, being cautious with the salt. But I didn't get that from Angela's kitchen. Instead, it made me think about what it would be like to live alone. The thought calmed me. It seemed to be an uncomplicated way to live and satisfying—maybe even empowering. At home, I was always negotiating Ruth's energy, competing with her effect on me and our space. Angela didn't have to do any of that.

I opened the fridge, peered inside. It had enough food for one. Vegetables in the crisper, a lone piece of salmon on one of the shelves. She drank whole milk and had two bottles of maple syrup, perhaps because she feared running out. There was also a plastic container of leftovers. I opened it up. Beef stir fry, slick with soy sauce.

"When did he say she'd be home?" Tom asked.

"I don't know. I don't think he did," I answered.

"This feels wrong."

I ignored Tom, wandering into the living room next. It was more cluttered than the kitchen. There were big books open on the coffee table, a throw blanket askew on the couch. On the mantle, there sat a series of framed photographs. Two young girls; an old man in a tuxedo; a woman wearing a beautiful pink coat. They must have been Angela's family. I could tell from their teeth: large, just like hers.

As Tom wandered off to find Caleb, I sat down on the couch to examine the open books. They were all gardening books, with sticky notes marking certain pages. As I flipped through one of the books, I found a piece of paper stuck inside with a meticulous, hand-drawn garden map. Every flower in her garden had been plotted out and planned in advance. It was drawn with such care and I was surprised by how beautiful I found it. I had never thought much about Angela, about her private life, or that she, too, might have passions and interests.

I looked up at the sound of Tom and Caleb rushing down the hall.

"We gotta go!" Tom said.

"What?"

"She just pulled in the driveway!"

Caleb was smiling, but Tom was pale.

The boys slipped out the back door while I struggled with my sneakers. My palms were sweating, the laces slipping. I could hear a car door closing. She'd be in the house any minute.

I opened the back door just as I heard her key in the front lock, then slid it closed behind me and crept around the back of the house. Caleb and Tom were waiting, already on their bikes.

"She's in," I whispered. "Let's go!"

We continued around the side of the house, heads bent in a silly attempt to appear smaller. The only way out was down the driveway, visible from the front windows. We would have to risk it, and hope she wasn't looking outside.

We went as fast as we could, pedalling and then coasting. I resisted the urge to turn my head and look back at the house.

༺❦༻

When I arrived home later that evening, Ruth was drinking vermouth on the front step, flipping through a magazine. The ice clicked in her glass as she raised it to her lips, pretending she didn't hear my footsteps. I felt grimy, dried sweat making me itch. I still hadn't had my swim. A cold shower would have to do. I sat down next to Ruth and took off my dusty sneakers.

"Hi," I said.

She gazed at me for a moment. She looked unhappy.

"What do you think you're doing, sending Mac Elliott to my studio?"

"Oh." I had forgotten. "It's for charity."

"You know I find him annoying."

"Yes, but I don't understand why." I stretched my arms overhead and then leaned back, resting on my elbows. "I was at the winery today picking up Caleb. Do you know they're a totally organic operation? He doesn't use pesticides, and he speaks so beautifully about the wine. He calls it a 'living organism.'"

Ruth ignored me, turning a page.

"What painting did you give him for the auction?"

She sighed. "The new one."

"The one with all the green?"

"That's one way of describing it."

"Why are you so mad?"

She looked up at me. "Giving him a painting is fine, but did you have to sign me up to plan the damn party?"

"I thought it would be good for you," I said, shrugging.

"I'm the parent. You're the kid. I decide what's good for the both of us."

I knew better than to respond, but what she was saying was laughable. How often had I taken care of myself while she was off with some slimy guy in the city? How often had I reminded her that it was garbage day, or that a bill was past due? I thought about Angela and how she got to return home to an empty house every day. To complete quiet and peace.

Ruth drained her glass and stood up. "You should shower," she said. "You smell."

I rolled my eyes as she walked away. She looked ugly when she was being mean.

AFTER

꧁꧂

The hall parking lot is already full. Paul Roberts stands at the entrance wearing a neon vest and shaking his head. He waves Ruth and me up the road, where others have parked their cars on the shoulder. Paul is one of those people who has probably never left the valley and will most certainly die here. He used to scare me as a child. The way he formed words as if with his hands, groping, searching, his tongue rolling around in the darkness of his mouth like a slug. He didn't finish high school and he's never had a real job. He still lives with his parents, Joann and Charlie. A housewife, a plumber.

"Morning, Paul," Ruth says, and he nods his head with his eyes closed, only opening them when Ruth and I have passed, watching us walk away.

"How old is he?" I whisper.

"Not now, Winnie."

In his thirties, I'd say, but it's hard to tell. Paul will never grow up. He'll look the same until he doesn't and then he'll be grey and hunched over and no longer our boy-man-about-town. Volunteering for this and that, stepping in whenever we need someone to do what no one else wants to. I hope when he dies, it's peaceful, in his sleep. Maybe even on the same day as his mother—otherwise, who would care for him?

Inside, the hall is packed and warm. The smell of coffee and body odour choking the air. We're wearing jackets and scarves but we take them off immediately, folding them over our arms, scanning the room for empty chairs. We're surrounded by people we've known forever but all of them look unfamiliar, confused and overly polite. How does one act? What does one say? They grasp cups of weak coffee and flash brief, uncertain smiles whenever someone says hello.

Chairs have been set up in untidy lines. Mac is sitting in the front row. He waves us over and we make our way through the crowd.

"Morning, morning," Ruth mumbles for both of us as we push past, everyone staring.

Mac grabs us both into a tight hug and I hug back with my eyes closed, trying to offer him some kind of comfort. He's teary when we pull away. We sit down and Ruth puts her hand on his thigh and squeezes.

We sit and wait. For whom, I'm not sure. Who will speak? What will be said? I force a cough.

"You okay?" Ruth asks.

I nod and lift one shoulder, a half shrug.

I hate sitting at the front, feeling everyone's eyes on us—even more so today. They all know. They all feel for Mac. I turn in my seat, look around the room. Sam and Jake are there, at the back, and through the crowd I see Tom's face in the doorway. Our eyes meet and I think his are saying sorry. About time. I blink and turn back around, feeling a bit smug.

Sam's mother, Lorraine, is on stage in her uniform. "Good morning, good morning," she says. "Please, take a seat if you can. I know it's full up. Find a seat if there's one to find." She pauses while the group settles.

I don't know Lorraine very well. Before she made chief, she used to come to the town events, but always on duty. Her mouth a straight, fuchsia line, her hands tucked into her belt. Sweating, usually—that uniform in the heat. She takes her job seriously and she seems to work all the time.

I remember once she came to a New Year's Eve party at our house. It threw me off to see her with a drink in her hand, sitting on the couch and laughing easily at something Jake's father had said. I don't think I had ever seen her sitting down before.

I've been going over to their house since I was ten years old, but she's never really warmed to me. Maybe she thinks it's odd, Sam hanging out with a girl, or maybe, as a police officer, she detects the part of me that likes breaking into houses.

Today, she stands tall like we need her to. She's not a tall woman but she has a powerful presence, seeming to inhabit more space than she actually takes up. She pushes her blonde hair out of her face, sweat shiny on her forehead.

Lorraine looks around and then speaks. "Okay. Everyone good?"

A few people nod.

She clears her throat, "We're gathered here today—" She stops and I resist a smile. She starts again. "We're here today because we've been struck by tragedy."

She pauses and clears her throat, as if considering her words. She must be nervous.

"We're here because of the loss our community suffered last night. I was asked to make a statement. Okay. I can do that." She glances briefly at her notes. "Today at 12:05 A.M., we received a call. A fire was reported on the River Road, around the area of God's Palm and the Elliott Winery. The fire department was already on their way. The flames spread quickly. It took five hours for the fire department to calm the thing down. Many of you were there. Thank you for showing up to help, but in the future, please listen to us when we tell you to stay back and go home. These are dangerous situations we're dealing with and it's our job to assess the level of danger. We have your best interests in mind, and you would do well to listen to us."

She waits a beat so that her point sinks in. I hate this about her, how she always finds a way to bring it back to procedure. The proper process and regulations. These people don't need rules. They need hope.

"At this time, we are investigating all possibilities. This means the area of God's Palm is a crime scene. Please do not cross the yellow tape at any point, as this will jeopardize our investigation. We all know what this fire means. We all know how many of us it affects. Let us do our work and find some answers."

She is finished but we don't know it. We all expect something more. She stands in silence and we wait for a comfort that never comes. Lorraine is not the reassuring type.

"Questions?" she says finally.

Angela speaks up first, our community journalist. She has her notebook open on her lap, a pen at the ready. All of this will appear in the next issue of the *Gazette*. "What are we talking in terms of damage, Lorraine?"

Lorraine jumps at the question, seemingly relieved to stick to the facts. "The agricultural land known as God's Palm constituted the main path of the fire. About 120 acres, all of which has been used to grow grapes for the last twenty or so years. Mac Elliott tells me the crop has all been destroyed. That means the grape crop for four of our seven wineries. The Elliott Winery itself also suffered damages. The main building, including the tasting room, an equipment room, the wine cellar, and the workshed were all destroyed by the flames."

The room falls into indistinct murmurs.

"Does this have anything to do with the recent break-ins?" someone asks.

"We're not sure yet," Lorraine responds, and I can feel frustration building in the hall, in the disappointed chatter moving around the room. These people came here for answers, but she's only telling them what they already know.

I am shocked to hear Tom's voice rise above the rest. "And this was definitely arson, Lorraine?"

I turn around in my seat. He has entered the room now, shouldered his way in so he can be heard. His voice sounds grown-up, like that of a man. The way he said her name. *Lorraine.*

"Nothing is definite," Lorraine responds. I notice she doesn't move her head much, not to nod or shake. It stays still, level. "We are investigating all possibilities."

"Any idea who did it?" someone else yells. They sound angry.

Lorraine shakes her head. "We are investigating all possibilities."

BEFORE

꧁ꕤ꧂

We fell into a rhythm. All five us now had summer jobs, keeping us busy during the day. When work ended we would reconvene, hours of freedom stretching before us. Caleb said we should lay low for a while, wait until everyone calmed down a bit about the break-ins before starting up again. I was disappointed, but I also knew he was right. I continued to follow where he led. Tom and Jake seemed relieved.

The boys and I often picked Caleb up from work at the winery. I liked crossing paths with Mac, who continued to speak passionately, telling us about winemaking. He taught us about the different grapes in his vineyard, how grapes for red wine darkened from shades of red to purple and even black as the fruit matured. Grapes for white wine were mostly green and yellow but could also be grey. All the grapes looked somewhat cloudy, covered in a waxy, translucent film.

Mac encouraged us to try the different grapes. They were bitter, tart and acidic on the tongue.

"Still a lot of ripening needed," Mac said, laughing at how my mouth puckered.

One day he took Caleb, Tom, and me into his cellar and showed us his latest experiment. It was called a pétillant naturel, pét-nat for short, which Mac explained translated from the French to "natural sparkling."

"This is an unusual method for sparkling wine," Mac said in the chilly, dark cellar. "Some people say pét-nat is the original way to make sparkling wine, perhaps a happy accident that occurred centuries ago."

We stood next to large wooden barrels full of aging wine lining the cellar's stone walls. At the back of the room, there was a case of wine and a few lone bottles on a table, and a shelf above with glasses. It took a moment for our eyes to adjust to the low-lit cellar.

"Typically," Mac continued, "sparkling wines undergo two fermentations. We ferment the wine in a tank, bottle it, and then add extra yeast and sugar. The yeast eats the sugar, leading to a second fermentation. That creates carbon dioxide in the bottle, which gets trapped, producing the bubbles we associate with sparkling wine." As he spoke, Mac lifted a bottle from a box to show us. "But with pét-nat," he said, "we only ferment once. We actually bottle the wine before the first fermentation is finished. No extra yeast or sugar. We let the wine sit, continuing to ferment, and the bubbles form. It's a low-intervention process. You don't really know what you're going to get at the end. It's completely unpredictable, but that's what I like about it."

Mac led us toward the table at the back of a cellar and opened the bottle in his hand. I noticed it had a metal cap rather than a cork. It popped loudly as he pried it open, the wine inside fizzing out the top.

He grabbed a wine glass from a shelf on the wall and poured a little for us to see. It was cloudy, a rosy-orange colour, bubbles flickering in the glass.

"See how it's a bit murky?" Mac asked. "That's not unusual for a pét-nat because it's often an unfiltered wine. There's a real funkiness to it. It has personality."

"Can I taste it?" Caleb asked.

Mac considered. Caleb had told us his work at the winery took place mostly outside. Mowing the lawn, raking between the rows of vines, tending to the flowers. Mac had him laying patio stones and shovelling pebbles for a new stretch of driveway. Nothing to do with the actual wine because Caleb was underage.

"No, I shouldn't," Mac said. "But you can smell it."

Tom and Caleb both smelled the wine. Tom made a funny face and then passed it to me.

I inhaled deeply. The smell surprised me. Funky was the exact right word for it. I smelled something bright and tangy, cut through with a bitter edge. Grapefruit maybe?

"I get grapefruit," I said, smelling more. "But there's also something in it that reminds me of soil, like clay or—rocks?"

"Rocks?" Caleb asked, skeptical.

"No, she's totally right." Mac looked delighted. "There's a minerality at the base of this wine that gives it an earthy body. I'm amazed you can smell that, Winnie. That's incredible! You have quite the nose."

I took a sip of the wine, delighted by Mac's praise. It was fizzy and sour and layered on my tongue. I tasted grapefruit and that lingering mineral flavour but also something floral, reminiscent of apple blossom. I immediately wanted more but I resisted.

"Sorry," I said. "I couldn't help myself."

Mac took the glass back, but he was still smiling. Just then, I felt a hot rush of envy. Caleb's job at the winery was so much more interesting than my own: familiar summer days at the U-pick, where I never learned anything new.

༺ꕥ༻

After work each day, we were faced with a decision: how to spend our free time. Before Caleb, this wasn't an issue. Tom and I liked to read in the shade and Sam and Jake often threw a baseball back and forth or fished in the river near my house. We all ended up going for a lot of swims, and of course there was tubing and biking. But Caleb grew bored easily. He always wanted to *do* something, and it had to be different from what we did yesterday. This need both annoyed and fascinated me. I was comfortable with our summer aimlessness and I didn't like having to come up with new ideas to entertain Caleb. But I also wondered what it would be like to always want more from life. To expect variety and excitement as a given. Was that an appetite he was born with, or could I wake up tomorrow and decide to live the same way?

The summer before, the boys and I had taken to playing a particular game every night. We called it Spotter. You played at dusk. The house (usually mine or Tom's) was the foundation of the game. Everyone but the spotter hid somewhere on the property. The spotter then took two walks around the perimeter of the house. While walking, the spotter had to keep close to the building. At each of the corners of the house, the spotter was allowed to stop and look around, standing in one place, scanning the yard for whoever was hiding. On the second walk around the house, those hiding had to try to run back to home base (usually the front door) without being seen by the spotter. When everyone was back at home base, the spotter divulged who had been glimpsed and where. The first person the spotter had detected was the spotter for the next round.

When we played the game with Caleb, he was underwhelmed. He didn't like all the rules, which he thought were arbitrary and silly.

"Why twice?" he asked flatly. "It seems like a game for little kids."

It probably was, but I realize now that that's why I liked it. I think I encouraged the boys to keep playing games like this because I thought it would keep them innocent, like they always had been, the opposite of the jocks at school.

To satisfy Caleb's restlessness, we found ourselves moving outward, beyond Gaspereau, looking for ways to keep our new friend entertained. We became desperate to prove we were worthy of his company.

We took him to the empty beaches under the cliffs of Blomidon where the water is ice-cold and the rocky bluffs loom above, casting long shadows on the beach. We watched the tide change while we ate a picnic packed by Ruth, the water swiftly receding and beaching a lone fishing boat. I expected Caleb to remark on how the beach had nearly doubled in size in the hour since we got there, the tide ebbing farther and farther out, but he offered no indication that he was impressed by this natural phenomenon. After lunch, we dashed into the ocean for a quick, bracing swim, feet stained ruddy from running in red sand.

We took him on hikes through dense woods and up our mountains, Caleb leading the way on trails he didn't know.

We invented new projects, which we would never finish. We tried to fix up the shed at the back of Sam's house, envisioning it as a hideout of sorts, a fort or a clubhouse. But Caleb grew bored after three days of sweeping and hammering, deeming it "childish," unworthy of our time. I understand now these comments probably embarrassed the boys, and whether he knew it or not, Caleb was already planting seeds to turn them against me. I was the one who had pressured them to remain boys, after all. Untainted by what I considered the degradations of adolescence.

The auction was a week away and Mac and Ruth were hard at work. To my frustration, they still weren't working much together. They made a list of donations to pursue and then Ruth divided it in two.

She spent a lot of time on the phone. Calling to confirm the donations, making sure they would arrive on the right day.

"How's it going?" I asked her.

She waved me away like I was a housefly, dialling another number. She frowned in the yellow light of the kitchen.

I had hoped she would have been converted by now, that she would have begun to see just how lovely Mac really was. It wasn't hard with the other men. All they did was ask her to dinner, flash a smile. It didn't take much to get her out, to get her giggling: the promise of sparkling wine, oysters. I thought if she spent enough time with Mac her feelings about him would change, but so far it seemed they had barely interacted.

She hung up the phone. "Goddamn Mac Elliott."

She mostly cursed him and always with both names, Mac Elliott. A mechanism for keeping him at a distance; he was not a close friend, and there was no intimacy between them.

"Everything going okay with the auction?"

She sighed. "Yes. Despite Mac Elliott's attempts to sabotage the whole thing. He has some strange ideas about how to throw a party."

"No one throws a party like you," I tried, offering her a compliment. I had decided I needed to take control of the situation. If I wanted Ruth to end up with Mac, I would have to proceed like Caleb, carefully reading the people around me and subtly nudging them in new directions.

"True," she smiled. She paused, looking down at the list of names in front of her. "I just hope this whole thing goes well."

"It will. Don't worry."

"How's your handsome friend settling in? He's working with Mac, right?"

My handsome friend. Why did that bother me?

"Good, I think. He and Mac have a lot in common in terms of personal philosophy."

"How do you mean?"

"Well, Mac's all about natural and organic with his winery," I said, seeing an opportunity. The more I learned about Mac's work, the more I liked him. Maybe Ruth needed to be exposed to Mac's core values too. "And Caleb is a bit of an environmentalist. Mac was telling us about terroir the other day. Do you know about that?"

Ruth shook her head absently, looking down at the list of names again. I feared I had lost her. I attempted to win her back by mimicking Mac's tone.

"It's a French term. It refers to the entire environment in which grapes are grown. The soil, the climate, the animal and plant life that surround the vineyard. All of that has an effect on the flavour of the wine. A Nova Scotia wine tastes different than a wine made in Bordeaux. Those unique geographical characteristics are the terroir of the wine. So, if you farm organically, you're making a choice about the environment and having a profound effect on the wine."

I sat down across from her, aware that I sounded a bit like an ad as I spoke to her bent head. "Mac says organic wine isn't only better for you, it has a more complex flavour."

Still, it was easy to be animated because I found it genuinely interesting. But Ruth stared up at me now, blank-faced.

"You're starting to sound like him," she said.

"Caleb?"

"No, Mac! Wine this, wine that. Isn't my vineyard special? Blah, blah, blah."

I sighed quietly. I was going about this the wrong way, trying to win Ruth over by parroting Mac's enthusiasm, which sounded awkward coming from me. Maybe Ruth liked the rich men from the city *because* they were vapid, lacking depth. She could drift along the surface, with no expectation of true intimacy or commitment. The truth was, I could see why that would be attractive. Despite my own feelings for Caleb, I was uncomfortable with the idea of a relationship. To be someone's girlfriend seemed too restrictive and binding. I didn't want that.

But it would be good for Ruth to settle down a bit. We might have the same instinct for independence, but she needed to be taken care of in a way I didn't. I would be leaving home in a couple of years, and I worried about her being alone. She needed someone to manage life so she could mess it up again, having fun, making art. Her wildness needed a container.

When I came home from work the next day and saw a vintage sports car in the driveway, I was angry. It was cream-coloured and warm to the touch. Ruth's studio door was ajar. I heard her voice, then that of a man. Laughter, exclamation, then long, mysterious, infuriating pauses.

I hated that I wasn't succeeding at my matchmaking plan. I wanted to prove to myself I could be as manipulative and clever as Caleb. I fingered the change in my pocket, making it jingle. I selected a penny and held it up, looking at its dull face. I hesitated, swallowing, but then I imagined Caleb standing next to me, watching. I reached out and scratched the penny against the car, above the right rear tire. It left a mark like a gash, dark and jagged.

⚜

By the night of the auction, I had decided to act. I had waited long enough for Caleb to make a move. It was unlike me to be so passive.

Scratching that man's car had reminded me how gratifying power could be. It was time to make a bold gesture.

I assumed Caleb knew how I felt. That I dreamed about him, imagining his hands on my body and mine on his. I wondered constantly what he was thinking, how he was feeling, and I was sure he could tell. He knew so much about everyone, it seemed.

But if he knew, what did that mean? Surely, if he wanted me at all, he would have acted by now. He wasn't one to hold back. The thought of his rejection terrified me, but also made me want him even more.

There had been enough signs to suggest he was interested that I remained hopeful. When we spoke just the two of us, his hands were always finding my body's most sensitive areas. The back of my neck; the inner line of my thigh; even, once, my ear lobe. These touches were so light, they could have been accidental, but that ambiguity itself felt intentional, like a tease.

I remember the first time I ever felt something sexual. The boys and I were watching a movie at my house. Ruth was out in the studio painting, though she wasn't the type to restrict what I watched anyway. Were we twelve? Thirteen? It was a typical serial killer flick. He was the bad guy and she was the detective, but you didn't know he was the bad guy yet. Maybe he was a detective too? The details are muddled and unimportant. What I remember most was the one scene.

She was in her hotel room. It was raining, at night. Dark windows and the glint of headlights on a soaked street. She was wearing a silk robe. She had thick brown hair and pouty lips. She didn't look like a real detective. He knocked on the door twice. Two meaningful raps. She knew who it was, and we did too. She turned the handle and she was in his arms. The same movement, the same moment. He picked her up and shoved her onto a table. It wasn't loving or soft. It was hard and fast. He untied her silk robe, the belt falling away. Weightless, forgotten. We saw one of her breasts. We heard her moan. She looked in pain, mouth open, gasping. I remember thinking *that is pain I want*. He was pushing into her and she accepted all of it, all of him. It was desperate and full of need. Briefly, it made me want to need.

We were all very quiet, the boys and I. No one laughed or made a stupid joke. I wondered if they felt what I felt.

The movie ended and the boys left. I could think only of the detective and the killer. His strength, and hers. I had felt, watching, that there was power in desire, in giving into it. Giving over, accepting lust and hunger. That it could be a kind of strength.

I couldn't stop thinking about them, lying awake that night. Her hand holding tight to the table. Her long legs, spread open, hugging him to her. It made me squirm. It made me hot. Thinking of it again, I pushed a pillow between my legs.

That's how Caleb affected me. I had never wanted anyone else; there had never been anyone else worth wanting. My boys, the kids at school: no one. But now, aching, wishing. A crushed pillow.

The night of the auction, I wandered into Ruth's room. The top of her dresser was a mysterious assortment of diminutive jars and bottles, all containing oils, serums, and creams claiming a different purpose: anti-aging, decongesting, plumping, smoothing. Ruth used them all. I had watched her applying thin, translucent layers of liquid, glistening damp until her skin drank them up. She had extensive routines for morning and evening, and I marvelled at her discipline. It was all quite exotic and confusing to me. I was a splash-and-go kind of girl and didn't wear makeup. I couldn't be bothered with all that time and effort.

When I was younger, I had spread one of Ruth's oils all over my face. It smelled of coconut and made my cheeks glisten. I turned my face back and forth in the light to admire my new glow. The next day, I awoke to a constellation of angry pimples on my chin.

"Not on your face," Ruth told me, shaking her head. "*Never* on your face. This one is for your legs after you shave them."

I decided to try one of Ruth's perfumes. I had read that men and women were naturally attracted to each other's odours but I feared my scent had had no effect on Caleb. A part of me knew I was buying into the same lie believed by so many women: the cruel delusion that simply being was not enough. Enhancement was required.

I didn't like that message, but it was worth a try.

Ruth had many perfumes, all for different occasions. I was drawn to the one that smelled of jasmine. It seemed feminine but not too girly. I spritzed it on the insides of my wrists as I had seen Ruth do and rubbed them together, then against my neck. I didn't hate it. I fluffed up my hair in the mirror, wondering if Caleb would notice.

This was not like me. I had never before even had a crush. I had never looked at a real-life boy as anything more than a friend. I knew I liked boys—I was attracted to male faces and bodies in movies and in magazines—but I had begun to think that true female desire was a myth, that what I had seen in that detective movie was make-believe. Maybe women were faking sexual appetite because it was just easier to play along.

I could see that men wanted women. Really, truly wanted them. I saw it in my friends. I saw it in the men that fell for Ruth. That hungry look, a thumping kind of need. But I hadn't seen the same lust from women and I hadn't felt it myself, until now.

"Ready?" Ruth called from downstairs. We were heading to the auction together.

"Almost."

I turned away from my reflection in the mirror and stared out the window, heat clinging to the brush, no movement in any direction. Everything waiting for the day to crack open, the air static and charged.

My skin blazed for Caleb. I felt dizzy, a strange combination of excited and ill, both full and lacking. I didn't like how he made me feel but I wanted him to make me feel more. I squashed a mosquito on the back of my calf. It was time to put an end to the teasing and uncertainty. I would grab him, pull him into dark corner, and kiss him. I shivered at the thought.

⚜

Ruth and Mac had spent the whole day setting up the auction. We walked into an event in progress, Ruth's touches obvious everywhere. There were no balloons or plastic tablecloths, like at other hall events. Instead, the ceiling was strung with hundreds of white fairy lights, emitting a pleasant, warm glow. Tables covered with chic, black fabric showcased the items for auction alongside vases of fresh flowers. The space smelled lovely, like lilies and sweet bee balm.

At the back of the room there was a trio—music students from Wolfville—playing quiet jazz and a long table bearing homemade pies, one dollar per slice. Ruth had baked all week, making many of the pies herself.

"This looks great," I said.

She nodded. "Not bad."

Mac approached us, practically skipping. His smile was huge and his eyes shone when he looked at Ruth. Apparently, my plan had worked on one of the parties involved.

"Isn't this amazing?" he said to me.

"Totally. You two clearly know what you're doing."

"Oh, I can't take any credit. This is all Ruth. Her idea, all of it. The Livingstons are in shock. They can't believe this is all for them."

"Hopefully people are feeling generous," Ruth said. "That's what this is for."

The three of us stood off to the side, watching people arrive. Jake walked in with his parents, Mona and Fred. They were a somewhat odd couple. Mona was a wacky free spirit while Fred had always seemed serious, quiet and reserved. But they had been together forever—since just out of high school, apparently—and I suspected they worked well together *because* they were different. I had been hoping the same would be true of Ruth and Mac.

Jake raised his eyebrows at me as if to say "hey" while Mona gazed upwards, delighted by all the lights.

Beautiful! she mouthed to Ruth. She looped one arm in her husband's and one in her son's. They began to walk around the room. With their backs turned to us, Jake and Fred looked like hunched twins, towering and awkward. When had Jake gotten so tall?

Tom arrived alone, Angela following behind him. She gazed around the room, in awe. None of her events had ever turned out as beautifully at this one. I remembered her gardening books and I wondered what she thought of all the flowers.

Tom and Angela approached us.

"What's up?" Tom asked.

Angela smiled. "Great job, you two. It's beautiful! Good turnout, too."

"Thank you, Angela," Ruth said. "We appreciate that."

I blinked twice when she said "we."

Angela continued to look around the room and I noticed the skin under her eyes was puffy, her complexion ashen. She looked tired and stressed.

"Are you okay?" I asked her quietly.

She glanced at me. Her eyes were very green.

"No, actually," she said, slipping her hands into the pockets of her pleated pants. "I'm currently dealing with a bit of a crisis at home. Someone has stolen my identity. Doesn't that sound ludicrous?"

"What does that mean?" Ruth asked, overhearing.

"Well, it started with my credit cards. Someone started booking flights under my name, charging them to my account. Flights to India and the Dominican Republic, expensive flights all over the world. The credit card company thought it seemed odd. I don't travel much. So they put a stop to it. I had to cancel the card of course but there was no actual loss in terms of money. It was more of an inconvenience."

Caleb, I thought. It had to be. I remembered how just before we'd left Angela's house that day, Tom told me he found Caleb sitting in her office, at her computer. But it didn't sound so bad. There were no real financial consequences. It seemed like more of a scare, a way to mess with her a bit.

"But now it's different," she continued, looking straight ahead at the crowd. "It's like someone has hacked into my email. They're sending messages to my family, my old colleagues. Very strange, upsetting things."

Angela gave her head a little shake. I tried to imagine the content of the emails. Threats? Suggestive messages? How far would Caleb go?

"The worst part is the humiliation. My family know I wouldn't say those things but some of the emails are going to people I worked with for only a brief time years ago. They don't really know me, so it's easier for them to believe the messages are coming from me."

"What do the emails say?" I asked.

Tom leaned closer, brushing my arm. He was trying to get me to stop talking.

"Bizarre things. They make me sound crazy and paranoid. I just keep wondering who would want to do this to me."

She seemed deeply hurt, her typical high spirits deflated. I noticed her shoulders were hunched forward, and her mouth drooped downwards at each corner, accentuating deep lines around her lips.

"I don't know," Angela gave her head another quick little shake. "I'm shutting down my email account so hopefully it will all stop. But now you'll understand," she looked at Mac and Ruth, "if you get a strange email from me."

She drifted off, looking unusually frail.

"How odd," Ruth said. "Who would want to hurt Angela?"

"We're going to go walk around too," I said, pulling Tom away.

"What did he do?" Tom whispered once we were out of earshot. "That's insane! Using her credit card? Isn't that fraud?"

My mind was buzzing. I genuinely felt bad for Angela. She had such a perfect, self-contained little world and we had broken into it, making a mess of her life. But I had to admit I also enjoyed knowing who and what was causing Angela's distress. Being involved in the secret made me feel entangled with Caleb, and superior somehow.

"We can't talk about this here," I told Tom dismissively. "Later."

Tom's parents had given him money to bid on the auction and I convinced him to forget about Angela for now and have some fun. I think he was pleased to have me to himself, like the old days. We bid twenty dollars on a massage from a woman who lived in a solar-panelled home on the far side of God's Palm. She was known for bringing her five-year-old son into her appointments. Magically, he kept quiet, sitting on the floor in the corner, playing with wooden blocks while valley bodies were kneaded into relaxation. Ruth once said it wasn't natural. "A boy that age should be hooting and hollering. Throwing the blocks, not stacking them into neat piles."

We bid ten dollars on a towering coconut cake, three layers stacked high with white icing. Giggling, we bid another ten on two bottles of wine donated from the winery we had broken into with Caleb. At my insistence, Tom also bid thirty on a wool sweater, hand-knit by the sheep farmer two doors down from my house.

"Now, we wait." Tom rubbed his hands together. "Pie?"

I had a slice of mixed berry and Tom went for pumpkin.

"It's so…unseasonal," he said. "I have to have it."

We made our way outside to eat in the warm breeze. Night had dropped and the stars were out.

We heard laughter immediately. Tom pointed to the parking lot, mouth full and chewing. It was Caleb and Sam. We hadn't seen them yet tonight and I had begun to think they weren't coming. An event like this wouldn't usually attract teenagers but we had all decided to go because of Ruth and Mac. Spotting Caleb, I felt a flutter low in my stomach. I told myself not to lose my nerve.

But they were standing with Paul Roberts. As always, he was in charge of parking. He wore his bright neon vest, his feet turned inward. He was carrying a flashlight, and though Caleb and Sam were talking to him, I noticed he was looking elsewhere, to the left and above their heads.

We walked over to them. Paul glanced at me and blushed. He stared even harder into the middle distance. I noticed Sam looked a bit unhinged and overly excited, like a little boy who knows he's doing something bad but can't stop himself. His eyes had a wild glint and he was trembling with quiet laughter.

"How many?" Caleb was asking Paul. "Tell us. How many have you had?"

I knew what this was about without needing to hear more.

"Two? Twenty-six? Come on," Caleb teased. "Spill."

Sam let out a loud spurt of laughter, clutching his stomach. Paul teetered side to side, foot to foot, staring elsewhere and trying to ignore them.

"I guess quantity doesn't matter. Quality is the thing. Who's the best you ever had?"

Another eruption from Sam. He wasn't used to this kind of talk. I looked at Tom, who stared at the ground, uncomfortable. He seemed to have stopped moving his mouth mid-chew. He swallowed loudly.

Paul grunted. "I-I-I," he stuttered. "I-have-to-work." He spat out the four words as if they were one. Literally spat, a wet, urgent utterance. All lips and tongue and saliva.

"The working man," said Caleb, laughing. "Okay, okay. But don't leave us with nothing. Give us a few juicy details before we go."

It should have been bizarre, that talk coming from Caleb. Polite, intelligent, inspiring Caleb. But he had shown us glimpses of this side before, usually when he was drunk. He wasn't afraid to talk about sex, to use the degrading slang of other teenagers, the vernacular I tried so desperately to shelter the boys from.

"That's enough," I said, and Paul looked like he might faint with relief.

Caleb seemed to be considering whether or not to challenge me, eyeing me as he bit his lower lip, amused.

"There's pie inside." I held up my plate. "Let's get some pie."

"Fine," Caleb said, as though he was bored all of a sudden.

We left Paul standing there, bouncing nervously on the balls of his feet. Sam was still snickering like a fool.

Inside, we joined up with Jake. The boys bought slices of pie (a second slice for Tom) and I stood behind them, arms crossed. I was annoyed. Stupid boys. Stupid Caleb for making my boys act like boys. I didn't understand it, the need to talk about bodies and fucking and jerking off. To humiliate. It should have been below Caleb—the environmentalist, the teenage philosopher—he who, until now, seemed to inhabit a rarified space above the rest of us.

I had always taken pride in the fact my boys didn't talk that way. They weren't like other boys. They didn't make crude jokes or use the vulgar language I heard bellowed in the hallways at school. I think they just knew. Winnie wouldn't like it.

But now, Caleb. He introduced us to social justice and post-modernism, but also that ridiculous wanking gesture. He talked about having balls (strength), and about being a pussy (frailty). I hated that distinction most of all.

Caleb turned to me and I re-crossed my arms. I couldn't believe I had started the night thinking I was going to throw myself at this person.

"What's up?" he asked, like nothing had happened.

"That was unnecessary," I said. "With Paul."

"We were just having a bit of fun, Winifred. The poor guy stands out there with no one talk to. We were keeping him company."

"You were degrading him. And I know you've been tormenting Angela, too."

His face lit up, he grabbed me by the arm and pulled me off to the side of the room. His voice was hushed but excited. "Is she talking about it to people?"

"Yeah. She's really freaked out. I think you might have gone too far there. What did you write in those emails?"

"Oh my god," he groaned, ignoring me. "You have to try this." He filled his fork with a bite of the pie and brought it to my lips before I could protest. It was the same mixed-berry pie I had chosen earlier. The juice filled my mouth. I chewed, trying to keep my lips closed. His face was right in mine.

"Good, right?"

I nodded, mouth still full.

"Almost too good." He grinned.

A part of me softened. It was his smile—wide, mischievous—but also the way he said "too good," like we shared a secret no one else could understand.

I hated him for having the ability to disgust and disarm me in the same moment. He drifted away before I could respond. I watched him buy another slice of pie, laughing with my friends.

AFTER

꽃⁓꽃

Angela is next to speak. She changes from fearless journalist to community matriarch. Lorraine stands off to the side, while Angela waits patiently for the crowd to finish the half-conversations just begun. The hushed comments, the questions.

"We don't know what this is," Angela begins once the room has settled. She scans the crowd while she speaks, eyes hinging on one person, then the next, chin raised. "We don't know if this was an accident—some strange twist of fate—or intentional. We don't know and we can't know yet. We'll leave that business to Lorraine. That's *her* job. What's our job? What we can do, what we can *always* do, is support each other. I know we're all feeling a bit broken by this. Mac and his winery and the work he's done there, all the other wineries with grapes in that vineyard, they've been the heartbeat of Gaspereau for a long time now." She smiles at Mac. "We used to be nowhere. Now, thanks to you, we're somewhere people want to visit. And that's not going away. If someone did this to us, we won't let them break us or make us nowhere again. There's a future in the distance that's much brighter. Trust me on that one."

Angela pauses, letting us absorb her message. She's never given us a pep talk before but it's obvious she's always wanted to. She's good at it. Her words are what we need.

For the first time in my life, I am thankful for Angela Lawson.

BEFORE

꧁꧂

Ruth's painting was the highest seller at the auction. Her work gave the Livingston family an overwhelming three thousand dollars. To my surprise, Mac himself bought the painting.

"That was nice of him," I said.

We were sitting on the front step at home with Mona, watching another summer day fade without a change in temperature. The heat was insistent, unrelenting. We fanned ourselves with our hands, a stray flyer from the mailbox.

"He's got a few of yours, doesn't he?" Mona asked.

"What?" This was news to me.

"Mac's been a fan of your mother's work since she moved here. He was buying up her pieces like crazy the first few years. I predicted he would make another big purchase soon. Didn't I, Ruth?"

"I don't remember that prediction," Ruth raised her eyebrows at me. "You must have forgotten to tell me."

"Must have. I said it, for sure. Mac Elliott with dollar signs hanging from his walls. Your name signed underneath."

I noticed Ruth chewing her thumbnail, glaring at the ground.

"What's up?" I asked. "You seem upset."

"Mac just annoys me. Now he wants me to come over and help him hang the painting. Doesn't he know how to hammer a damn nail? It's ridiculous."

"He probably wants you to help him pick a good place for it," I said, grinning. "It's nice. You always say people hang your art in the worst places."

"I'm sensing you will become great friends," Mona piped up. As usual, Mona didn't have things quite right.

⟨⟩

Caleb knew about my failed plan, my attempt to bring Mac and Ruth together. He brought it up a week or so after the fundraiser, when the boys and I were listening to music in his bedroom. It was another searing day. Wicked hot, the promise of an instant sunburn. After a quick swim in the river, we sought shelter inside. Caleb suggested his house; it was closest. We followed him upstairs to his bedroom on the third floor, the house dark and tranquil. We flopped down, Tom and Sam on the bed, Jake and I on the floor. Caleb sat at his desk and turned on his computer, playing more of the esoteric indie music he insisted was the height of artistic evolution.

With my back against the bed, I glanced around at the walls, Caleb's things. It was my first time in his room and there was much to absorb. The full bookshelf, the neat closet. The pencil sketches of birds pinned on the wall above his desk. I was very familiar with the bedrooms of teenage boys, having spent countless hours in Tom's, Jake's, and Sam's rooms, but Caleb's was unusually tidy. No posters on the wall, no dirty laundry or used dishes waiting to be cleaned up by his mother. It lacked that teenage boy smell, too: a strange mustiness, like spoiled fruit juice and unwashed sheets.

The large window next to Caleb's bed framed a view of leafy maple trees in the backyard. I fingered the edge of his bedspread, a navy quilt, and wondered what it would feel like to crawl beneath the covers. Between the cool sheets.

We listened to the music and Caleb played around on his computer. I watched him type with alarming speed, not looking at the keyboard. Occasionally, his computer made a *ding* sound, announcing the arrival of an instant message. I had heard the same sound on Tom's and Sam's computers. They used instant messaging too, though I knew little about how it worked and who they might be corresponding with. Tom assured me it was just for keeping in touch with his cousins in Toronto, but I once caught Sam chatting to a girl in the grade below us, attempting to flirt.

I wondered who Caleb was messaging. He didn't know anyone here but us, so it must be people from Vancouver. There had been vague mentions of Caleb having an older brother and sister. Maybe he was talking to them. Or maybe girls back home.

Tom and Jake stood up, announcing they were hungry.

"The cupboard next to the fridge," Caleb told them, continuing to stare at the computer screen. "She's always got something in there. Pretzels, maybe."

Was Sylvia home? I knew she worked from an office on the ground floor of the house, with the occasional meeting out of town. She often left Caleb alone for days at a time. I had once heard her on a conference call in her office. The door was closed but her low voice had a power that carried. I stood outside the room, bare feet on a soft rug, listening. She spoke about search engines and algorithms and code, things I knew nothing about. She sounded like her patience was endless, but also like she knew she was smarter than whoever was on the other end of the line.

"Winnie, you want water?" Tom lingered in the doorway and I felt he was watching us, Caleb and me. I noticed this was happening more and more, as if he recognized the change in me. A glowing, evolving warmth. My gravitation towards another body.

"I'm good."

We heard him pad down the stairs.

Caleb didn't waste any time. He turned away from the computer, towards me.

"Mac and your mother," he said. "What's going on there?"

I glanced at Sam. I was reluctant to share my secret wish about Ruth and Mac with anyone, but Caleb dismissed my hesitancy with the tilt of his head, a *come on, what do you care what he thinks?* frown.

"Nothing," I sighed, conceding. It was stupid to pretend with Caleb. He was unnervingly perceptive, more aware of others than they were of themselves. And he was right. I didn't really care what Sam thought. "I want there to be something," I said, "but she's childish. She doesn't know what's good for her."

Caleb frowned. "I don't think your mother is childish."

"No?"

"She's...resolved. Ruth is incredibly independent and she fears losing that independence. She likes her life and she doesn't want it to change. That's why she has one-night stands. That's why she dates men she can suffer for only a few hours at a time."

I looked up at him. How did he know that about Ruth? Tom and Jake were the only ones who knew what Ruth did in the city and Jake would never share that information with anyone. It must have been Tom. I didn't like that he was divulging the private details of my life and I didn't like that Tom and Caleb were having private conversations. When had this happened? Where had I been?

"I don't know if I'd call them one-night stands."

"Flings, then? Is that more palatable?"

"Maybe that's all she needs." I shrugged. "That's okay too." It sounded true when I said it. I didn't want to be a prude. It wasn't the fleetingness of her encounters I hated; it was the type of men she chose to have them with.

"Is it, though? I'm guessing you put this whole matchmaking plan into action because you want something more for her."

"What are you guys talking about?" Sam yawned, his words drawn out. He was laying on the bed, dozy from the heat.

"Nothing," Caleb said. "Why don't you go find the others?"

Sam nodded obediently, yawning again. He left us alone in the bedroom.

"I respect your instinct to take care of her," Caleb said, moving off the chair, sitting next to me on the floor. He placed a hand on my bare knee. His touch radiated heat and I sat perfectly still.

"And I'm going to help you," he said.

"What?"

"It was a valid effort, Winifred. But you went about it the wrong way. We'll sort this out."

"Sort what out?" Tom was back, Jake and Sam behind him. Tom spotted Caleb's hand on my knee and frowned.

"Nothing, nothing," Caleb said. He removed his hand. "What did you find to eat?"

"Pretzels, like you said."

Tom tossed the bag at Caleb.

"Next time take some initiative," Caleb said, a hint of disgust in his voice. "Put them in a bowl."

⁂

A couple days later, we were hanging out at the canal when Caleb brought up Ruth and Mac again. Work had ended for the day and we all met up for a swim. We weren't alone; the oppressive weather had inspired many folks to put on their suits and go for a dip. The river was crowded, a funny combination of kids splashing and old people floating serenely.

Caleb and I sat on the riverbank, our hair dripping. We watched the boys swim and I exhaled deeply, refreshed by the water.

"The first thing you need to realize," Caleb told me, leaning close, "is that Ruth's disinterest in Mac has little to do with Mac himself. It's not his looks or his personality that are the problem. We both know he's attractive and a good person. A catch, really. The problem is Ruth, how she *sees* Mac."

I glanced at Caleb. His eyelashes were wet and dark, making his grey eyes look slightly blue.

"Okay," I said, unsure exactly what he meant.

"She wrote him off long ago as just another local guy. Boring, uninteresting. And she's never had a reason to reframe that thinking."

"I tried to change that," I said. "I told her about how passionate he is, all the good work he's doing at the winery."

Caleb nodded. "Yes, but I'm guessing it had no effect because, to her, it was just more of the same. She sees Mac as a valley boy, through and through."

"Okay. Then how do we help her see him differently?"

Caleb grinned. "That's where we need to get creative. Outwardly, Ruth seems quite superficial. She goes after these rich, old guys, but why? She's gorgeous. She's relatively young. She's a talented artist. She could have anyone she wanted."

I looked away, annoyed that Caleb had called Ruth gorgeous.

"Well," he said, poking my bare leg with a finger, calling me back to him. "What do rich, old guys represent? They represent wealth and power, status in society. Their expensive cars and flashy suits signify their status. When Ruth goes out with them, she feels special, a part of that world, even if only for a night. That's what she *thinks* she wants."

What Caleb was saying made sense. Ruth's vanity was really an expression of her deep insecurities. Those nights in the city were part of an endless loop: seeking and receiving flattery, wanting to feel envied by others.

"But Mac will never be like that," I said. "He's not materialistic and he'll never be rich. He's so humble."

"Right. And, like you, I believe Ruth would be a lot better off with someone like Mac, someone who doesn't indulge her vanity."

"Okay, but I still don't understand. How do we convince her Mac is what she really needs?"

"It's not about convincing. It's about reframing."

I was growing impatient, tired of playing student. "Right. But how?"

"Let me show you," he said.

He nodded in the direction of a silver car that had just parked on the shoulder of the road. The car was blasting horrible hip-hop music and I recognized Amber and Jess immediately in the front seats, both wearing skimpy bikinis. A boy from school named Kyle, rumoured to be sleeping with Jess, was in the back. We watched them get out of the car and walk towards us.

Amber and Jess both did a double take when they saw Caleb. I wondered if they had met him before, but he didn't nod at them or seem to recognize them, which was a relief. Amber whispered something to Jess, who nodded. I wondered if it might look to them like Caleb and I were together.

"Those girls," Caleb said in a low voice only I could hear, "are completely one-dimensional. They're sixteen years old and their only real concern is finding a boyfriend. You know them?" he asked.

"Yeah, they go to our school."

"Am I right about them?"

"Absolutely." I loved that he was talking about Amber and Jess this way, the way I had always seen them.

"Thought so. And the boys they go after are typically what? Jocks? Ripped and popular?"

I nodded, laughing a little.

"Perfect. Here's what I want you to do: get back in the water and start flirting with Tom."

"What?" My laughter stopped.

"I'm serious," he said. "Get in the water and, I don't know, start splashing him and laughing at what he says. Make it seem like you find him funny and hot. Trust me," he added to soothe my bafflement. "It'll be fun."

I hesitated. Flirt with Tom? What good would that do?

Caleb reached over and tucked my hair behind one ear. "Just pretend he's me," he whispered.

I gazed at him for a minute and then stood up, propelled by the thought of Caleb wanting to see me flirt. It felt like a game, exciting and performative. I just had to pretend, like he said. What did I care how it looked? I was always telling the boys to ignore what other people thought.

I plunked back down in the water and swam towards the boys. They weren't far from Amber, Jess, and Kyle but there was no conversation between us and them, which was normal. At school, the various cliques didn't mix much; people tended to stick to their own kind. Amber, Jess, and Kyle were considered popular, which meant they were either good-looking, wealthy, or athletic.

As I moved through the water, I noticed Sam was eyeing the girls, their barely covered breasts. I resisted telling him to stop drooling. When I got close to the boys, I splashed some water at Tom with my hand.

"Hey!" He smiled.

I did it again. He splashed me back. I laughed, like Caleb said I should. Soon, we were splashing each other, water flying everywhere. I swam close and pushed Tom's head down underwater. He resurfaced quickly and then did the same to me. He looked confused but also grateful, like he had the day I kissed him all those years ago. We were both laughing now but I made sure my laughter was feminine. I thought of Ruth and how she laughed with the men who visited her studio. I mimicked her pitch, high and inviting.

When we stopped splashing, I reached out and wiped the hair out of Tom's face.

"I like your hair long," I said. He had been growing it out, too lazy to get a haircut. "You should keep it this length."

"Okay," he said. He was blushing a little, pink bright on his cheeks.

I continued to swim close to him, unsure how to keep this flirtation act going. Jake and Sam looked thoroughly confused by my behaviour but I noticed Amber and Jess watching us, curious.

The boys and I soon got out of the water. Caleb winked at me and I shrugged. I wasn't sure what was happening but apparently Caleb approved.

We dried ourselves off and I noticed Amber looking Tom up and down. She whispered something to Jess, who nodded.

"Did you see that?" Caleb asked me. We hung back while the others got on their bikes.

"They want what I have."

"Exactly. Those girls are grasping. Vapid strivers." He spat the words. "They know nothing about true desire."

I stirred. True desire. Was he talking about me, about us?

"But Ruth isn't a teenage girl," I pointed out. "It can't be that easy with her."

"You'll see."

❦

Peach day was always a Saturday in mid-August. Peaches were Ruth's favourite summer treat and so we dedicated one whole day of the season to that ephemeral fruit, its flesh tender and intoxicating. For the last few years, the boys had joined us. They came with us to the farmers' market, helped us carry out the laden bags, contributed to the peeling, the slicing, the freezing. We worked all afternoon, chatting, the radio on in the kitchen. When we finished, Ruth and I made the boys a peach cobbler as a thank you. Bubbling hot, with melting heaps of vanilla ice cream on the side.

That summer, peach day was exceptionally warm and sticky. It was thirty-two degrees when I woke up, which meant the afternoon was sure to scorch and blaze. It was hard to believe the weather would ever turn, that in a few months winter would arrive, long and bleak. I tied my hair in a ponytail, high off my neck. I was already sweating.

When I came downstairs, Ruth was dropping ice cubes in her coffee. She had laid out cutting boards and paring knives, zip-top freezer bags and aprons.

"Don't let me forget ice cream," she said, her forehead glistening.

The windows were open but the curtains didn't twitch.

⚶⚶⚶

When we pulled up to the farmers' market Caleb and the boys were waiting for us, all four of them leaning against Jake's truck. Ruth laughed.

"Boys," she said, shaking her head.

The market was quiet, nearly empty. Most of the valley had fled the heat, escaped to the beaches that line the surrounding coast. Red sand and cold water.

Ruth had her favourite spot, the farmer she always bought peaches from. We walked straight there, not stopping to talk to anyone. He wasn't our regular produce guy—I never even learned his name—but he sold the best peaches in the valley and always gave Ruth a good deal.

She bought the peaches and then told us to find breakfast. Everything on offer seemed heavy and unappetizing, given the weather. We settled on a box of blackberries, a few slices of banana bread, and iced coffees for everyone. We found Ruth again, then went outside to sit in the shade and eat in silence, too uncomfortable to talk.

More people trickled in and Ruth eventually broke the quiet, asking Tom about his family. How were they doing? She hadn't seen his mother in too long.

Tom's mom, Elaine, was a math professor at the university, recently retired. She was a mousy woman, slight-limbed and fuzzy-haired, with a high voice. Nothing like Tom. He took more after his father, Peter, also a math professor, but easygoing, with a loud laugh and a warm presence. He had the same ruddy hair as Tom. Peter often teased me about spending too much time with his son, though it didn't bother me like it did when other people said it.

"Retirement is an adjustment for my mom," Tom said, "but so far so good. She won't really feel it until September when school starts up again. She's been going back to school every fall her whole life."

Ruth sipped her iced coffee through a straw. "I always hated school. Too much structure. Even in art school, all the classes and the timetable nonsense. I don't like being told how to spend my time, where to go and when."

Jake made a noise, indicating agreement.

"I guess I shouldn't be surprised Winnie took after me." Ruth sighed.

Caleb's head whipped in my direction. "You hate school?" he asked.

"I don't hate it," I said. "I just don't like it much."

"But you're *smart*," he said.

"So?"

"You should use your smarts. They can help you get out of this place."

I shifted awkwardly in my seat. Caleb was studying me. I avoided the pull of his gaze because I feared what I might find there. Disappointment? Pity? I wanted to leave the valley eventually—most people did—but I also didn't see much point in trying hard in school. The classes were easy and boring, undeserving of my effort. Surely Caleb would understand that. School was about routine. Compliance. The opposite of everything he seemed to want. But a part of me worried he was right. Maybe I had I been short-sighted—too careless with a future I could only half-imagine.

"I'm hoping she never leaves," Ruth teased, easing the tension of the moment and Caleb's obvious judgment.

I smiled at my mother, grateful. The boys looked uneasy too. Caleb's words had implications for them as well. Where were they going, if anywhere, after high school?

"Empty nest syndrome," Caleb nodded at Ruth sympathetically. "My mother fears it too. Both my siblings already left home. I'll be the last to go. Not sure what she's going to do all by herself."

"She can drink wine with me." Ruth grinned. "I've been meaning to have her over."

"She's been saying the same," Caleb said. "I think she's planning to throw a barbecue next weekend, invite the neighbours. You should come."

"I'd love that," said Ruth.

Back at home, slicing peaches, the juice ran down our arms and sweat beaded on the furrows and ledges of our bodies: the ridge of an eyebrow, the pronounced curve of a top lip. Caleb stood next to me, working through a pile of fruit. He kept us entertained with a story about a broken-down moped on a Greek island, he and his brother stranded on the side of the road after midnight. They ended up walking for two hours in the dark, back to their vacation villa. Along the way, they came across an orchard of peaches and devoured the ripe fruit to quench their thirst. "Even better than these!" Caleb said, slipping a wedge of peach between his lips.

Every so often, Caleb bumped his hip against mine, affectionate, taunting. Once, I noticed Tom cast a dirty look my way but I ignored it. I wasn't even the one flirting. Why was he scowling at me?

We froze sixteen large bags of sliced peaches, finishing late in the day, tired but triumphant. Ruth made us a dinner of grilled sausages and corn on the cob, simple food that didn't require the stovetop. Instead of turning on the oven, she baked the peach cobbler in a skillet on the barbecue, which Caleb said was ingenious.

Ruth served dessert in chipped bowls. The ice cream had already melted before we could attack it with our spoons. The boys all agreed, though: melted ice cream was just as good.

꿈꿈꿈

Sylvia held her barbecue the following weekend. Ruth and I were both invited, as were the boys and their families and a few other neighbours. Both Mac and Angela were there, plus the people who lived close to Caleb and Sylvia on Slayter Road.

Ruth wore a floral, summery dress and strappy sandals, her red hair wavy and sun-streaked. When I saw Ruth's outfit, I thought about dressing up too. But then I thought of Sylvia, how she always looked polished without trying too hard. I stuck to my T-shirt and cut-offs. I tucked one section of my hair behind my ear, like Caleb had done at the canal.

We left for the party a bit late because Ruth took too long getting ready. She kept changing her sandals, trying to decide between two different options.

"Who cares?" I asked, impatient to see Caleb. "It's just a barbecue up the street."

"Sylvia always looks so good," Ruth mused. "I don't want to show up underdressed."

I rolled my eyes and told her I'd be waiting in the driveway. I wondered if Sylvia ever envied other women, wishing she looked more like someone else. I thought it was unlikely. She seemed almost too confident and self-assured, like her son.

Caleb was serving food off the grill when we walked around the side of the Taylor house, to the backyard. The day was just starting to darken. Lit torches burned bright, scattered within the garden. The party guests mingled: the boys with Caleb at the grill; Mona, Fred, and Tom's dad Peter sitting at a patio table with Angela and a few other neighbours; Mac and Sylvia speaking over by a cooler stocked with drinks.

"We're here!" Ruth called out, too loud for such a peaceful gathering. Her voice halted the various clusters of chatter and everyone stared. Mona grinned and waved.

Sylvia left Mac to welcome us. "So glad you could make it," she said, taking the bottle of wine Ruth had brought. "Ruth, I love your dress. Winnie, you look stunning, as always."

I beamed in response.

"There's plenty of food. Way too much! I got a bit carried away. Help yourself. There are cold drinks too. I told the boys they could have one beer each, if it was okay with their parents. Same goes for you Winnie, if Ruth doesn't mind."

"Of course not," Ruth said. "Go ahead, Winnie."

I grabbed a beer from the cooler, saying a quick "hi" to Mac, and joined the boys. The beer was called Poseidon's Sister, and the bottle had a colourful blue label with a drawing of a sea goddess on the front. She had long, flowing, blonde hair, a trident in one hand. I tasted the beer and was surprised. It was light in the mouth, bitter in a way I liked, with a fruity, tropical aftertaste. Not like any beer I had ever tasted before. I noticed the boys had beers with cool labels too, all with different names.

"This is good," I said to Caleb.

"Right? I told you that stuff we've been drinking is hillbilly beer. That one's from a microbrewery in Quebec."

I had never heard of a microbrewery before, but I nodded and took another sip.

The boys and I sat in the grass, watching the adults socialize. It wasn't an especially fun party, but it was something to do. Tom and Sam argued quietly about a book Caleb had insisted they both read, a graphic novel about World War Two in which the different sides were depicted as various animals: mice, pigs, cats.

Caleb poked my bare thigh.

"What?"

"Look," he nodded his chin in the direction of the drinks table.

Mac and Sylvia were talking again. Mac was pouring her small glasses from the different wines in the cooler. We couldn't hear what they were saying but it was clear they were having fun. Sipping and giggling, talking close. I watched Sylvia laugh and place her hand on Mac's upper arm. They almost looked like a couple.

I glanced over at Ruth, sitting at the patio table with the others. She was watching Sylvia and Mac, unsmiling. She looked lonely, her mouth slack. It occurred to me how seldom I saw her like this.

"I'm not sure about this." I asked Caleb. "Did you know this would happen?"

He ignored my uncertainty. "It's perfect," he said. "Just like those girls at the canal. I wasn't sure Sylvia would be interested, but clearly...."

My gaze drifted back to Sylvia and Mac. She looked so happy. Mac did too.

"You don't think your mom really likes him, do you? I don't want anyone to get hurt."

"She'll be fine. She's tough," he said, unmoved.

I continued to watch Sylvia and Mac, and Ruth sitting glumly off to the side. Could it really be so simple? Were people that easy to manipulate? Or was Caleb just that good at it?

AFTER

꧁ꕥ꧂

Mona is dismayed. She doesn't remember that she saw this coming. She smelled smoke—she anticipated destruction—if only she knew how to interpret her own visions. If only she had connected the dots. Change, smoke, Winnie. Caleb, the mediating force. The missing piece. If only she had put it together. But really, what good would that have done?

I've always struggled with the idea of predetermined futures, of decided fates. We seek to learn what comes next, but why? If it's yet to come, preordained, then it can't be changed. That's why, besides a few readings to mollify Mona, I avoid anything mystical.

Mona is dismayed and to make up for what she calls her "catastrophic failure" to protect the community, she has volunteered to run the tip line. A dial-in number for anyone who knows anything about the fire, a way to call and share. I doubt they'll get any useful information. Lorraine must doubt it too. That's why the tip line's sole volunteer is also its manager. Mona's home phone is the number to call if anyone knows anything.

BEFORE

⊱❀⊰

I knew Caleb's plan was working when, one day the following week, Ruth suggested we stop at the Elliott Winery to pick up some wine. We had never done so before.

"Yeah?" I said to Ruth. "You need some wine?"

"Yeah," she nodded. "I do."

The winery wasn't busy. The sky was grey that day. Migraine-inducing clouds teasing rain that would never come. I scanned the grounds for Caleb but didn't spot him anywhere on the property. Maybe he wasn't working today.

"Am I frizzy?" Ruth asked as we walked in.

"No," I lied. We both were.

The tasting room of Mac's winery featured a long wooden bar with a massive window behind it, looking out over God's Palm. Lush lines of leafy green unfurled across the vineyard, some of them Mac's grapes, some grown for other wineries. On the opposite wall, there were bottles of wine on display. I was shocked to see one of Ruth's landscapes hanging in the centre of the shelves of wine like an anchor, drawing your eye away from the window view. I had been in the fields and the cellar with Mac and the others, but never the tasting room.

"When did you paint *that*?" I walked over to see it up close. The texture and heavy strokes were unmistakable, but it was so unlike her other work: full of intense colour, nothing faded or subdued. The valley fields were rendered in lemon yellows and electric greens and a royal purple. I was shocked by all the fuchsia.

Ruth stared at the piece fondly. "Years ago. When you were just a baby."

"Mac bought it?"

"Yeah, I totally forgot. I had a show in our front yard. 'En Plein Air,' I called it. I was desperate for the money. You went through diapers like you wouldn't believe. This was the largest piece for sale. If I recall, Mac was the first to arrive and the first to buy. He took one look at this painting and said he'd buy it, and then he hung around waiting for the other pieces to go. He said he knew the impact of the larger works could help to sell the small ones. I guess he didn't want to take it away too soon."

"It's beautiful."

"Thanks."

Mac appeared, carrying boxes. "Aren't you two a sight for sore eyes!" he said.

I was pleased to see Ruth gave him a warm smile, inviting and uninhibited.

"Buying some wine?"

"What's good?" Ruth asked.

Mac walked over. "What isn't?"

He grabbed a bottle from the shelf. "This one, our 2003 L'Acadie, is one of our best, maybe ever. It surprised me. When you pour it into a glass it's like water, it's so clear. But the complexity will astound you. It's like the flavour is hiding in there. Invisible layers, and so smooth."

"Can I try it?" Ruth asked.

"Of course."

Mac walked us over to the bar.

"Tara, can I get a chilled bottle of L'Acadie and two glasses?"

"Sure. Hey, Winnie," Tara said.

"Hey," I said back.

Mac poured two small glasses of wine, one for him and one for Ruth. He was right. It looked like water. Weightless, with only a hint of gold.

"L'Acadie blanc is our main grape here in Nova Scotia. You'll find a few wineries in Quebec and Ontario that also plant it, but it's really our claim to fame. It's a hardy vine, able to cope with our cold temperatures in the winter and spring, which is why we like it. It also produces a gorgeous, crisp white." He held the glass up to the light, examining the liquid inside. "I like to smell it first," he told Ruth.

It was a suggestion, not an order. That was good; Ruth didn't like being told what to do.

"If you put your nose right in the glass and inhale, you'll get it."

"Get what?" Ruth asked. She had long been a wine drinker, but it occurred to me she was more of a gulper than a sipper, and never seemed to remark on the flavour of wine. It was strange, given her obsession with food and cooking.

"Whatever you're going to get," Mac said, patient. "I believe drinking wine should be an entirely individual experience. We make a point of not putting tasting notes on our labels. I don't want to influence people's interpretations of our wine. I just want them to taste it for themselves. See what it means to them."

Ruth looked impressed, which surprised me. Last week, that kind of comment from Mac would have been tuned out, quickly classified as another example of Mac's egotism. But now, just like Caleb said she would, Ruth seemed to be perceiving Mac through a new lens. I was struck again by Caleb's insight, his astute reading of Ruth's needs. But I was also unnerved. If he was that discerning, what subtle games was he playing with the boys and with me?

"I get gooseberry," Ruth said, inhaling deeply.

"How do you know what gooseberry smells like?" I teased.

"I just do."

"What do you get, Winnie?" Mac asked, handing me his glass.

I smelled the wine as Mac had taught me, sticking my nose deep in the glass, tipping the wine at an angle to expose more surface area.

"There's something tart, like lemon," I said, smelling more, "but there's also a hint of pear. With," I inhaled again, thinking, "I don't know, grass maybe?"

Mac howled, delighted. "That's remarkable!"

"What is?" asked Ruth.

"She's spot on." Mac took a sip of the wine. I could see him rolling the liquid around his mouth between parted lips. "Not just spot on. She's smelling angles I can barely taste."

Ruth took a sip too. "I definitely taste the citrus," she said. "I can see where she gets that."

Mac grinned. "Now, how about some rosé?"

Mac led Ruth through a full wine tasting. She tried five different wines and I smelled each one. Mac continued to praise the genius of my nose, occasionally prompting me for more: did I smell the black pepper? What about the red licorice? He marvelled when I came out with a note that he himself had only caught a faint whiff of. Tara joined us, listening in.

An hour or so later, Ruth left with a full case of wine and flushed cheeks. She said nothing on the drive home.

⧉

Ruth's first date with Mac was soon after. I lay on her bed while she brushed her hair then curled her eyelashes. She seemed uncharacteristically nervous. Shaking slightly, talking too much. She poured herself a vermouth but didn't touch it. The ice melted and when I snuck sips later on, it was tepid and weak-tasting.

"What's with you?" I asked.

"Anxious," she mumbled, distracted.

"How many dates have you gone on this year? How can you be nervous?"

She shook her head. "This is different."

"You're going to be fine."

She returned a weak smile. Watching her apply pink blush to her cheeks with a light hand, I considered whether her penchant for jerks was less about superficiality (Caleb's take) and more about a lack of confidence, and how little she valued herself. Did she not think she was worthy of a real relationship, of someone like Mac? Maybe those trips to the city were a twisted form of self-punishment, a periodic reminder that she was a woman who only deserved an insincere kind of affection. Shallow and fleeting.

I was sure Ruth could thank the man who fathered me for that particular baggage. I wondered what it felt like, to be pregnant and alone. To love someone and to leave them, or to be left. She never talked about that time. She made it seem like she was better off without him. But what had their rupture done to her?

It was a relief to think Caleb might have got it wrong, that Ruth wasn't as uncomplicated as he had presumed. No one knew Ruth like me. For so long, it had been just the two of us. Now, there might be three. I had helped engineer their relationship and I was happy for them. For all of us. Ruth deserved more than she ever gave herself.

Mac picked Ruth up in his Jeep, right on time. I watched from the upstairs window. A car door opened by a strong hand, his smile glinting white. The soft hem of her floral dress trapped in the door as they drove away. The light was pink and weakening but their day was just beginning.

He dropped her off just before midnight. I heard their footfalls on the gravel. Slow, careful steps, drawing out the evening. A few moments of silence and then the opening of the front door. She closed it and ran upstairs.

"Winnie!" she said excitedly, bursting into my room. She lay down next to me on my bed, buzzing. She couldn't wait to tell me all about her night. Unlike in the past, I let her.

Mac soon started coming round for supper. It was the first time she had ever invited a man she was dating into our house. The others were restricted to the studio, the boundaries of professional space.

Mac always arrived with a bottle of his wine. He talked to her about the grape, the year, the process, while she stood at the stovetop and I listened in from the living room or the kitchen table. Now, it seemed, Mac's work talk was sexy to Ruth. She asked him questions. She took a real interest. He chatted away, watching her make dinner.

Ruth was a very physical cook, bodily and unapologetic. She would dip her fingers right into the salt bowl. She would pour wine from her own glass into the stew. She tasted relentlessly, always with the same spoon. I'm sure, for a man, it was pure foreplay. Her food and her cooking were an extension of her body.

Occasionally, I sat with them at dinner and wondered if they had had sex yet. I didn't want to picture it, but I did. I wondered where and when. I wondered if I might overhear. I knew this wasn't normal, but I was curious. At least with Mac, I was able to wonder. With those other men from the city, there was a hollow certainty.

I had known Mac my whole life but suddenly he was there, in front of me, all the time. It gratified me to see how right I had been. About Ruth, about Mac. They were good together. Maybe Caleb could take the credit for making it happen, but it had been my idea.

The summer crops dwindled. The last of the berries turned too ripe in the heat, making the U-pick fields smell overcooked and vaguely rotten. Sid the farmer thanked Tom and me for another summer of work. Picking season was over; school would start soon. We spent our last days of freedom feeling aimless and a bit melancholic. We wanted to make the most of the time we had, but the sweltering temperatures limited our movements. I thought ahead towards the school year with a lurking sense of dread, depressed that I would soon be stuck inside all day and have to see my classmates again. What would this year be like, with Caleb at our school? I was sure the other kids would be pulled toward him like we were, but how would he feel about them?

꿯

At this point, Sam seemed to be completely beguiled by Caleb. He followed Caleb around like Caleb was a big brother, someone he idolized without question. He remained endlessly agreeable, jumping up to refill Caleb's cold drink, quick to endorse whatever theory Caleb espoused. It was a bit pathetic, but I figured it was a passing fixation. Sam had always been a follower. At school, I had noticed him stare longingly at some of the popular boys in our grade, the captains of various sports teams. He was drawn to them, eager to fall in line behind a letterman jacket. I would much rather Sam worship Caleb, whom I approved of, even if that meant Sam and I drifted apart for a while.

Of course, we all idolized Caleb in a way, but Tom, Jake, and I weren't quite as shameless as Sam. We didn't lose ourselves in our admiration; we still resisted him on occasion.

Whenever Caleb flirted with me, Tom sulked, giving me dirty looks and an icy silent treatment. Occasionally, though, he also took it out on Caleb. He was reading all the books Caleb had assigned, but he didn't consume Caleb's world view uncritically. Sometimes, when Caleb spent too long trying to make me laugh or pulled me into a tight hug, Tom would announce he had doubts about the value of protest-style activism. Was marching in the streets really doing anything these days? A debate ensued, with Sam backing up Caleb's convictions while Tom remained firm, glowering and contrary.

Jake didn't like to argue, but I don't think he ever got past feeling intimidated by Caleb. He often stared at the ground or off into the distance when Caleb spoke to him, as if trying to deflect Caleb's intense gaze. The rare times Jake answered Caleb's questions, he tended to stutter, toppling over his own thoughts. Mostly, he remained silent. Quiet laughter was his main contribution to any conversation. In this way, Jake's admiration of Caleb seemed cautious, even fearful.

But on a particularly humid day near the end of August, we took Caleb to Three Pools, a series of swimming holes in a sister community. Ruth and Mona had often taken us there when we were kids. They used to sunbathe on the rocks while we cooled off in the still pools. As we got older, we began venturing upwards, to the tops of the rocky cliffs where you could jump off and plunge in.

The day we took Caleb to Three Pools was the day Jake's relationship to Caleb changed.

The walk in took us through deep woods. The sweet smell of sap and pine needles stuck to our heels. It was a well-worn path, known only to the locals. When we reached the end of the trail, we found a group of people already in the water. We set our towels on the rocks and started undressing.

I had tried to find another bathing suit, finally accepting my old one-piece just didn't fit me anymore. Riding up my bum, cutting a sharp line across my chest. I searched through Ruth's drawers, but all of her suits were bikinis, stringy little things in bold colours. I tried a few on, fiddling with the ties, standing in front of the big mirror on her closet door, but I didn't recognize myself. I tried to imagine wearing one of the bikinis out in the world and knew I couldn't go through with it. Tom and Jake would look confused and embarrassed. Caleb might like it, but then again, I had no idea what Caleb really liked.

"Is that where we jump off?" Caleb pointed to the highest cliff.

"Some people do," said Tom.

"Not you?"

"Nah." Tom kept his gaze upwards.

"I've been thinking about it," Sam offered weakly.

We had never gone to the top. For Tom, Sam, and I, the second-highest cliff offered enough of a thrill. Jake, terrified of heights, still preferred to wade into the water. Slow, careful steps with his eyes on the bottom of the pool.

We all watched a man jump from the top cliff, arms flailing as he fell. He disappeared into the dark water, his splash erupting in a high, shimmering arc. His children clapped enthusiastically. "Go, Daddy!" one of them yelled.

"Looks like fun," Caleb said.

Jake nodded, frowning.

Leaving Jake on the rocks below, the four us of climbed up the cliffside, feet bare. Caleb was behind me. I wondered where he was looking. It took all my willpower not to pull down the bottom of my bathing suit, which was riding up higher with each step.

We reached the top of the second cliff and stopped.

Caleb turned. "You're seriously not coming?"

"You go first," I said. "Tell us what's it's like."

He rolled his eyes and shook his head, hiking up the last bit of cliff. He stood above us, tanned and looming. He looked otherworldly, like a Greek god.

"Pretty high," he said. "Hope I make it."

Sam laughed nervously.

"You watching?" Caleb called.

Then he jumped, running and soaring, without hesitation. We watched him fall and then plunge and splash. The children below clapped again.

"Amazing!" Caleb yelled when he surfaced. "Now we'll all go together."

Tom and I searched each other's faces. He bit his lip, uncertain. I wasn't actually scared of jumping from the top, but I suspected Tom was. He has never been much of a thrill-seeker. I had always kept to the second-highest cliff because I knew it was all he could handle. I didn't want to push him too far or make him feel weak.

"We can't," Tom whispered. We watched Caleb get out of the water and pat Jake on the back, talking into his ear. "*He* can't."

"Looks like he is," I said.

We watched Caleb guide Jake up the cliff, one hand on his back as if he was propelling him from behind. When they reached us, Jake's face was pale. His arms dangled awkwardly at his sides under tense, hunched shoulders. He glanced at me, a furtive, pleading look.

"Are you sure about this?" I asked, sounding more panicked than I would have liked. It was safe to jump—lots of people leapt from that same cliff all the time—but Jake looked like he might faint. I wanted to protect him, and Tom too.

"Come on, Winifred." Caleb grinned. "It's not so high. We'll be fine."

He continued to push Jake along the path up the side of the cliff and Sam followed close behind. Tom looked at me and groaned a little. He followed them, scrambling up the rocks. I guess he figured if Jake was doing it, he had to as well.

I watched them climb up to the top. I'm not sure why I didn't just join them, but I really hated being told what to do, and a part of me thought Jake and Tom wouldn't jump. I'd be there waiting for them if they needed me.

I was stuck on the second cliff, unsure, feet beginning to burn on the hot rock. My friends were now stepping to the edge. Caleb was whispering to them, words that weren't for me. Jake was visibly trembling.

Before I could decide whether or not to go to Jake, Caleb yelled, "Now!" and they were falling. I couldn't believe it. I blinked as they splashed. I took a few running steps and jumped off the second cliff without thinking, fuelled by concern. I wanted to get to them.

When I emerged from the water, the boys were already climbing up the rocky bank. Was Jake crying? I swam to shore with long, desperate strokes, the water in my way.

"Are you okay?" I huffed, slipping on the wet rocks and skinning one knee.

They all looked at me. Jake wasn't crying; he was laughing. Hooting, delirious laughter. They were all laughing; Tom too. For a brief moment, I thought they were laughing at me because I'd slipped. I blushed.

"We're fine," said Tom, giving me a hand, helping me up. "Better than fine! That was amazing!"

Caleb started hollering, calling out to the trees, the sky, the day, like a wild animal. The boys joined in. I stayed silent, unsure how to make that sound come out of my throat. I stood amongst them, confused, left out. Jake's roaring was the loudest. The usual slump of his posture was gone, his shoulders broad, his back straight, face to the sky. I barely recognized him.

Tom's alignment with Caleb came at the very end of summer.

The northern lights would soon be visible from the valley. Tom had been talking about it for weeks. The best night for viewing would coincide with the last weekend before school started, a final late night before many early mornings.

"I stole a bottle of vodka from my parents," Tom whispered to me. "They won't miss it. I thought we could toast the summer while we watch the lights."

We were biking, the five of us, after picking up Caleb from work. Tom and I rode behind the others, coasting down an empty road.

"Vodka, you say?" Caleb asked, glancing back at us.

Tom and I looked at each other.

"Are you two drinking without us?" Caleb asked.

"We're watching the northern lights tonight," Tom said.

"Where?"

Tom waited a beat.

"God's Palm," I said. There was no point hiding it.

"Are you two going?" Caleb asked Sam and Jake.

They shook their heads, looking forward at the road.

"But it's the last real night of summer," Caleb said. "We should all be together."

Tom glanced at me. "We're not leaving anybody out," he called. "It's just something we do."

"Just the two of you?" Caleb asked.

"Yeah," Tom said.

Caleb frowned.

I liked that he was interested, maybe even jealous. The idea of Tom and me and a bottle of vodka, alone under the stars.

"Well, maybe you can make an exception this once," Caleb said, slowing down so his bike was in line with ours. "It's our last night of freedom. We should we make the most of it."

I shrugged. The prospect of another night of stargazing with Tom was nice but predictable. The truth was, our traditions were growing stale. I knew exactly how the night would go if it was just the two of us, but I had no idea what would happen if Caleb joined us.

Tom looked disappointed but said nothing.

⛈️

Tom's bottle of vodka was just the beginning. Caleb stole all manner of booze from his mother. Tequila, rum, an assortment of unusual beers like the kind I'd had at the barbecue. There was also some kind of blood-coloured cherry liqueur that I wouldn't touch. It smelled cloying, thick and syrupy in the bottle.

Sam and Jake were eager to try everything. After each sip, they gave tasting notes in hoity-toity accents, making fun of my nose for wine.

"Aromas of cactus and scorpion piss," Jake laughed.

"The last cherries of the season. Fallen, not picked," said Sam. "Base notes of rot."

Caleb and I laughed too. The sharpness of the tequila made me feel loose, awake and exhilarated, the stars above beaming with new energy.

"You have to try it with salt," Caleb told me. "And lime. Makes all the difference."

Tom was close-lipped, refusing to say much or try anything besides the vodka he'd brought. I found it harsher than the tequila. It burned my throat and made me sputter.

"Gross," I said.

He looked defeated. I knew this wasn't what he wanted. He would have much preferred it to be just the two of us. He lay on the grass and stared up at the sky, his bottle clutched in one hand, waiting.

"Let's play hide-and-seek," Caleb suggested.

We were all drunk by then.

"Yes!" I said. I stood up and fell back down in the same moment. Everyone laughed, even Tom.

"But it's going to start soon," Tom said, nodding upwards.

Caleb gave me a hand, helping me back up. "We'll keep an eye on the sky. We won't miss it."

Caleb volunteered to seek; the rest of us had to hide. There weren't many good places. You just had to go as far as you could, find a dark patch in the vineyard where the light of the moon didn't betray your shadow. I set off into the night, my stride mismatched and too fast, propelled forward by something other than myself. When I finally managed to stop, I was out of breath and dizzy. I knelt down behind a post at the end of a row of vines, one of the lifelines of God's Palm.

I waited forever. I must have gone farther than I thought. Caleb couldn't find me, which was the goal of the game, but I wanted him to seek me out, to discover me, my face half-hidden by grape leaves.

I kept looking upwards, expecting the lights to perform their dance at any moment. I was hungry. I craved the salty chips I knew were stashed away in my bag. I thought about heading back but I wasn't sure where back was. He'll find me, I told myself. He's Caleb.

And he did. Suddenly he was there, tapping me on the shoulder. Had I dozed off?

"Look," he said, his face turned towards the night sky.

I stood up; there it was. Aurora borealis. Purple, pink, green. Radiant and pulsing against the sky. It reminded me of Ruth's painting, the one at Mac's winery. Caleb grabbed my hand. His face was turned towards mine, partly shadowed.

I closed my eyes and decided to kiss him. His mouth was soft and hard in the same instant, overwhelmingly warm. I fell into it, an unrehearsed back and forth. Where were my feet?

He had a hand in my hair. He tasted slightly sour, boozy. My whole body ached for more of him.

I remember thinking: finally.

But really, it was just the beginning.

AFTER

꧁ꕥ꧂

Tom pushes his way towards me. The crowd opens around him. Everyone else is leaving but he's moving inwards, towards the front of the hall. I look at my feet. I can't look at his face or I'll smile.

Without speaking, he hugs me. Tight and close. I feel his strength, my face in his chest. The smell of soap from his morning shower.

His arms loosen just slightly and he leans back. He looks right into my eyes. I think he might start to tear up but then he shakes his head. He looks disgusted. He pulls me back towards him, whispers in my ear.

"I know it was him," he says.

I smile into his shoulder, relieved. Tom was always smart enough. Why did ever I doubt him?

BEFORE

꧁꧂

T he first day of school was bright and noisy. Upon waking, I could already imagine the slap of late footsteps echo down an empty hallway, catch-up chatter bouncing around the cafeteria at noon. I lay in bed and stared up at the ceiling. The light shifted above me, a trace of unknown movement outside. My stomach fluttered. I was nervous. It occurred to me I had never been nervous for the first day of school before, which I knew was unusual. You were supposed to be nervous, the day fuelled by adrenaline and anticipation. Even if you knew exactly what to expect—where your classes were, which teachers you had, where you'd sit in the cafeteria—the moments were still meant to pulse, signalling a beginning.

In the past, the most I had felt about the start of school was a resigned disappointment. I dreaded the end of summer. It meant the boys and I had to face the other kids, giving up the precious seclusion of the summer months.

This year though, an unwelcome apprehension crept into the dark corners of my mind. Caleb remained an unknown, unknowable. Even after our kiss, a new closeness, I had no idea what the day would bring because he would be a part of it. I looked down at my stomach, willing it to stop churning.

"First day of school," Ruth said, beaming, when I arrived downstairs. She tucked one side of my hair behind my ear.

I shrugged her off, annoyed. The gesture reminded me of Caleb, how he had once reached over and done the same. I wanted that gesture from him, not her.

Jake picked me up in his truck and we made the rounds, gathering the others. The two of us sat in silence as we drove, a prickly discomfort between us. The other night, when Caleb and I returned to the boys, Tom had been visibly angry, his hard gaze avoiding my eyes. He stormed off ahead as we collected our backpacks, the bottles, while Jake had stood off to the side, awkward and wordless. Sam and Caleb were the only ones to talk, rattling on drunkenly like nothing had happened, singing some stupid song together as we wandered through the vineyard to return home. I wasn't sure what Jake knew or what he suspected, but it felt different between us now—strained somehow.

"Who are we getting first?" I asked, knowing the answer.

"Caleb," he mumbled.

My insides swayed once again. Yesterday had been brutal. I had woken up hungover, lips peeling, and waited all day for contact. It was the first time I wished I had a computer or a cellphone. Caleb was always texting and instant messaging other people. Surely I was worth a quick message, some reassurance. Instead, I waited. I thought he might call or stop by, but he didn't.

To occupy my time, I had washed and folded laundry, preparing for the start of the school year, and wondered what he might be thinking. Before Caleb, insecurity was unfamiliar to me, but I realized now these feelings had been building all summer: self-doubt and uncertainty, confusion over a boy. Who had I become?

I had considered calling Tom but I was too anxious for any kind of peacemaking. He would be grumpy, unrelenting. Making amends would require a tricky combination of cajoling and distracting, and I hadn't been in the mood, not yesterday.

Jake and I idled outside of Caleb's house. He appeared on the front step, wearing new clothes. A crisp white shirt that accentuated his tan, with dark jeans and cool sneakers. He looked like he could stop your heart from beating. I briefly touched my chest.

"Morning," he said, hopping in the truck's back.

"Morning," we called.

Why didn't he sit next to me? I had slid to the middle of the truck bench to make room. An empty space, waiting for him.

I turned around to face him. Caleb was looking elsewhere, out at the day. He seemed completely relaxed, a still expression on his face, his hands loose in his lap. I turned back around. I wasn't sure what I was expecting. A wink, perhaps, literal or figurative. Some sign of recognition that things had changed between us.

Sam joined Caleb in the back and Tom had to squeeze in with me.

"Hey." His voice sounded cold. He was still upset.

"Grade eleven," I said, faking excitement. I was trying to be light.

"Grade eleven," he said distantly. He turned towards the window and stayed that way the whole ride.

We walked across the parking lot towards the school. Other kids stood around in clumps, hugging, laughing, swinging new backpacks. The boys walked fast, leaving me behind. Or maybe they were trying to catch up. Caleb was leading the way, as he tended to do. I rushed to follow.

It felt like everyone in the school looked at us when we walked in. Maybe that's what I had been feeling nervous about. The new member of our group, the attention he would attract. The secretary turned her head sharply as we passed the front office and the janitor stared at us under heavy eyelids. I smiled at my favourite teacher, Mr. Wheeler, in the hallway but he only squinted, looking at me and then Caleb and then me again. Social math.

The cafeteria was the worst, hundreds of craning heads.

I guess I knew it would be this way. I knew as soon as they saw him, they'd want to take him away from us.

৻৵৵৲

Tom and I had chosen all the same classes back at the beginning of summer. We couldn't have anticipated that there would ever be a reason not to navigate our days together, in and out of classrooms. Sam and Jake appeared in a few. Caleb as well. Right from the beginning, Caleb asked a lot of questions, his raised hand punctuating the teachers' monologues. Constant interruptions, no surprise to us.

"Is there a reason the final essay is only 750 words?"

"Is there a reason why we're spending two whole units on Nova Scotia geography?"

"Is there a reason why we're using an out-of-date textbook?"

The teachers answered his questions as best they could, flustered and mumbling. I felt bad for them. *Is there a reason?* wasn't really a question. It was an interrogation. A judgment. He was pushing them to justify their decisions and they seemed to have nothing compelling to pull them back from the edge he had chiselled off.

"Was it this bad last year?" he asked me. It was just the two of us now. The hallway crowd had swept the others ahead.

I shrugged. "Guess so."

"You really don't care, do you?"

I shrugged again.

He stopped and I stopped too. He put a hand on my arm, and I held my breath. "Self-education is important, Winifred, but it will only get you so far."

He sounded so sincere, I found myself nodding.

After English class, which Caleb, Tom, and I had together, we walked towards the cafeteria for morning break. Cliques of students wound familiar pathways to the same tables where they sat last year. Despite having reputations for wild spontaneity, teenagers are really creatures of habit. We passed a table of people I would usually ignore, but Dylan Sawyer whistled, loud and sharp, snagging our attention. A few others turned to look as well.

"Winnie, is that you?" Dylan asked, eyebrows raised. He wore a goofy smile.

I would usually disregard a comment like that, but I didn't mind Dylan, one of the more tolerable athletes in our grade. He lived up on the mountain with his many sisters and brothers; there seemed to be a Sawyer kid in every grade. They were all tall and slender with faces like teen movie stars. Angular cheekbones, and oddly straight, white teeth. Great legs too, because they all played on multiple sports teams. They had little money, but they got by on charm, which they had plenty of. They were known to be big flirts, but harmless. Good people.

"My god, you're beautiful," Dylan said, leaning his chair back on its two hind legs, his head resting in his hands, interlaced behind him. He wore a neon orange shirt made of a sporty, quick-dry material, and black running shorts. Dylan always looked ready to run track.

I wasn't sure how to respond. Ruth thanked men when they admired her appearance out loud, but I thought that was absurd. Why thank *them*? Thank them for what?

"Good summer, Dylan?" I asked instead.

"Great summer. Worked like a dog at my dad's garage. Finally made enough to fix up that old Camaro I've been holding on to." He looked at Caleb. "Who are you? The new kid?"

"I'm new to the area, yes." Caleb's voice sounded stiff after Dylan's mountain accent.

"What's your name?" Dylan asked.

"Caleb."

"You got a last name, Caleb? Or are you one of those eccentrics, like Prince or Cher? Maybe you take after Madonna." Dylan laughed at his own stupid joke.

"I don't think I have anything in common with those individuals, no."

Tom and I glanced at each other. It was obvious to everyone but Dylan that he was rubbing Caleb the wrong way.

We found Jake and Sam at our usual table in the back corner of the cafeteria. Jake was eating a banana. Sam was playing with a cellphone, typing madly with both thumbs.

"What's that?" I asked, sitting down next to them.

"Caleb gave it to me," Sam said. "He got a new phone. This is his old one."

I took an apple from my backpack. I didn't like seeing Sam hunched over a phone, communicating with god-knows-who—a private world, inaccessible to me. But maybe it was just a matter of time. Sam had always been the weak one. I said nothing, taking a large, loud bite of my apple.

"So, what's the deal?" Caleb asked.

"What?" I said.

"You really don't hang out with anyone else?"

I shrugged. "Not really."

"Never?"

I looked at the others. It wasn't something we really talked about.

"That's weird," Caleb said. "You guys are weird."

"We just don't get along," I tried. "Why force it?"

"You ever get in fights with them?" Caleb asked. "Disagreements?"

"Not really," Tom offered. "It's just, we have...different priorities."

Caleb looked unsatisfied, which irritated me. Why didn't he get it? He knew what it was like to distinguish yourself from the herd.

Sam tried. "There are the jocks, you know, the popular kids. Then there's the mountain dudes. See all that plaid?" He pointed to a group of guys who looked a bit like lumberjacks a few tables away. "Then there's the artsy farts, the nerds. The list goes on. We just don't fit in any of the groups. We do our own thing. It's cool." Sam didn't sound very convincing, perhaps because he himself wasn't entirely satisfied with our social arrangement.

"Is it?" Caleb asked.

"It's worked out okay so far," Jake mumbled.

Caleb left it at that, but only for a short time.

Later in the day, we had to participate in the annual school photo. The entire school gathered outside on the baseball field and a photo was taken from above to document the beginning of the year. The boys and I usually lurked at the back, uninterested in having our class membership captured on film, but Caleb walked directly to the front of the crowd. He didn't turn back to see if we would follow him, but we did. Sam certainly wanted to be pictured standing next to Caleb and I was starting to feel territorial, irked by how the other girls were eyeing him, and worse, how he was eyeing them.

Earlier, I had seen him talking to Amber and Jess in the lunch line, making them giggle. I didn't want to believe he would be interested in girls like that—girls he had dismissed as shallow just a few weeks previous at the canal—but why else would he talk to them? They should have been beneath him, but he was spending precious moments engaging them in conversation, coaxing out their laughter.

The boys and I crowded together with Caleb at the front of the group, looking up at the camera. The photographer was taking a number of shots and we were encouraged to "keep smiling" for several minutes. I kept my face impassive. When the photographer told us that it was time for the last shot, I grabbed Caleb's hand without thinking. I guess I wanted something about us to feel solid and real. Maybe if there was photographic proof of our connection, it would crystallize, adopting the form I wanted it to. Maybe it would be less confusing.

Caleb squeezed my hand but quickly let it go. The photographer told us we were done, and the crowd dispersed. Everyone wandered back inside. Caleb walked with the boys. I remained a few steps behind, frustrated. I had thought that night at God's Palm was the beginning of something new for him and me, but now things felt the same as before.

⧫

The last period of the day was Canadian History, which the boys, Caleb, and I all had together. Dylan was in that class too. He wasn't known for being very smart, but I often wondered if his difficulties with school might be less about intelligence and more about attention span. In class, he was easily distracted and often spoke out of turn, jumping from one subject to the next, stealing the attention of the class whenever he felt bored or couldn't follow the lesson.

Our teacher, Mrs. Sanford, droned on about the Acadian settlement in Grand Pré—Acadian history would be a major unit this semester—when Dylan put up his hand.

"Yes, Dylan?" Mrs. Sanford blinked behind thick, grandmotherly glasses.

"I caught a baby raccoon yesterday," Dylan said, with no acknowledgement of the subject change. "Saw it trampin' around the backyard. I baited it with my peanut butter sandwich. It walked over to me like it was nothin'. Ate the whole thing, right out of my hand."

Mrs. Sanford blinked again. Caleb, sitting next to me, looked sideways, baffled by Dylan's outburst.

"I've got it trapped in a cage," Dylan went on. "The one we use for the dog in the summer so he can stay outside all day. What do you think raccoons like to eat?"

The class laughed and Mrs. Sanford looked down at her lecture notes as if maybe they held the answer.

"Do you think the momma's gonna come looking for her baby? My brother Chase says raccoons can be vicious, especially if you take their young."

"I—I don't know, Dylan," Mrs. Sanford stuttered. "I can't say I've ever been in that situation before."

"That guy," Caleb whispered to me, "is fucking *nuts*."

We saw Dylan again in the parking lot at the end of the day. He was showing off his newly refurbished car, red with silver stripes. I recognized it immediately. That car had passed Caleb, Tom, and me in a cloud of exhaust when we were biking up to Angela's house, the day we broke in.

"That thing is an environmental hazard," Caleb said, disgusted.

Dylan revved the engine. The smell of gassy fumes surrounded us and Caleb coughed dramatically. Dylan didn't notice but he probably wouldn't have cared anyway. He loved that car. I could see it in his face: a bursting kind of smile. Pure joy.

Because he was one of the few kids outside the boys who I occasionally chatted with, I knew Dylan wasn't much of a partier.

In that way, he was different than the other boys in our grade. He chose physical labour instead. I guess because money was scarce and there was work to be done. He was clearly proud of his new ride. Caleb would never understand that.

⟨ℰℴ⟩

In school, Caleb answered as many questions as he asked. He quickly rose to the top, overshadowing the other A students, inspiring both awe and fear in his teachers. They seemed to respect his ability to answer every question posed, to push class discussions into unfamiliar territory, but the fact that he challenged and corrected them clearly also made them nervous. One day, he disputed Mr. Minglewood's definition of corruption.

"It's more nuanced than that," Caleb explained. "You're only thinking about corruption in a very traditional sense. What about subtle forms of corruption, like how advertising is corrupting young minds, making kids think they need to buy things to feel whole?"

Better teachers would have welcomed engagement from a bright student, but Mr. Minglewood blushed a deep red, shooting back a retort.

"We're not talking about that kind of corruption, Caleb. This is economics class."

"But aren't advertising and capitalism central to our economy?"

The class broke into murmurs.

Did Caleb really care about doing well in school or was he just trying to make a point? I knew our school would be easy for him, given his elite, urban education (he once told us he'd gone to a private school back in Vancouver), but instead of blending in, he used his intelligence to stand out. I couldn't quite figure out why.

Was he attempting to raise the tone at our rural school, or was he just showing off? Maybe a bit of both.

⁖⁖⁖

The first dance of the year was held on Thursday. Dances happened on weeknights, likely to discourage drinking. If you had to get up and go to school Friday morning, you would be less likely to drink the night before. The theme for the first dance was always *Welcome Back!* Every year they hung the same banner, threadbare and yellowed, in the cafeteria.

I looked up at it and groaned. It was early in the day, before the first bell. Amber and Jess were standing on tiptoe on top of two chairs. They wore short denim skirts and as they reached up to hook the banner in place, their skirts appeared to shrink, their legs to grow.

I hit Sam on the arm. "Stop staring."

Jake looked down, embarrassed, when I said it. Tom laughed.

Despite their diminutive clothing and general ditziness, Amber and Jess were heavily involved in school activities. Together, they signed up for dance committee, school council, and planned various fundraisers. For this, the principal and teachers loved them. If only they knew.

I had heard stories—we all had. One in particular stuck with me. The cops had raided a party up on the South Mountain the year before. The police officers stormed through each room in the house, flashlights held high, and kids stumbled out of the house in a mass frenzy, clutching their half-drunk beers, staggering into the woods. The story I heard was that the cops happened upon Amber and Jess in the upstairs den. Both bent over the same couch, topless, two hockey players behind them. When I first heard the story, I tried to picture it. Bouncing breasts, pink faces. I couldn't imagine stripping down in the middle of a party, bending over, and spreading wide in front of my best friend. In some ways, I envied their closeness. What level of intimacy would it take to do that? But I also felt sorry for them, a sickening kind of pity. The two officers walking in: breasts quickly covered, faces burning red.

We watched Caleb smile at the girls as he entered the cafeteria, checking out the banner, looking at their bare legs. Tom was still giving me the silent treatment, but I refused to give in and apologize. I had done nothing wrong. Why was he acting like a teenage girl, anyway? Holding a ridiculous grudge.

"Morning, boys," Caleb said, joining us at our table. "What's this I hear about a dance?"

"Just some Welcome Back thing." Tom yawned. "A bunch of drunk jocks and their girlfriends."

I rolled my eyes. "Don't tell me you want to go."

Caleb mimed zipping shut his two perfect lips.

⟡

By lunch, the boys had decided they were all going to the dance. Tom, Jake, Sam. I couldn't believe it. How could three people change so quickly?

"You're kidding," I said when they told me. I honestly thought they were.

"Why?" asked Caleb.

We were firmly anti-dance and always had been. We made fun of the kids who went to dances. We thought of dances as the lowest and most laughable of high school rituals. But all of a sudden our shared, fixed opinions were becoming irrelevant. Caleb was changing them.

"Because school dances are lame."

"Have you ever actually been to one?"

I shrugged. "No."

"Well, then how do you know they're lame?"

I looked to Tom for support, but he wouldn't meet my eyes.

༒

Later that night, Ruth asked me if I was staying in. She was making supper while Mac and I sat at the kitchen table. Mac combed through spreadsheets related to the winery while I tried to lose myself in a new book. I still hadn't made it through the stack Caleb had loaned me, but I wasn't in the mood for one of his recommendations. I'd returned to my old detective genre, comforting in its familiarity.

"Mm-hmm," I mumbled.

"Isn't there a dance tonight?" she asked.

"Uh-huh."

"Full words would be appreciated, Winnie."

I looked up from my book. "Yes, Ruth, the Welcome Back dance is tonight."

"You don't want to go?"

"Have I ever?"

She asked me to get a jar of pickles from the cellar. I closed the book and yawned. I opened the hatch in the kitchen floor and climbed down the ladder, breathing in the cool scent of must. I liked it down there. Dark and serene. Unseen critters spinning webs or building nests in the far corners, along the rafters. It seemed like a whole, contained world that we just rented shelf space from.

"Mustard pickles or chow?" I called up.

"Mustard," she said.

I grabbed a jar of bright green pickles and re-emerged in the light of the kitchen.

"So, you and the boys are still in your anti-dance phase?"

"It's not a phase, Mother. At least not for me."

"I hate it when you call me that."

"That's because I only call you that when I'm annoyed."

She was dredging haddock fillets in flour, then egg, then breadcrumb. Once breaded, she laid the fish in a hot, buttered pan to cook. I had watched her do it a million times before.

"And why are you annoyed?" she asked.

"So many questions." I rolled my eyes at Mac, who chuckled quietly.

"I'll stop."

"No, it's okay." I sat back down at the table, folding one leg underneath me. "It's Tom and the boys. They're...going to the dance."

"Hm," Ruth muttered, arranging the crisp, golden fish on a platter and squeezing lemon overtop.

"Full words would be appreciated, Ruth."

She briefly stopped squeezing but didn't look up. "I assume this has something to do with girls?"

I considered. "Maybe."

Maybe it *was* about wanting girls. Maybe a platonic friendship with a girl was no longer enough. They were hormonal teenage boys, after all.

"Is Caleb going?"

"Yup."

"Caleb's going and you're not?"

I shrugged, feeling my face heat up. "Yeah, so?"

Ruth understood she shouldn't press it. I noticed Mac glance up from his papers, curious. He knew Caleb from the winery, after all.

A part of me wanted to tell Ruth. To take her into the other room and tell her everything. The kiss, the northern lights, and nothing since. Caleb treating me like I was just one of the boys again. How did it all work? She would know what to do. But as I watched her scatter chopped parsley over the fish, I couldn't bring myself to ask. I didn't want to resurrect her past dating life. She was happy with Mac. He had practically moved in by that point. He spent every night at our house and kept a toothbrush in the bathroom. It was odd at first, a third person in our small world. I sometimes stirred at the sound of his footsteps in the hallway at night, a heavier tread than Ruth's. But I liked having him there. It was what I wanted for Ruth and they got along so well. It might be dangerous to remind Ruth of the chase, of how to win. Her old ways.

We ate the fried haddock with mashed potatoes and sweet, crunchy mustard pickles. I imagined Caleb dancing with Amber and Jess. With both of them at the same time.

"You don't like it?" Ruth asked, always eager for a compliment.

I took another forkful. "No, it's great."

"It's amazing!" Mac said. "Here, Winnie, why don't you try it with some wine?"

He got a glass from the cabinet and splashed some white wine inside. "You don't mind, right Ruth?"

She shrugged.

I held the glass up to the light. The wine was pale yellow with a subtle green tint.

Ruth snorted. "You look like a professional," she said.

"She practically is," Mac beamed. "What do you get from this one, Winnie?"

I stuck my nose in the glass. Immediately, I smelled green apple, sour and plump. Underneath, layers of minerality. Earthy, damp, then something salty like the sea. When I told Mac, his eyes shone.

I took a sip. The wine rolled over my tongue, pooling in the sides of my mouth. It was weightless, soaring. All the flavours I had smelled, and more. I thought of waves unfolding and crashing on the shore. Light movement with a strong finish.

"It's wonderful," I said, after I swallowed. I quickly took another sip. "What is it?"

"This is a blend of white grapes I've been working with," Mac explained. "Some L'Acadie blanc, some Chardonnay, a few lesser known grapes. I love that it tastes a bit like the ocean. It's so Nova Scotian. Goes great with fish."

I drank slowly, savouring each mouthful. The wine accentuated the humble haddock, playing off the richness of the buttery breadcrumbs and tangy lemon. It was so good that in that moment, I forgot to be mad about the boys, about Caleb. I forgot to think about the dance and what they might be doing there.

⁂

Jake was late picking me up the next morning. He was always at my house by 8:20 A.M. to drive to school, but it was 8:32 and there was still no sign of him.

I was sitting on the porch, waiting. Ruth came out with a fresh cup of coffee. She had a day of painting ahead of her and she looked alert and energetic. Mac had already left for the winery.

"Not here yet?" Ruth asked.

"Nope."

Ruth checked her watch. "It's getting late, Winnie. Want me to drive you?"

"You're about to start working."

"Someone's gotta take you."

"Give it a few more minutes."

We waited a bit longer and then I gave in. The drive to school was fast and silent. I think Ruth knew that questions wouldn't help. I was already internally asking them myself.

I was relieved to see Jake's truck wasn't in the school parking lot. The thought had formed that they might have forgotten me. But that was silly. It was one night, one dance. I was still Winnie, their oldest friend.

But where were they?

First period was English with Mr. Wheeler, a class I had with both Tom and Caleb. I arrived just as the second bell was ringing, the final warning to get to class. I couldn't see Tom, but Caleb was there. He waved me over. I slid onto the seat next to him as Mr. Wheeler started taking attendance, making little checkmarks on his list.

"Where's Tom?" I murmured.

Caleb's eyes were so wide you could fall right into them. "You didn't hear?"

I shook my head, heart paused.

"They got suspended."

Heart on fast-forward. "Who did?"

Caleb lowered his voice, his face serious. "Thomas and the others. Samuel and Jacob."

"Suspended?" I couldn't believe what I was hearing. "For what?"

He winced. "Drinking on school property. We all had a few beers before the dance. I guess the principal smelled it on them. I was lucky."

Caleb nodded at Mr. Wheeler who was giving us the look. He was ready to start class. I shut up, my head full with the news.

Drinking at a school dance got you a five-day suspension. Your parents were called to pick you up and you weren't allowed back on school property until your suspension was served. I was vaguely aware of this fact—everybody was—but it felt completely unattached to my high school reality until it stole my three best friends away from me for five whole days. Suddenly, I was implicated in the mundane dramas of the student population. Associated with school dances and suspensions.

The worst part was they hadn't told me. Tom, especially. I knew things had been strained between us but the betrayal I felt was acute. It was a gasping, sputtering kind of abandonment that left my insides feeling vacant.

I didn't call. I didn't check in. I stayed quiet that whole weekend and the days that followed. The sense of their falseness combined with my fear of being forgotten left me cut off. Because they were a bunch of cowards, their five-day suspension turned into exile from me, too.

"You're back," I said to Jake on Friday morning the following week. His truck appeared at 8:20 A.M. like nothing had happened. Idling, waiting, the radio on.

Ruth and I were on our way out of the house. We both assumed she would have to drive me, like she had every other day that week.

I climbed into the truck and he nodded, wincing. "I'm back."

Sam was more enthusiastic when we picked him up "Winnie, my man, long time no see!"

I laughed. "What's it been? Six years?"

"At least! Fill me in. What have I missed?"

Tom only grimaced.

"Hey," I said to him, trying for lukewarm.

"Hey," he said, a degree warmer.

One of the best things about boys is it's very easy to pretend. To move on, like nothing ever happened.

※

The tension between Tom and I eased up when the boys returned to school. I'm not sure if he was keeping some kind of score, my supposed wrong in kissing Caleb vacated by his experiment in adolescent shame, or if he, like me, realized nothing between Caleb and me had changed post-kiss. Caleb was still frustratingly flirty but nothing more. Whatever it was, I was relieved Tom's tedious grudge had ebbed.

In the cafeteria, it felt good to laugh with Tom, uninhibited, at Sam's discovery he had grabbed his little brother's lunch instead of his own. A meagre serving for a much smaller boy, and tuna salad to boot (Sam's most hated of all sandwiches). Our laughter had a cleansing effect, washing away some of the complications Caleb had introduced into our friendship. It felt good to look over and meet Tom's eyes throughout the day, to communicate without speaking, as we had always done before. I realized how much I had missed him. I could tell he had missed me too.

At the end of the day, I expected us all to pile into Jake's truck and do something fun together. It had been a whole week, longer than we'd ever gone without hanging out, and the day was sunny, calling to us from outside the stuffy school. I envisioned us biking down the valley, maybe going for an ice cream. But when the bell rang, Tom seemed in an unusual hurry to pack up his things.

"Where are you off to?" I asked, watching him stuff loose pages into his backpack.

He fumbled with the bag's zipper. "We actually have tryouts today."

"Tryouts for what?" I gazed up at him, puzzled.

He seemed to wait a beat before meeting my eyes. "Football."

I laughed and shook my head. "Come on. We don't even have a football team."

"They're starting one this year. We're all trying out." He shrugged and smiled meekly. "It could be fun."

"But it's such a mindless sport," I said. "And you'll be playing with all the jocks."

"We're allowed to do things without each other," Tom said slowly, carefully, as if someone else had prepped him for this exchange. "I don't have to do everything with you."

"Right," I said, nodding. "But is this really the thing you want to do without me?"

"I'm gonna be late." He swung his book bag onto his back. "Let's hang out tomorrow. I probably won't even make the team."

I watched Tom rush out of the classroom, feeling dazed. First the dance, now this. Tom had said they were all trying out. That meant Jake and Sam too. Caleb was pushing them farther into the mob, away from me.

❧❧❧

They all made the team. It was the first year for football, so no one was particularly good. They would have taken anyone.

Practices took place before and after classes. It was all the boys seemed to do and who knew if they were getting any better? Ruth had to drive me to and from school because they were all too busy and I refused to take the bus. Our school was a hub for a large area of valley communities; they transported kids in from thirty minutes away. I had no interest in mixing with the civilian population on a meandering, bumpy drive through the countryside.

The boys looked absurd in their football uniforms, top-heavy and uncoordinated. Tom tried on the full outfit for me the day before their first official practice. We were in his bedroom and I was lying on the bed, looking from poster to poster, stargazing. The Milky Way, Saturn's rings. He emerged from the bathroom wearing those tight little pants and the ridiculous shoulder pads.

"Do I look stupid?" he asked.

Yes.

"No," I said. "You look great."

Sometimes I would linger after school to watch them practice, catch a ride with Jake when they were done, but I soon learned football was as dull as I had imagined. I didn't know the rules of the game and didn't care enough to learn. It seemed like a lot of starting and stopping and unnecessary whistle blowing. The coach was Ms. Vaughan, the biology teacher. She had short grey hair and a voice like a bark. She blew her whistle as though her life depended on it.

Caleb spent a lot of time talking to Ms. Vaughan. Squinting together, pointing at the others. I assumed he had played football before. After they spoke, she would blow her whistle and shout instructions I didn't understand. In response, the team rearranged themselves on the field in complicated formations.

Despite Caleb's intensity, he was not the team captain. Dylan was. I took a quiet pleasure in this fact. Within the first few days of school, Caleb had singled Dylan out as someone to hate, probably because Dylan was one of the few people immune to Caleb's intelligence and charm. Like the boys and me, the kids in our grade quickly fell under Caleb's spell, the girls eager to enchant, the boys hungry to impress. What did Caleb have that the rest of us didn't? Any list of traits fell short. His looks, his intellect, his urban sophistication. All of those were important, but did they really add up to greatness? I decided some people must have a kind of magic about them. My attraction to Caleb certainly felt supernatural, defying reason and expectation.

Dylan, however, remained indifferent. By this point, Caleb was flitting between social groups, spending recess with us and eating lunch with the jocks, his teammates. While the other boys on the team appeared enthralled by Caleb (rapt attention while he spoke; roaring laughter when he teased or joked), Dylan seemed to tune Caleb out, uninterested in his stories from a life lived elsewhere, of travels and adventure. I watched the jocks gather around Caleb at lunch, leaning in to listen, while Dylan chomped away at a sad sandwich he had probably made himself, gazing up at the ceiling. I'm sure this drove Caleb mad. Even if he hated Dylan, Caleb would still want to be able to manipulate him. That's why the idea of Dylan bossing Caleb around as team captain—acting superior, getting all the glory—was so satisfying.

I still wanted Caleb, but I also wanted, just once, for him to be put in his place. I wanted to watch someone dominate *him*. He was corrupting the boys, leading them away from me. He was also mixing with the other kids, which disgusted me. We were better than them! I started to feel ashamed that I had followed him so blindly all summer long. I needed to break free, to be on top again, and to take the boys with me.

I smiled quietly to myself when I imagined Dylan vetoing Caleb's suggestions at practice or staring blankly, unmoved, in response to Caleb's attempts at influence. Those fantasies made Caleb seem less powerful, less attractive. But then I wondered what it would mean, to no longer want Caleb. A return to my old life, commonplace and pale. I knew I didn't want that, but I also missed the sense of control I once had.

In addition to Dylan, the football team was made up of a bunch of boys I had known my whole life and mostly ignored. Watching them run up and down the football field, I realized I hadn't said a word to many of them in years. It really started in middle school, back when the popular boys made a list ranking every girl in our grade by her hotness level. The list was passed around, a shared secret between classmates, hidden carefully from the teachers. By that point everyone already understood who was considered hot and who wasn't, but the meticulous ranking seemed especially cruel and noxious.

Since then, I had shunned the popular crew and the boys had stepped in line behind me. We had always been somewhat of a closed group anyway, so it wasn't a major adjustment.

Now though, I watched the boys huddle on the field with the pigs who had written that list years before, and who had done much worse in the years since. To my endless annoyance, their girlfriends joined me in the stands. I sat separate from them, in a far corner on the top row of the bleachers, a book on my lap. They ignored me and I tried my best to ignore them. It's easy to ignore quiet girls. The high-pitched and giggly ones are harder to tune out.

At one point, I heard Jess whisper to a girl named Katie about me and Caleb. "Are they together? Kyle said they were."

Katie turned around in her seat and looked at me. "No way," she hissed back. "She's been with Tom for, like, ever."

I stared down at my book, pretending I'd heard nothing. Let them think what they want.

Soon the team started playing actual games, at our home field but also at schools in neighbouring towns and counties. The first game was an away game. I watched the boys pile into a bus with their teammates after class. Jake gave me a small wave from the window as they drove off, his face pale. I could tell he was nervous.

But by some miracle, they won.

Things changed after that. Winning seemed to bond the team together. Like Caleb, the boys started sitting with their teammates at lunch, leaving me to fend for myself. Tom explained that this was expected of them. They needed to sit together to strategize about games to come.

I sat at our old table, watching them from afar. They didn't look like they were discussing football. Caleb was talking, face animated, hands flying, while the others looked on eagerly, waiting for the punchline. When it finally arrived, Sam spit out his drink through raucous laughter. I flinched when some jerk named Chris slapped Sam on the back affectionately, as if they were old friends.

I decided to attend their first home game. I told myself I was trying to be supportive of my friends but really, I was desperate to understand how and why they were slipping away from me. Was this solely Caleb's influence, or were the boys actually drawn to the game of football, its promise of male fellowship?

I took my seat on the bleachers, which were nearly full. I had to squeeze between a teacher and another student. The day was cloudy but still unusually warm. It was nearing the end of September. I wore short sleeves and the teacher next to me smelled bad, like sweat.

The game was even less interesting than practice. It seemed to me they stopped and started even more in actual games. I grew bored quickly, squinting to make out Tom, Jake, and Sam, confusing them with others on the team. The only person who remained distinct on the field was Caleb. Even from a distance, he seemed to radiate heat and energy.

At one point, Coach Vaughan called a time out. I could see her speaking with both Caleb and Dylan on the sidelines, their helmets off. Soon, Caleb was yelling, pointing at the field. Dylan crossed his arms and shook his head. Coach Vaughan shrugged. From what I could tell, Dylan prevailed.

They ended up losing the game. Later, I would find out that their loss had everything to do with Caleb and Dylan's confrontation. Dylan's strategy had been wrong; supposedly Caleb's suggestion likely would have changed the course of the game and led to a win. I would hear all about it later that night at our first high school party.

The boys were feeling defeated by their loss and Caleb convinced them the party would help.

"We can commiserate while we drink," Caleb said. "It'll be good for you."

Dylan offered to the host the party, possibly because he felt guilty. I had never heard of him hosting a party before. There was a field in the back of his house. He told the team he would build a bonfire; we could gather around the flames to drink.

"Please come," Tom urged me after the game. "I'll be extra bummed if you're not there."

I agreed, but only because it felt good to feel wanted, to be the centre of Tom's world once again.

When we got to Dylan's, we could smell the fire immediately. Dylan and his family lived in a small house up on the mountain. Peeling blue paint, an overgrown lawn. The yard was full of cars and only a few of them looked functional. I spotted Dylan's red Camaro parked off to the side, away from the rest.

"Back there." Jake pointed.

We could see the bonfire crackle in the distance, flickers of light against a darkening sky. Night descended quickly. It didn't feel like fall but the days were getting shorter.

We stepped carefully in the dark, heading for the field. Caleb led the way and I followed, nervous about being at a football party, about what people would think when they saw me there. A part of me wanted to hide behind the boys all night.

When we reached the party a few kids glanced our way, but no one remarked on my presence. Most of the team had already arrived. They stood around drinking cans of beer, unusually quiet, staring into the blaze. The bonfire was huge, and Dylan kept adding more wood. The flames swelled, sparking in response.

Tom handed me a beer. I drank it quickly, wondering if all parties were this quiet, this awkward. Maybe no one was drunk enough yet. I looked up to find the stars, but they were hidden by clouds.

"What do we do now?" I asked Tom.

"Not sure," he said, and we both laughed quietly.

Luckily, more people soon arrived. As the crowd grew, it also loosened. The team was depressed. They needed Amber and Jess and the other popular kids to lift and lighten the mood. Soon, people were yelling and laughing, chugging beer and cheering each other on. *This* was what I thought their parties would be like, though I had never envisioned them in a field.

I drank another beer, and then another. I stood with Tom and Jake. Sam had wandered off, following Caleb.

"Caleb's pissed," Tom said, slurring his words a little.

"About the game?" I asked.

"Yeah. He thinks it's Dylan's fault we lost."

I took a sip of my beer. It tasted awful. "Do you agree?"

"I don't know," Tom said. "I barely know the game. But Caleb seems certain. He says we should vote Dylan out as captain."

Jake frowned. "Seems a little harsh. It was just one game."

"Do you guys even like playing it?" I asked.

They looked me.

"Of course," Tom said. "What do you mean?"

"It looks so boring. I thought maybe you were just doing it because Caleb told you to."

I could feel both Tom and Jake bristle. I knew them so well; any change of energy was easily perceptible.

"We *want* to play," Tom said, his face serious. "Those guys aren't so bad, you know. You've been telling us for years they're these horrible people but they're actually pretty good guys, right Jake?"

Jake nodded. "Yeah," he said. "Tom's right."

I didn't know what to say.

"And you know, what right do you have to tell us who to hang out with?" Tom asked. He suddenly looked angry. "We can do whatever we want."

"Of course," I said. I took a step towards him, a pleading look. I wasn't sure how the conversation had turned so quickly. "I just thought, I don't know, that we'd be better off without them."

Tom's face softened slightly, but he still looked upset. He shook his head. "I'm just mad about the game and I'm taking it out on you. Losing sucks. Maybe we *should* vote Dylan out."

I nodded, though I didn't agree.

Later, Caleb and Sam emerged from the crowd. Caleb stood in front of the fire and pulled bottles of wine from his backpack. He opened them up and passed them around. Grateful, people took large swigs and then handed them to others. As the bottles got closer, I recognized the labels with a start. They were from Mac's winery.

I barely had time to process that Caleb was stealing from Mac when I heard someone yell in the distance, towards the house. It was non-verbal, more of a howl. A male voice. People started running toward the sound and I followed, joining the crowd. We saw flames on the front lawn. For a moment, I thought it was another bonfire but then people were yelling at us to stay back. It was a car. Dylan's red Camaro, in flames. I saw Dylan at the front of the crowd. He was crying, cheeks wet and glistening.

I glanced at Tom. His mouth was open, his brow crumpled. I wondered if he was thinking the same thing as me. Caleb.

A door slammed open and one of Dylan's brothers burst from the house, announcing he had called the fire department. He slung an arm over Dylan's shoulders to comfort him. Dylan was still crying. People looked at each other awkwardly. No one knew how to handle a crying teenage boy.

I searched the crowd for Caleb. Eventually I spied him at the back of the crowd, standing next to Sam. His arms were crossed and he wore a satisfied smile, close-lipped and arrogant. He caught my eye and his smile opened. He nodded at me, with a look I couldn't quite read—almost as if I were a part of this somehow.

AFTER

❦

We decide to visit God's Palm. Jake has his truck and it's a short drive from the hall. We pile in like we used to. Tom and me up front with Jake, Sam in the back. No fifth member to accommodate.

Jake is unusually chatty. Sam, eerily quiet. The fire has revealed unknown sides of these people I've known forever: how they respond to crisis, to chaos. Jake mumbles about this and that: the weather, what he'd like for dinner, how many trick-or-treaters they got last year. With a jolt, I remember today is Halloween. Jake keeps talking. He sounds almost manic, spewing more words in a few minutes than he has in the last three months combined. I feel dizzy. His words are coming out so fast and he leaps from topic to topic, avoiding the fire but prattling on about everything else. Tom glances at me, worried, and then turns on the radio. It's the local station. A cheery pop song fills the truck, at odds with our mood. Jake shuts up at the sound, but it looks like a real effort.

Sam sits in glum silence in the open back. Knees clutched to his chest.

We drive up to the vineyard. The auto-tuned, perky voice of the singer on the radio makes the moment feel surreal. I gasp. Before us, black stretches in every direction. The vines, once a sign of life and promise, are indistinguishable, part of the never-ending darkness. The scene is far worse than I imagined. God's Palm looks larger somehow, now that it has been destroyed. The damage is so vast, I can't make out where it ends.

The winery itself is a mere skeleton. Caved in, blackened. Collapse imminent.

"Fuck!" Jake yells for all of us, silencing the music with the turn of the key.

We emerge from the truck and Tom is holding my hand. We walk to the yellow tape. I don't know how long we stand there, just staring. I want to do anything but look, but I know it's important for them to see what Caleb has caused.

Sam finally breaks the silence. "This was him?" he asks, staring me right in the eyes. His are flecked with amber. Has he ever looked at me so directly?

"Of course," I say. "Who else?"

"Maybe it was an accident? It's been so hot," Sam says.

"Something had to start it. Fires don't just spontaneously ignite," I reason.

"I just can't believe he would do this," Sam says, staring out at the charred wasteland.

"You can't?" Tom laughs in a way that almost frightens me. "I can. Look at what he did to Angela, to Dylan."

Sam grows teary. I squeeze his hand with my free one.

"So what are we going to do about it?" Jake asks. His voice is so loud, so clear.

BEFORE

✿

At the beginning of October, Mac offered me a job at the winery. I had more free time now that the boys were busy with football, and maybe Mac sensed I needed a distraction. After school and on weekends, I had been spending a lot of hours on the couch in the living room, reading and watching movies. Mac sometimes walked by and asked politely about the book in my hands, but I felt his eyes on me as he walked away, a kind of quiet worry. I wasn't sure what concerned him more, my laziness or all that time alone. Either way, work was a good solution, and I liked the idea of learning more about wine.

My position at the winery consisted of odd jobs, most of them related to cleaning and upkeep: scrubbing the bathrooms, weeding the flower beds, putting labels on wine bottles. I felt like I was constantly sweeping. The steady flow of foot traffic in the tasting room brought in plenty of dust and dirt from the parking lot and the vineyard itself, and Mac wanted it all promptly whisked away.

"Wineries are very dirty places," he said, "but our customers like everything to feel sleek and clean. They don't realize a vineyard is actually a farmer's field and a vintner is a farmer. It's the great secret of the wine world. Everyone thinks wine is this pillar of elitism but it's born of good, old-fashioned hard work in the soil."

All the cleaning left my limbs heavy and tired at the end of the day, but I liked feeling I was contributing to the production of Mac's wine, however peripherally.

I expected to see Caleb at work, but he was never there during one of my shifts. I figured he had cut back on his hours because of football or maybe he and I fulfilled the same role in the ecosystem of the winery: he worked when I didn't. We hadn't really spoken since the party at Dylan's. I was certain Caleb had set the fire, but I didn't know what to do about it.

I was growing concerned about what Caleb might be capable of. His reactions to interference from others seemed to be escalating. What he had done to Angela had been troubling, but what he had done to Dylan seemed worse, perhaps because it was such a violent, exhibitionist kind of revenge. A fire that could have spread, that could have hurt more than Dylan's car.

Another part of me admired Caleb's lack of inhibition and remorse. While I worked, bent over and scouring the sinks in the bathroom at the winery, I kept seeing his face that night at Dylan's, the way he had looked at me. I was sure he was trying to tell me *he* had lit the fire. Almost as if he was showing off, performing for me. I didn't tell anyone. Did that mean I was his co-conspirator? That I needed to protect his secret?

Sometimes I worked with Tara, the girl I had seen around the winery in the summer. She liked to talk, which helped our working hours pass quickly. Tara was nineteen. Last year, she had been kicked out of her university dorm in Halifax the first week of school for doing mushrooms, banned from returning until frosh week was over. She couch-surfed for a few nights and then found herself back in the valley, under her father's roof. I knew her dad, Les, from around Gaspereau. He was a valley hippy of the old guard. He lived in a crooked house covered in solar panels that he had built himself, up on the mountain. Their home was a jumble of awkward renovations and haphazard rooms. I had never been inside, but from the road it looked like it might fall down if the wind blew too hard.

Les had dropped Tara off at university that first week, and then woke up a few mornings later to find her eating cereal at the kitchen table.

"What did he say when he saw you?" I asked.

"Nothing really." She shrugged. "'You're back. Pass the corn-flakes.' He didn't care."

I wondered what Ruth would do in the same situation. She probably wouldn't be mad like most parents, but she'd at least ask a few more questions than Les. *Why are you home? Is everything okay?* Tara's story made Ruth seem almost responsible by comparison.

In addition to her frosh week shenanigans, Tara also flunked out of first year.

"I kept sleeping in, missing class," she said. "I couldn't afford the textbooks, so I was always behind. It just wasn't for me."

I quickly grew comfortable around Tara. She required little of me, and I wondered if I had been wrong about girls, about their universal need to share feelings and dreams. Maybe they weren't all as bad as I'd once thought.

"Do you ever fantasize about putting the wrong label on a bottle?" I asked Tara one day, pressing a sticky square of paper onto a bottle of Chardonnay.

She laughed. "No, but I love that you do."

"They wouldn't even know the difference. They would drink their Chardonnay and think it was a bottle of L'Acadie."

"So why do it then?" she asked.

I considered, thinking of Caleb. "Sometimes it's fun to play with people."

Tara blinked twice, grinning.

"Okay, let's do one," she said. "Let's send a mislabelled bottled of Chardonnay out into the world. It'll be our secret."

Tara held the bottle while I spread the label on its front, both of us laughing. I briefly thought of Mac, but the thrill of defiance, however small, won.

⁊⧉⧉⧉⧉⧉⧉⧉⧉⧉⧉⧉⧉⧉

I was fortunate that I was too young to serve the wine. It meant I rarely interacted with customers. While I loved Mac's winery—his philosophy, his natural approach—the clientele was predictable. Familiar locals shopped there, of course, but they were outnumbered by tourists from away and visitors from other parts of Nova Scotia. There were far too many bachelorette parties from Halifax, groups of twentysomething women usually wearing hot pink or floral dresses, the bride crowned with a cheap, plastic tiara.

I wasn't allowed to sell the wine, so I got to pass the customers off to Tara, who hated them just as much as me. We loathed the middle-agers too. The groups of ladies who wore T-shirts with stupid sayings like *Sip Happens!* and *Where's the Finish Wine?* They were all so loud and excited. I often pretended to count our stock while I closely observed these women. What was their connection to one another? Sometimes they held hands while they pranced around the tasting room like little girls. I watched them mill around the winery, making too much noise, and saw through their sad attempts to make sure everyone else knew how much fun they were having.

With each group, I waited for cracks to reveal themselves. Disagreements and low-lying resentments. They were there; they always are. The one left out. The two who compete. The three who should really be two. It looked like a lot of work to sustain all that giddy, false joy alongside envy and insecurity.

"How can eight women actually be such good friends?" I asked Tara, my chin in my hands as I leaned on the tasting bar, watching a group of women leave the winery.

"They're not," she said, wiping the bar clean with a cloth. "They're only here because it's someone's birthday or someone's engagement. One woman brings them together and then they take photos and call each other girlfriends, but really they only ever see each other when they're all dressed up and looking their best for outings like this. You think these people call each other when they need a ride home from the hospital? When their father dies? No way."

It was nice to know I wasn't the only one who saw through it. It made me wonder, though, if any friendships were truly genuine. I thought I had that with the boys, but look how quickly they had turned away from me, tempted by someone else. Maybe that was because I was forcing them into something we had all outgrown. I considered my budding friendship with Tara. It felt natural, but what if we no longer worked at the winery together? Would the connection falter? Maybe friendship was always partly contrived, a choice you had to keep making. Maybe that's why I had been so drawn to Caleb. Desire wasn't a choice. It was as involuntary as hunger. A kind of spell.

On breaks from work, I'd wander outside and sit on top of one of the picnic tables, gazing out at the vineyard. The leaves around us had turned—the colours of burning embers—but the vineyard was still a brilliant green. Mac had decided to delay the harvest that year. He said any other year, they would have already started picking, but the strange summer weather had prolonged the growing season. The hotter, the better, he told me.

"You want the vines to fight to live. You can taste that fight if you let it happen. This will be the best year for valley wine yet."

Not everyone who visited the winery was insufferable. Occasionally, a man would show up who caught my attention. A man or a boy on the verge of manhood. From away, always. Was that my type? He—whoever he was—would look at me and I would feel it. Not as strong as with Caleb, but yes, I wanted. Licked lips and unblinking eyes. The skin on my neck craving touch, closeness. I imagined his hands in my hair. I imagined the heat of his breath.

I was pleased by this. It diluted Caleb's power. I hadn't had these feelings until Caleb, but they weren't *only* for Caleb. There could be others. I could desire more than one.

They always had dark hair. They were always tall. I never wanted anyone too manicured or perfect. There needed to be an edge for me to feel it. Stubble or dark eyes. Hands that looked calloused. They couldn't smell like cologne or have gel in their hair. They couldn't appear to be trying.

꧁꧂

After a couple of weeks, I began to suspect Caleb no longer worked at the winery. I still hadn't seen him there and no one at work ever mentioned him. I considered asking Mac, but I remembered how Ruth had asked about Caleb and me at the beginning of the school year: if he was going to the school dance, why wasn't I? That question had seemed to intrigue Mac and I didn't want to feed that curiosity. Despite having interfered with Ruth's and Mac's personal lives, I wouldn't allow them access to mine.

I could have asked Caleb, but I rarely saw him or the boys outside of class at that point. During free hours, they were occupied with their new crew of guys from the football team. I decided to ask Tara instead.

"You worked with Caleb this summer, right?"

We were in the wine cellar. I was mopping the floor and she was sitting on the cellar steps, making an intricate string bracelet in her lap. She was on a break, keeping me company. I sensed the movement of her hands behind me while I worked. A flurry of left over right.

"Yup."

"What's the deal? Does he still work here?"

The stir of movement stopped. Tara looked up. "You don't know?"

"What?"

"He got fired."

"For what?"

"Stealing," she said.

I thought of the bottles Caleb had passed around at Dylan's party.

"Mac caught him?" I asked.

"Hard not to. Apparently, he stole upwards of three cases of wine during his time at the winery. Mac was noticing product disappearing over the summer, but you know Mac—he always wants to see the good in people. It took catching Caleb in the act for Mac to finally fire the asshole. He found Caleb in the winery after hours, stuffing bottles into his backpack." Tara paused. "I thought you must have known. You replaced him. Aren't you guys friends?"

I shrugged. "I don't know. Kind of. Not really anymore."

It was true. Our connection, whatever you wanted to call it— friendship or something else—felt precarious at best. I'd spent no time with Caleb for weeks, and beyond that, he seemed to be changing. Not long ago, he represented an alternative path: intellectualism, sophistication. But lately he was choosing to follow another, more conventional route.

Tara continued her bracelet-making. "That guy is trouble."

"Yeah?"

"Bad news bears. The stealing was only one part of it. He was always stirring shit up."

I dunked the mop head in the bucket. Water sloshed onto the concrete floor. "Like what?"

"Like...that time with Sarah."

My pulse dashed. "Who?" I had never heard about a Sarah.

"Girl who worked with us this summer. She's about my age, I think. Nineteen or twenty. Here for the summer on a co-op placement from university. She rented an apartment in Wolfville. She was okay, a little flighty. She was our *marketing assistant* for the summer, whatever the fuck that means."

I pushed the mop mechanically. "What happened?"

Tara laughed. "I'm the one who caught them, actually. In the bathroom, if you can believe it. Gross. They didn't even lock the door."

"What? Having sex?"

"No. But close enough."

Did I nod? Laugh? Inside, I felt blank. A void. People talk about jealousy as if it fills you up with heat and spite. But not for me. Jealousy drained me of all colour and feeling. I forgot about the mop in my hand and all that was left was a ringing in my chest, the distant thump of a heartbeat.

"I didn't tell Mac," Tara continued. "What was I supposed to say? Yo, your yard boy is getting a BJ in the ladies' bathroom on the second floor. Not a conversation I wanted to have."

"He's disgusting," I said. I knew it was true, despite how I still felt.

"Yup. Like I said, *trouble*. I keep my distance from those types. Too smart for his own good, and too reckless. Could talk his way out of almost anything. I find if you get too close to people like that, they blind you. Best to keep your shades on and your eyes averted."

We laughed at that, but something inside me was still ringing.

Tara invited me over that night after work. I accepted immediately, anxious for a distraction. The story about Caleb and Sarah continued to haunt me. What did this Sarah have that I didn't? Why was he only kissing me and doing *that* with her?

We closed up the winery and I sunk into the soft seats of Tara's old beater. The radio in her car was broken, so we sat in silence as we drove down quiet valley roads. Eventually, we turned to crawl up the South Mountain, Tara's car struggling on the incline. We twisted onto a heavily wooded dirt road. The trees looked moody in the fading light.

"Not sure if Dad's home," Tara said when we arrived at her house. She slammed the door of the car and I feared it might fall off.

Their home was even more ramshackle up close. The renovations and additions appeared to be drunken afterthoughts. Built without a plan, mismatched and shoddy. It was like a hobbit hole, held together by sheer will, maybe some magic. I liked it immediately.

"Dad?" she called, opening the front door, which, I realized, with a start, was round.

"Up here!" He was in the loft above the main floor, looking out over the open living room and kitchen. Tara and her father had similar voices. They looked alike too. Small in stature, with slim faces and a dreamy look.

Les and two other men were up there, drinking beer and playing guitar. I recognized one of them from the farmers' market, where he sometimes performed.

"Ruth?" Les squinted down at me, surprised. "Is that you? You haven't aged a day."

Tara laughed when most daughters would have groaned. "This is Winnie, her *daughter*."

"Right, right. Of course," Les scratched his chin, fingers disappearing in a wiry grey beard. "Welcome, Winnie. Welcome to the hovel! Make yourself at home. Beer in the fridge. Chicken on the stovetop. I got one of those rotisserie ones at the grocery store, Tare Bear. You and your friend can help yourselves."

"Thanks, Dad," she said. "We're gonna go hang out in my room."

I stepped carefully. The house was dirty and dark, cluttered rooms in every direction. It smelled stale like cigarette smoke.

"He forgets I'm vegetarian," Tara shrugged, throwing her bag down on the floor of her room. The space was small and bright yellow. She seemed to have a hammock instead of a bed. I wondered what that was like.

"He keeps buying those chickens. He thinks I like them because they disappear so quickly. But he and his buddies get high and devour them, then forget about it later. I'll have some quinoa when they pass out."

I nodded as if I knew what quinoa was.

"He's a good one, my dad. We get along."

We sat down on the floor, cross-legged, and Tara pulled embroidery floss in every colour out of an old paint can: purple, green, yellow, bright red, sky blue.

"He's really just a big kid." She started to braid the string, concentrating. "Not sure what he did when I was away at school. He needs me to take care of him. I don't mind though. What else am I doing?"

"I take care of my mom, too," I said. I picked out some string the colour of grass and wound it tight around my thumb. "Or I used to. Mac does that now, which is a relief."

"Mac Elliott. Valley hero! You know he and Dad used to be friends?"

"Really?"

"Hard to imagine, right? Funny how people drift apart and change. And then you're all stuck in the same small town, waving politely at people you used to like and now only kind of tolerate."

"Yeah," I said. "Strange."

"What about your dad?" she asked. "Where's he?"

"I don't know," I said. I leaned my back against the wall, discarding the string back into the pile. "I only met him once, when I was ten. He doesn't live close, but he came to Halifax for some work thing, said he wanted to meet me." It wasn't an encounter I thought much about. "He took me out for lunch," I continued. "Insisted I get a milkshake even though I didn't want one. I think he was trying to live out some idealized father–daughter narrative. Buying me a treat he thought my mother wouldn't let me have or something."

Tara didn't look up from her bracelet, which I liked. It made me feel less exposed, like we were just talking about any old thing.

"What did you talk about?" she asked casually.

"Nothing really. He asked me a few questions about what I liked to do, my friends. He wanted to know if I liked drawing. I told him I didn't, and he looked disappointed. He seemed really old. He would have been in, like, his sixties or something. I remember he got teary at one point. He apologized for not being a part of my life, for not staying in touch. For some reason, I pretended to be mad about that. I crossed my arms and looked out the window, like I was pissed, holding a grudge. But really, I didn't care, and I still don't. I'm not sure why I wanted to make him feel worse about it. I guess I was just being mean."

"You were ten," Tara said, looking at me then. "You probably *were* upset. That's perfectly normal."

"But I wasn't," I said, insistently. "I remember very clearly watching his eyes well up and thinking, *oh god, here we go.* But I felt nothing."

"You never wished he was around more?"

I shook my head. "Maybe if I'd gotten to know him better and liked him. Maybe then I'd wish he was a part of my life. But I don't know him at all and I have no innate desire for his company. I know *that's* not normal," I added. "I'm *supposed* to want my father in my life, supposed to feel wounded that's he's not. But I really don't. I think it's good for Ruth to have someone. And I like Mac. If Mac left, I would miss him. But that man I met in the diner years ago was a stranger. He's nothing to me."

Tara nodded like she understood. I had never shared that story with anyone else. I had never wanted to. And even if I had, I would have worried I might sound too cold. I knew it was strange to feel the way I did about my father. But it didn't seem to bother Tara and it was a relief to say these things out loud.

⁊ᔕ᙭᙭ᔕ᙭

Thanksgiving approached, the light changed. Though the heat remained, the lingering haze of summer lifted to reveal clearer, brighter days. Thanksgiving was a huge deal in our house. It always has been, for as long as I can remember. Ruth put on a full spread. Turkey and all the sides, homemade rolls, multiple pies. The boys always came, and Jake's family too, plus some hungry stragglers Ruth rounded up from the community. The deal was that she cooked while we stacked firewood. There was a great pile of it in the backyard that needed to be stored in our woodshed for the winter. As a group, we did the heavy lifting. Then, as a group, we sat down to feast. Tom had nicknamed it Thank-stacking years before.

Ruth cooked for days in advance. The pies were always made first, early in the week. Pumpkin and apple and pecan, maybe a pear-cranberry, making the whole house smell like a bakery. Then came the vegetables, endless pounds of potatoes, and on the day itself, the turkey. I've never understood those people who say turkey is dry and tasteless. Ruth's turkey was amber-crisp on the outside and juicy on the inside, the meat scented with lemon and garlic. Her stuffing was legendary.

If the day was fine, we ate outside. Mona and Fred would bring over a few folding tables, line them up in a row, and cover the whole thing in fabric the colour of Cortland apples. It felt like a grand harvest table, worthy of the feast we lay upon it. Ruth would place squash and fall foliage in the middle: thrown-together centrepieces that looked like they'd been arranged by Mother Nature herself. Dinner lasted until the stars came out. Then we would huddle under blankets and eat second slices of pie in the candlelight.

That year, I was more excited for the event than usual. The boys were all coming and Caleb wasn't. He had his own dinner to attend. For the first time in months I would have the boys to myself for a whole day. I wouldn't be distracted and neither would they. It would be like it used to be, or so I told myself.

Jake arrived first with his parents. Then came Tom and Sam together. I hugged them all like I hadn't seen them in months. Jake blushed when I pulled away.

The stacking was yet to begin. We were waiting for Mac, who had run home for more wine. There was a new bottle he forgot to bring, a Riesling, which he said would pair well with the turkey. Sam was in the kitchen, probably trying to flirt with Ruth, while Tom and Jake and I sat on the back step watching Mona and Fred arrange chairs around the dinner table.

It felt awkward between us immediately. Had we spent too much time apart? All that football? Something had changed and conversation no longer came easily. I couldn't think of what to say. Football came to mind, but how low had we sunk? Chatting about last week's away game wasn't us.

"I've been working at the winery," I tried. "After school and on Saturdays."

"I heard that," Tom said, as if I were an acquaintance whom he got the occasional word about through others.

"How do you like it?" asked Jake.

"It's all right. I mostly clean the place. But I like working with Tara. She's cool."

Jake and Tom nodded, faces blank.

I was thankful when Mac returned. "Ready to start?" he asked. I couldn't take much more of this uncomfortable quiet and bringing in the wood would give us something to do.

We formed a line from the woodpile to the shed. Tom and Jake always did the actual stacking. They knew how to line up the logs to make them fit neatly in the wood shed. The rest of us fed them wood, passing logs between our hands until they reached the end of the line. That year, the line consisted of Mona and Fred, Mac, Sam, me, a chatty university student named Libby who worked at the art gallery in town where Ruth showed her work, the gallery owner, Robin, Robin's husband, Oscar, and Flynn Lewis, a newly widowed garlic farmer who looked like he hadn't eaten a good meal since his wife had died five months earlier.

Robin and Oscar joined us every year and I liked them. They were in their mid-thirties and seemed hipper than most in the valley. Stylish and easygoing. Oscar was a stone sculptor. We had one of his pieces in our garden. Flynn and Libby were new. Flynn was quiet but Libby insisted on whistling while she worked. I rolled my eyes and made a face. Tom smiled.

The work went faster now that we were older. When we were kids, we slowed the whole process down. Small hands dropping logs, fussy voices complaining that it was too hot or too cold. When Fred announced that we had reached the halfway point, we decided to take a break. I gulped down some icy water from Ruth's makeshift bar (an old chest of drawers she put outside and topped with beverages) and wiped sweat from my upper lip.

What did the boys and I used to do at break time? I couldn't remember because I had never had to think about it before. *We just were.* Existing together was enough. It always felt like we were doing something because we were together, telling stories, laughing. I looked at my feet and tried to remember. What did we used to talk about?

"Caleb's brother is in town," Tom said, and I looked up.

He wasn't talking to me. He was speaking to Jake and Sam. Turned just slightly towards them.

"The famous Sebastian," Sam said. "You get to meet him?"

"Nah," Tom mumbled. "Maybe later."

"Where does he live, again?" I asked casually. I felt the need to act like this wasn't new information, maybe just information I hadn't bothered to fully remember.

"Boston," Tom said. "Visiting from university. He's in his last year."

So, Caleb had a brother whom Tom might meet. Caleb had a brother visiting and Tom was the one to know all about it. Not me. Not us. I felt my stomach sway.

Mac told everyone it was time to get back to work, and while we finished the second half of the wood heap our conversation became easier. I learned how unhappy Caleb was about getting fired from the winery from Sam, who had always liked to gossip.

"He's *pissed*," Sam whispered.

"But he did *steal* from Mac," I said under my breath.

"He says he didn't. And now he's really angry. Like, more than Dylan angry."

"Do you think he would—?" I started but Tom overheard and stopped me.

He shook his head. "He would never." He sounded so certain.

When we finished stacking all the wood, Ruth rang the dinner bell that hung just outside the back door, leftover from previous owners. We kept it for this event alone.

We all helped bring out the dishes: a platter of carved turkey and buttery mashed potatoes; roasted vegetables sprinkled with thyme.

I sat down next to Tom because I always did. Libby was on his other side and I noticed how pretty she was. Blonde hair the colour of new cream, cut into a soft bob. A pale face and perfect pink lips. She wore black jeans and cowboy boots that seemed too heavy for this weather. A tattoo on the side of her neck. She was sweet, with an edge.

Ruth stood up at the head of the table. She looked tired, but triumphant. "To the harvest," she said, raising her glass.

"To the harvest," we repeated, our glasses clinking like wind chimes.

Everyone around the table fell into happy concentration, staring down at their plates. In between bites, Tom asked Libby what she was studying.

"Everything," she said, eyes wide. She finished each mouthful before talking, cleaning the front of her teeth with her tongue. "Arts mostly, but I can't decide what I want to focus on. Philosophy, politics, history. There's just so much to learn."

Tom was nodding as if he understood completely.

"Where do you go?" she asked. "Somewhere in the city?"

Tom laughed, his face red. "I'm still in high school."

"Are you? You look older."

Didn't that tongue of hers get tired? Sam winked at Tom across the table.

"Mac," I hollered. "Can I try the wine?"

Mac looked at my mother, who shrugged and nodded.

Mac disappeared into the kitchen, returning with a tall, slim wine glass, different from the ones the other guests were using. He had told me before that the taste of a wine could be affected by the glass you served it in. The shape mattered: the height, the curve, the width of the rim. I beamed while he poured this special glass half full, just for me. I guess he wanted me to experience the Riesling, which I hadn't tried before, under optimal conditions.

I held up the glass while the others watched me. The wine looked like morning sunlight. Shining, pale.

"Remember to let your nose lay the groundwork," Mac said gently.

I inhaled with my eyes closed.

"There's definitely some citrus there. Lime maybe?"

Mac nodded. "Anything else?"

"Something spicy. Ginger? And something sweet too, fruity. I can't quite...."

I took a sip. I could feel the eyes of the others fixed upon me. The wine rolled over my tongue. I thought of slicing peaches in the summer, Caleb standing beside me, a tingling between my legs, at the back of my neck.

"Peach," I said, taking another sip. Wanting to feel more of whatever that was. "This is really quite good."

"Quite good," Mac laughed. "Ruth, your daughter thinks my Riesling is quite good."

"Great, I mean!"

Everyone laughed, and for a moment Tom looked at me like he used to, a kind of knowing admiration shining through his gaze, like he was proud to be my closest friend. I smiled back, warmed by his affection.

We worked up an appetite for pie by walking around the yard, looking up while Tom pointed out constellations above us. Night had fallen and the temperature had dropped just slightly. I began to settle down. Relaxed, full, and sleepy, I felt my frustration and discomfort with the boys slip away. Nothing was different. Nothing had to be.

Ruth brought the pies out. Six in total. Six pies for twelve people. Ruth's worst fear was that there wouldn't be enough food. Mac had taken to teasing her about it. She cooked enough for eight even on those nights when it was just the three of us.

"Pumpkin, Tom?" Ruth knew which pie Tom liked best. She always gave him the first slice.

"Actually, Ruth, we have to get going." He was looking at Jake and Sam.

"What? Where?" My voice sounded surprised and desperate, louder than I wanted it to be. I was just starting to feel secure and now they were leaving. I closed my open mouth but I couldn't take back my reaction, sloppy and embarrassing.

"Thanks so much for everything, Ruth," Tom said, ignoring me. "It was amazing, as always."

Sam also thanked Ruth, and Jake said goodbye to his parents. They hugged me, looking away, and then they were gone.

<hr/>

When had I lost them? Where did I go wrong? Maybe I should I have gone to the dance, should have better hidden my feelings for Caleb. If it wasn't for him, could we have held on longer?

AFTER

꧁꧂

We are looking out at the remains of the vineyard when the clouds finally come. One minute there are blue skies, the next, stiff peaks of white. Flat-bottomed clouds float as if on an invisible surface. We look up and blink. The sun and the clouds seem to produce a new kind of light. Will rain follow, at last?

We retreat back to the truck to discuss our options. Sam continues to press down on the corners of his eyes, wiping away new tears. We leave him outside. He lies down on the truck bed with his hands on his stomach.

"What do we do now?" Jake asks me. "Should we tell someone about Caleb?"

I pause, considering. "I'm not sure that's the best idea. Caleb's incredibly smart. He likely would have covered his tracks. There might be an investigation, but I doubt it would come to anything. Arsonists are really hard to convict because the evidence is burned along with everything else. They would probably find traces of the accelerant, but not who did it."

Tom nods. "We tell Lorraine. She follows up and finds nothing. Then Caleb gets to feel all the more satisfied for fooling the cops."

"Do we confront him, then? Tell him we know what he did?" Jake asks.

"That's an option," Tom says, nodding slowly. "But I can't help but feel like we're somehow responsible. We knew what he was capable of. Dylan's car? That was fucked up and we did nothing."

"What could we have done?" I ask. "Intervene? How? He doesn't exactly respond well to criticism."

"Winnie's right," Tom says. "It would have been too dangerous."

"We're his friends," Jake mumbles. "He wouldn't just turn on us."

"He turned on Winnie!" Tom says. "She was his friend."

Jake looks over at me, frowning.

"The thing with Caleb is," I say, "he's always going to put himself first. You're his friends, sure. But what does that really mean to him? You're these people he can spend time with, but does he actually feel anything for you? Would he have your back? Not if it conflicted with something he wanted."

I watch Tom and Jake carefully. Jake rubs the back of his neck, his eyes closed. I can feel him wanting to fall back into our familiar roles, to let me tell him what to think.

"Take me, for example," I say. "All summer he led me on, even though he knew it would hurt you, Tom. He just wanted to have some fun and he didn't care if it meant fucking with us. He likes messing with people. He gets off on it."

Tom swallows.

"And what was I doing? Letting him distract me and get away with it. He has a way of confusing people. He's a manipulator."

"You really believe that?" asks Jake. He looks thoroughly depressed by the idea.

"He doesn't have limits," I insist. "He just keeps pushing. He doesn't care who he hurts."

I can tell they're starting to doubt. Jake keeps blinking, a sign he is trying to absorb uncomfortable information. Tom, meanwhile, is looking out at the blackened vineyard, biting his lip.

"This time, he was mad at Mac," I continue, speaking slowly so they hear it all. "Mac fired him because Caleb was stealing wine. Mac was in the right, but Caleb just couldn't let it rest. He always has to be in control."

Tom sighs, shuddering on the exhale.

"So, he's dangerous," Tom says. "Maybe even sociopathic. We go to Lorraine and whether she finds proof or not, we're screwed. He's gonna retaliate, take it out on us. Who knows what he'll do?"

"Man," Jake shakes his head.

"I think the only option we really have," I say, "is to freeze him out. Caleb is power hungry. He wants to feel in control, but what happens if we just start ignoring him? Not aggressively, but quietly. The key is not to motivate him to seek revenge. If we drift away without conflict, he'll eventually find new friends to push around. Maybe we can try to go back to how it was."

Jake looks dissatisfied but Tom is nodding. "Winnie's right. Let's just go about our business like we never met him."

"But—"

"No," Tom cuts Jake off. "It's the only way."

We are all quiet. The rain picks up. The windshield blurs.

"Okay," Jake says, finally. "I'm in."

There's a knock on the passenger's side window. We all jump. We forgot about Sam. He stands outside, a drowned rat, and we all laugh. God, it feels good to laugh with them again.

BEFORE

꿏

"**W**hat are your plans this fine Friday evening?" Tara asked me.

We were waiting out the end of a boring work shift. Thanksgiving was the last real tourist weekend in the valley and business at the winery was slowing down. After the harvest, the winery would close until spring and we'd all be without a job for the winter months. But the timing of the harvest was still uncertain. Mac walked out into the vineyard every day and tasted a few grapes, sometimes bringing me along. The grapes were much sweeter than those I had tried in the summer, ripened and bursting with more juice. Mac said they could start the harvest any day but he believed waiting would produce superior wines. It was a risk—a rogue frost could destroy the vines—but this kind of heat wave was incredibly rare. He didn't want to pass up such a unique opportunity to allow the fruit to reach its full potential. The other wineries with fields in God's Palm held off as well, following Mac's lead.

"Hanging with your boyfriends, I assume?" Tara teased. She knew all my friends were boys.

"No," I said. "They're going to some party with the other kids at school."

I had seen a flyer passed around English class, eventually landing on Tom's desk. Jeremy Weir was hosting a "bling"-themed party that night. I wasn't exactly sure what "bling" meant but the flyer boasted obnoxious dollar signs, so I suspected the guys would probably dress like rappers and the girls would dress like the women draped on rappers' arms in music videos.

"Party?" Tara said. "I could go to a party."

"Not you, too," I groaned. "I've already lost my other friends to the dark side."

"I don't want to go to the party to actually *go* to the party," Tara said. "I want to crash. We can drink their beer and make fun of their slutty outfits. I used to do it all the time when I was in high school."

I laughed. Since Thank-stacking, the boys had seemed so far adrift, I worried they might be lost to me for good. We hadn't hung out and we had barely spoken, save for a few words in class. But I felt no real impulse to try to win them back. It seemed to me I had been competing with Caleb for their attention since the summer and he had finally won. I was tired and resentful. If they wanted to waste their days spending time with that group of utterly average teenagers, that was their choice. I had given up.

But going to Jeremy's party to make fun of them all (the boys included) sounded fun, a bit like revenge. I imagined Tara and I walking in together. Crashing, as she called it. I would look powerful in the company of an older girl. Maybe it would give the boys a sense of how they had made me feel these last few months. Outside, replaced.

"Okay," I agreed. "We'll go. But I'm warning you, it'll be lame."

"Of course it will!" Tara grinned. "That's the point."

Tara came over to my place after work. Ruth made us grilled cheese sandwiches for a quick dinner and Mac told us not to drink anything that anyone else gave us.

"You can't trust these kids," he said, across from us at the kitchen table. "You don't know what it is they're handing you, what they might put in your drink."

Ruth was standing at the stovetop. She rolled her eyes behind his back, winking at me.

"I know what you're doing, Ruth," Mac said, without turning around. "But date rape is nothing to joke about. Here, Winnie," he stood up and opened the fridge. "Take a bottle of wine. That way, we'll know you're safe."

"Thank you!" I grinned, genuinely grateful.

"Let's make sure it's good and chilled," he said, sticking it in the freezer. "We don't want you drinking warm white just because you're in someone's smelly basement."

Tara laughed. She had eaten two sandwiches and was now tucking into a bowl of chocolate ice cream. She spooned the cool dessert into her mouth so quickly, the next time I looked over it had disappeared. She was clearly hungry. From what I had seen at Tara's house, Les was useless when it came to food, but I figured Tara was used to looking after herself. She had always seemed so independent and I envied her for it. But maybe that wasn't the case. I watched her enthusiastically scrape the last of the ice cream from the bottom of the bowl with her spoon and felt embarrassed for her. She looked like a child. I made a mental note to pay more attention when Ruth tried to teach me to cook. I wouldn't rely on anyone when I was older. I wouldn't go hungry either.

Jeremy lived beyond Gaspereau in a village called New Minas, a fifteen-minute drive from home. It was the commercial centre of the valley but its biggest claim to fame was that it had a Walmart, which had opened a few years ago. I didn't have the address for Jeremy's house but Tara used the computer at work to chat with a few people online, retrieving the details. I had watched her type—fast and assured, not looking at the keys—with bewildered curiosity. Maybe I really had been living under a rock these last few years. For Tara and Caleb, the online world seemed like second nature. I felt slightly left out watching her scroll through a long list of contacts, people she seemed very comfortable messaging a quick "hey" to start an exchange. But just like in the past, feeling left out offered me a kind of empowerment. I had chosen this other path.

Ruth dropped us off at the party and reminded me to call when we needed a ride home. I was surprised to see Jeremy lived in a small, shabby bungalow. He paraded around school like he had money. Flashy sunglasses and a loud voice that rang through the cafeteria. His home clashed with this persona: king of the castle; loud-mouthed football star. He always had a girlfriend and she was always blonde and glossy. He chewed tobacco and put his feet up on top of the desk in class. Entitled. I was surprised he wanted us here at his house. It seemed to be an unveiling, a lifting of the spell. I wasn't sure if I should be impressed or not. Did he just not give a shit?

From the driveway, we heard loud, bass-heavy music playing inside. I went to knock on the door but Tara pushed it open before I could. You didn't knock at parties, apparently. You walked right in. I recalled all the times that summer when I had feigned ownership of the places I entered without knocking. This felt way less fun.

Everyone was there—everyone from school I usually ignored. The Ambers and the Jeremys. They stood around, leaning slightly forward or back or to the side, limbs like cooked noodles, unable to keep themselves fully upright. Everyone held a cup or a bottle with loose fingers, their eyelids heavy.

Wordlessly, Tara opened me a beer. There were a bunch of them on the kitchen island and I felt self-conscious about bringing out the bottle of wine, still cold in a tote bag slung over my arm. The beer was warm and tasteless but I wanted something to do, something to hold. Tara and I stood in the corner of the kitchen, looking around. No one expected us to be there so no one saw us at first. If they did, they probably thought they were imagining us.

I was happy for the quiet, the space to observe. There was no one I wanted to talk to anyway. We were in one big room. The small kitchen opened up onto the living room, which had a heavy brown carpet. There were already multiple dark spots from where kids had spilled their drinks. Or maybe those spots were dry and permanent, the marks of neglect.

The room was dominated by a large sound system and big-screen television. It took up a quarter of the space, which amazed me. Ruth and I had an old TV from god knows when, the kind with antennas and dials. We liked to cover it with a piece of floral fabric when we weren't using it. We stuck a plant on top sometimes. It was something to hide, not showcase.

The TV wasn't on but the sound system was blasting. Pop and hip-hop and the kind of music I imagined they played at the school dances. The girls were all dressed up. They wore tight, short dresses made from a clingy material that reminded me of bathing suits. Metallic or pastel pink. High heels that wobbled on that thick carpet. Plenty of costume jewelry, satisfying the "bling" theme.

I gulped down my warm beer.

I couldn't see the boys anywhere, but there was a crowd of people in the backyard, smoking and yelling over each other, visible from a sliding glass door in the kitchen. Maybe they were out there.

"The kids are getting worse," Tara said.

I nodded in agreement, watching them dance.

Caleb soon emerged from a hallway off the kitchen. He tripped over one of his own feet and he wore a silly smile he couldn't wipe away. Behind him, a brunette. I squinted across the room and recognized Allison Levy. I had known her since elementary school. She wasn't so bad; she wasn't wearing a bathing suit to a party in October. I remember once when we were young, we went on a field trip to the zoo down the valley and Ruth had forgotten to pack me a lunch. The boys all ate their food in record time and so they had nothing to share with me. Allison gave me an apple from her purple lunch box and I was grateful.

She wasn't dressed like the other girls at the party but she was just as drunk as they were. Maybe more. Her hand grabbed for Caleb's. I couldn't tell if it was a gesture of affection or pure survival instinct. She was having trouble standing. He held on for a beat but then pulled away, like he had done with me during the school photo earlier in the year. Caleb was heading for Tara and me, blinking excessively when he spotted us. I wondered what was down that hallway.

"What on earth are you doing here?" he cried, grabbing me into a hug. "And you!" he lunged for Tara as well. He knocked over a bottle that fell to the floor and smashed. "Oops!" he laughed and so did everyone around us, looking over. They noticed Tara and me at last. Out of the corner of my eye, I saw Jeremy get a broom and sweep up the mess.

Caleb finally let Tara and me go but kept one hand on my shoulder to keep himself upright.

"Seriously. You two are the last people I expected to see, and together?"

For a moment, his sloppy drunkenness subsided as he assessed this new alliance, the beginning of a friendship. I don't think he liked it, probably because he preferred controlling where I stood in the social hierarchy: off to the side, alone, where he could always retrieve me if he needed to. He frowned.

"Winnie?" I heard Tom's voice behind me.

Tom, Jake, and Sam moved into the house from the back door, smelling of cigarettes. I wrinkled my nose.

"Smoking now, are we?" I swigged my beer.

"What are you doing here?" Tom asked.

"Why does everyone keep asking her that?" Tara said. "She's here because she wants to be. She doesn't need to answer to any of you." Tara pointed a finger at Tom's chest.

"I'm just surprised," Tom mumbled.

I shrugged. I didn't know what to say.

"Come on, Winnie. Let's par-tay." Tara grasped my hand and pulled me away.

I didn't look back at Caleb and the boys but I imagined them staring, dumbfounded by my behaviour. Good. Let them see what that feels like.

We sat down at the kitchen table, joining some others who were playing a drinking game with cards and complicated rules. Jess sat across the table wearing a sparkly, low-cut dress and long, acrylic nails with tacky white tips. There were also two senior boys from the football team and a girl in our grade named Stacie, who smiled at me when we sat down.

With each round of the game, we grew increasingly tipsy. I was the only one who had never played before, and I suffered as a result, being told to "drink!" by the others whenever I messed up a rule or missed a direction, which was about twice as often as everyone else. Tara and I opened our bottle of wine and shared it between us. The more I drank, the less I tasted, all the nuance and subtlety I had been learning to decipher, lost. But drinking helped counter the disorientation I was feeling, of being at that party, of sitting at that table and playing that game.

Occasionally, I glanced around to see what the boys and Caleb were up to. I was horrified to see Sam dancing with the crowd in the living room. A girl named Brittany was grinding against him, her butt wiggling against his crotch. I watched my friend sway to the music and felt completely estranged from him. I recognized his face, but it was like his body had been possessed, seized and controlled by the norms of our sad generation.

I also spotted Jake, smoking on the deck outside with a group of his teammates. He was laughing like he was high, giggly and unable to stop. I had nothing against smoking weed but it bothered me to see Jake doing it. He was now governed by other people's expectations.

Even worse, when I got up to go to the bathroom, I caught Tom making out with Allison, the brunette I had seen stumbling around with Caleb at the beginning of the party. I happened upon them attacking each other in the hallway and I was so shocked, I laughed loudly, a bit of a squawk. Tom broke away and looked at me, frowning like he was hurt. He left Allison in the hallway and returned to the main room. Allison, oblivious to what had just happened, asked me for the time. I told her it was getting late and then went into the bathroom where I took a deep breath, gazing at my knees, sitting on the toilet. I felt no jealousy seeing Tom with Allison but my earlier sense of alienation—from Sam and Jake— intensified. I had not only lost them; they had lost themselves.

I ditched the card game and wandered outside. Tara was very drunk and seemed to be warming to one of the seniors at the kitchen table, leaning in close to talk to him. What was this sickness, infecting everyone good? Why did it take so little to convert unique individuals into faceless members of the crowd? I saw no appeal in the party or the people who were there. The drinking game had been fun for a while, but mostly just because it was a quick way to feel tipsy. But the music was so loud. It was hard to hear and you had to yell and there was nothing interesting to say anyway. No one wanted to talk or listen. They just wanted to *be* at a party, like unthinking zombies.

I passed by the horde of smokers and walked to the back of the yard, feeling drunk and frustrated. I didn't want to be here anymore.

I was surprised to see Dylan sitting on a lawn chair by himself. He had been laying low since his car was torched. I hadn't even seen him in the cafeteria much at school.

"Hey," I said.

He looked up at me, a tepid smile. "Hey, Winnie."

"You look like the only other person besides me who doesn't want to be here."

Dylan chuckled. "Yeah, not really my thing."

I pulled a lawn chair over to join him.

"Why did you come, then?" I asked.

"Why did you?"

I nodded. "Yeah, not sure. Kind of got dragged along. I've been regretting it since I arrived."

"Same here," Dylan said. "And I have to work at five tomorrow morning."

"At your Dad's shop?"

"No, I have a second job on a farm. I work there on Saturdays. It doesn't pay as good but it's still money."

"I'm guessing none of them need to get up early tomorrow," I said, gesturing towards the house.

"Definitely not," Dylan said, looking at me for a moment. "What's up with you and your friends? I never see you together anymore."

I inhaled sharply. "Yeah. We seem to be moving in different directions."

"Caleb have anything to do with that?"

"Maybe."

"Maybe not?" Dylan asked.

"I don't know," I said. "It's easy for me to blame Caleb but a part of me wonders if this was all inevitable. People grow up and apart, don't they? Maybe we made more sense as friends when we were younger."

"But you were inseparable."

"We were." I nodded. "But maybe I've been trying too hard to keep it that way. Maybe it's good to be alone sometimes."

Dylan laughed. "Alone. Never heard of it. Too many siblings for that."

"I can't imagine," I said. I really couldn't.

We grew quiet, listening to the party noise behind us.

"You know, I always had a crush on you," Dylan said suddenly, grinning. "Since we were, like, seven."

"What? Really?"

"Yup," Dylan said. "I wanted to ask you to our grade-eight dance but I overheard you tell Tom that dances were stupid and you weren't going. I lost my nerve."

"That's crazy," I laughed. I wondered, if he had asked me, would I have gone?

"Winnie." A deep voice behind us.

I turned. It was Caleb.

"Nice talking to you, Winnie," Dylan said, standing up. "I'm gonna head out. I've served my time."

"Thanks for keeping her company, man," Caleb said. He reached out a hand to shake Dylan's. Dylan didn't take it. Instead, he nodded at me and walked away.

Caleb scoffed. "What are you talking to him for?"

I stood up. "What do you care? And I don't need a chaperone. I'm not your pet, Caleb."

"Come on," he said, putting an arm around me. "Everyone thinks we're together."

"Do they?" I asked. "Why would they think that? We're clearly not." I shrugged his arm off my shoulders and took a few steps back.

Caleb frowned and then lunged forward, kissing me. I let him continue for a moment. He tasted like breakfast cereal. He must have been eating some inside the house. But then I pulled away. The kiss was sloppy, not like the first time in God's Palm.

"What?" he said, smirking.

"What?" I said back.

"Don't tell me you're interested in *him*?"

"Dylan?" I asked.

"I saw you out here, flirting."

I laughed. "Please."

Caleb went to kiss me again but I took another step back. He had never seemed less attractive.

I went inside and told Tara I needed to go home. She said she wanted to stay a bit longer—she was practically sitting in the lap of the senior boy at that point—and I agreed, begrudgingly. I couldn't leave her there, without a ride. I sat at the kitchen table with my arms crossed, one eye on the clock, drinking a glass of water. I decided I would give Tara half an hour and then I would call Ruth. Around me, the party roared. The drunker the crowd got, the harder they danced, the louder they sang. Everyone on the dance floor seemed to be making out and everyone who wasn't dancing was watching. It was like one giant orgy.

I watched the party, disgusted, and eventually stood up. "I'm going to the bathroom," I told Tara, "and then I'm calling Ruth. You can either come home with me or find your own way back to Gaspereau."

She mumbled something and I squeezed past the heaving mob back towards the bathroom. It was the only place to find some peace. My buzz was wearing off and I was desperate to splash water on my face.

The bathroom door was ajar and from the hallway I could see there were a few people inside. I realized with a jolt it was the boys: Tom, Jake, Sam, and Caleb were all in there. They had their backs to me, turned towards a fifth person, shorter with brown hair.

I took a step closer to the bathroom and saw it was Allison. She was so drunk she looked barely conscious, her heavy-lidded eyes ringed with smudged mascara and her hair a messy tangle.

In a clear voice, Caleb told Allison to take off her top. She complied without protest, almost robotically. I watched, alarmed and frozen with shock as she removed her tank top and then her clean, white bra. Caleb took one of Jake's hands and placed it on Allison's left breast. Then he took one of Sam's hands and placed on her right breast. Tom was silent, watching our friends.

Allison looked like she was half-asleep. I took a few steps backwards and then ran outside through the front door. I asked someone if I could use their cellphone and called Ruth to come get me. I didn't want to go back inside but I also knew I couldn't leave Tara with those animals. Moving swiftly, I went into the house and yanked her away from the party. We passed Jess in the kitchen where she was pouring vodka into a red, plastic cup. At the last moment, I turned and told her Allison was sick in the bathroom.

"She needs your help."

ᘏᘏᘏ

I slept until noon, then Ruth made me bacon and eggs and pancakes. Mac had already left for work at the winery. I was happy he wasn't there when I woke up. I was feeling fragile and confused. Too many voices or questions would overwhelm me.

"There's coffee," Ruth said, not looking up from the stovetop. The bacon fat popped, splattering onto her wrist. "Ouch."

"You okay?"

She nodded. "What about you? How was your night?"

I splashed coffee into a mug and sat down at the table. I didn't know how to answer. How was my night? Terrible? Terrifying? Scenes from the party appeared in loud, obscured flashes that hurt my head. I kept seeing Allison's bare breast, pale and plump, the hard nipple like a bull's eye. Jake's hand moving to cover and squeeze.

"Fine," I mumbled. I felt nauseous but not from the alcohol.

"You look rough. First hangovers are nothing though, Winnie. Savour it while it lasts. I recommend eating your breakfast and then going for a walk. You have to change your physiology if you want to feel better. That's my trick."

A walk was the last thing I wanted but I sipped my coffee and nodded. No part of me considered telling her what I had witnessed. Not only was the overt sexuality of it embarrassing to describe, but I feared saying it out loud. I would be calling out the boys, identifying them as something vile. If I didn't say it, maybe it wasn't true.

I also kept asking myself: why didn't I stop it? I was right there, outside the door. I could have barged in and put an end to it. Ruth would probably ask the same question, which I was too ashamed to face.

After breakfast, I took Ruth's advice. I put on some clothes and went outside. I was thankful the air had cooled overnight, feeling more like October. My face was refreshed by the wind. The clouds above were damp and heavy but they moved too quickly, passing us over without rain.

I turned left at the end of our driveway, towards God's Palm. I didn't want to pass Jake's house or the turnoff to Caleb's. I didn't want to happen upon Sam driving with his parents. Or even worse, Tom out for a bike ride. In this direction, there was nothing and no one. Farm land and a few cows and endless vines. That was what I needed in that moment.

The night before continued to skip in my mind. Blinks and flickers that I tried to connect together into some sort of linear narrative. Everything prior to catching the boys in the bathroom felt oddly dream-like, hard to delineate. But Allison was crystal clear. She kept emerging, interrupting my vision of sweaty bodies dancing, of Tara sitting on that gross guy's lap. Of Caleb kissing me outside when I hadn't wanted him to.

How was Allison feeling this morning? They had passed her around, shared her between them. What would she remember? What would she forget? I knew, if it weren't for Caleb, the boys would have never treated her that way. They had been safe with me: safe from being hurt, from hurting others.

Caleb was the problem. He had always been the problem. He had insinuated himself, coming between Tom and me in the summer and then taking the boys away from me when school started. He had altered them so much they were now unrecognizable.

The summer came back to me in flashes. Caleb exploiting Sam's deep fear of inadequacy. He coldly watched Sam grovel and fawn without ever giving my friend the praise and acceptance he needed. Caleb kept Sam feeling lesser and wanting. Dependent.

Jake pushed to the edge of terror on the cliff at Three Pools. In that moment, he abused Jake's fears, his sense of shame, making him feel like he would be a coward if he didn't jump. And when Jake leapt, Caleb rewarded him with possibility and potential: a glimpse of the man Jake could be. He had felt indebted to Caleb ever since.

But the biggest change was between Tom and me. Had Caleb only flirted with me to make Tom jealous? He had exposed dormant feelings and raised new questions in Tom's mind about our relationship. Caleb must have known Tom would blame me. I was his best friend, after all. I should have known better, *been* better.

Even adults were vulnerable to Caleb. He sent Ruth running into Mac's arms. He had used her most profound weakness—her insecurities—against her, manipulating how she saw Mac. And it worked.

And then there was me, of course. I had been confused for months about why Caleb kept me at a distance, longing. He knew he could have me, so why didn't he want me? Even if only for one night, one time. *Use me*, I kept thinking. Against me, ambiguity was his best weapon. I didn't like the anticipation, the uncertainty, but maybe, deep down, I wanted it. The destabilizing pleasure of never knowing exactly how he felt, of waiting for him to act.

But why? Maybe he was unnaturally cruel and it was all just for fun. It almost didn't matter, because his strength was also his weakness: the need for control.

I'm not sure how long I walked but when I finally got ahold of my skittering mind, I was standing in the middle of God's Palm. The wind had picked up and every leaf around me was vibrating. The clouds above the vineyard rumbled and I knew I had to get started. Who knew how much longer the rain would hold.

AFTER

꧁꧂

We decide to go to my house. We all squeeze into the front of the truck, Sam sitting on my lap like a little boy. Jake starts the engine. The rain is driving down in sheets now. Mac's Jeep is in the yard. We tumble out of the truck and run. Back-kicking footsteps and arms shielding our heads. By the time we reach the porch, we're already soaked. Sam saunters along behind us, pretending to enjoy it. A nice shower. We all laugh again and the laughter feels cleansing, a relief.

"Hello?" I say once we're inside the house.

"In here," Ruth calls.

They're in the kitchen, sitting at the table, having tea.

"Hi," we mumble.

"Hi," they mumble back.

"Quite the rain," someone says.

"Boy, do we need it."

I feel awkward. *We needed it last night*, I think.

But Mac only closes his eyes and nods. He looks oddly peaceful.

"Is it okay if we hang out here?" I ask.

"Sure," Ruth says. "You can help hand out the Halloween candy."

"Think we'll get many kids in this weather?"

"A few. They always come. Can't waste their costumes. Only one chance to wear 'em."

We leave Ruth and Mac alone. I run upstairs and change, leaving the boys in the living room.

I husk off wet, heavy layers and stand naked and shivering. The boys are here, and though I have won them back, I have never felt so alone.

BEFORE

꧁꧂

mber and Jess watched every football practice. Hip-to-hip on the bleachers, tying braids in each other's hair. The Monday following the bling party, there was a whipping wind as I headed for the football field after school. I knew where they'd be.

By the time I reached the bleachers on the sideline, the wind had stolen my breath. I perched on the end of the bottom bench, wiping my hair from my face. Amber and Jess were sitting a few seats away. I coughed. I kept my gaze forward. The team was out there running laps. I spotted Tom, Jake, and Sam. Caleb. And there was Dylan.

I could hear Amber and Jess giggling to my right. I snuck a glance sideways. They had a magazine open across both their laps, conjoining them, its pages even shinier than their lips and trembling in the breeze.

While the boys ran in circles around the field, I listened to Amber and Jess silly-laugh through an article called "Seven Sex Positions Guaranteed to Make You Orgasm." I wondered how many times they had had sex. With how many guys?

The boys broke into two teams and Amber and Jess moved on to their horoscopes. I learned Amber was an Aries, Jess a Libra. The predictions were ridiculous, filtered through the steamed lens of sex and love. *A good month to experiment in the bedroom. The time is now to pursue your crush.*

Even they saw through it. "They said the same thing last month," said Jess, scrunching up her nose.

There. An opportunity.

"You know who's really good at that prediction stuff?" I ventured.

They glanced at me, wary. They probably feared I was making fun of them.

"Jake's mom, Mona."

"Isn't she a psychic?" Amber chirped, face opening up.

"Yeah, but she also does astrology readings. Birth charts, or whatever. Pretty cool."

It wasn't, of course.

"I've always wanted to see a psychic." That was Jess. She leaned across Amber, towards me. Her eyes were dark brown and heavily lined, mauve sparkles on the lids.

"I had a reading last summer," I told them.

"You *did*?"

"What did she tell you?"

I thought back to the reading. It had been vague, and as I told Amber and Jess about it, I couldn't remember much of what Mona had said.

"She told me I would be involved in a love triangle," I lied.

Their eyes looked round and hungry. I knew what they were thinking. Me, Tom, Caleb. Was that what I meant? They wanted more.

"You should go to her," I looked back out at the field, hair flapping around my face. "She's good."

⧉

At the next practice, Amber asked if I wanted some candy.

I eyed the bag in her hand. Multicoloured somethings, coated in sugar. The kind of stuff I hated. But I knew accepting the offer was important. People are always looking for an opportunity to feel generous.

"Sure, thanks," I said, reaching over and grabbing two of them, an orange and a green. I didn't even like them being in my hand and touching my skin. I could smell them. They were printed with tiny faces, one scowling, one grinning.

Amber and Jess weren't watching me closely, but I still popped the orange one in my mouth anyway. I was going for authenticity.

It was worse than I imagined. Pure sugar injected with artificial sour. Nothing orange about it. No wonder Ruth banned this junk. She always used to go through my pillowcase full of candy on Halloween and remove anything too colourful or "sickly sweet." The chips and chocolate bars were okay, in moderation.

I watched Jess stuff three little faces into her mouth at once. She chewed slowly, cheeks full. They were always eating stuff like this. Maybe that's how they remained perfectly plump. Baby fat clinging to small frames. Sugar hips.

"Can I have another?" I asked.

Amber smiled and passed me the bag. She looked pleased, just as I had predicted she would. They were already warming to me. It didn't take much. I wondered if they had always wanted to be my friend. What had Caleb said? Girls like Amber and Jess want what they can't have. I had always been the friend they couldn't make, too distant and unimpressed by their popularity. I imagined they saw me as a white whale of sorts. The elusive, disinterested girl they needed to hook to feel like they had truly dominated the school.

I grinned at them both and asked if they understood anything happening out on the field. They shook their heads and laughed sympathetically. It amazed me that they didn't seem to question my new warmth towards them. But then again, they had never been very smart.

"Hey, Winnie, can you give us a hand?"

Amber and Jess were pulling Halloween decorations from out of Jess's car the next day. Ruth had just dropped me off at school.

"Sure."

I hooked my arms under the straps of my backpack and joined them, reaching for a box from the back seat. Jess's car smelled like her. Baby powder and coconut.

Jess closed the trunk with a soft thud and we headed towards the school, arms weighed down by bags and boxes filled with orange and black.

"What's all this?" I asked. I knew, of course.

"Halloween dance." Amber grinned.

"You going?" asked Jess.

I laughed out of habit but they just looked at me, waiting for an answer. "Maybe." I shrugged. "I don't know."

"You should totally go. It's gonna be awesome. Well, not *awesome*. But something to do."

I was impressed that Amber realized the limitations of an event she herself had planned. Not awesome, just okay. I wondered if she ever felt dissatisfied with her painfully normal life, always doing the expected, never deviating from what was required of her age, her gender. Maybe she stayed so involved to distract herself from an inner sense of doubt—the subtle cracks in her complacency.

We had to take the decorations to the student council office. That meant walking through the cafeteria. I wished the boys weren't away, playing a football game elsewhere. I wished they could see me, walking in with these unlikely companions. What would Caleb think? What would he say?

A few people smiled and waved at Amber and Jess. Some looked intrigued at the sight of me with them. A few double takes.

With her free hand, Jess dug her keys out of her purse, unlocked the office door, and flicked on the lights. A big calendar hung above a small desk with school events marked in different colours. Someone's shoes in the corner, a filing cabinet with a broken drawer hanging open.

"Just set them down there, thanks."

I did as I was told and turned to go, but Amber stopped me.

"Let us know if you're going to the dance," she said nonchalantly. "You can get ready with us, if you want."

"Okay, cool," I said. "Thanks."

I didn't tell the boys or Caleb. I thought a surprise would be more effective. Shock him, unnerve him. Make him see that I was no longer under his control. Caleb hadn't liked it when I showed up at the bling party with Tara. What would he think when I showed up to the dance with Amber and Jess?

⁊᠍᠍᠍᠍ᢤ᠍᠍᠍᠍᠍᠍᠍᠍᠍᠍᠍᠍ᢤ᠍᠍᠍᠍⁋

Ruth was shocked when I told her I wanted a ride to Amber's house on the day of the dance.

"But why?" she asked. We were out in her studio. She was still wearing her work clothes. Paint-splattered. Red hair heaped on the top of her head and tied in a knot, a pile about to tumble.

"I'm going to the dance," I said. It took real effort to make sure the words sounded whole and clear, without any shame in them.

"The *school* dance?"

"No, Ruth. The dance at the seniors' home."

She didn't laugh. "Okay, okay."

"Is six all right? She lives in Wolfville. I've got the address."

"Yeah, sure." She sounded distracted, like she was still trying to figure out a riddle I had forced her to abandon too soon.

"What?" I asked.

"It's just...first the party, then the dance. Is everything okay?"

I considered. "Not really," I said. "But don't worry. It will be."

Amber lived in one of the Wolfville neighbourhoods up on the hill, overlooking town. A swirl of smooth pavement dotted with houses, hidden in the trees. Walking up to her front door, I noticed the creepy quiet. Virtually noiseless compared to Gaspereau. Not a single owl hooting; trees without secrets. I imagined the cul-de-sac was muffled by a large hand wearing a black, leather glove.

Amber's mother, Michelle, answered the door. I had seen her before, but never spoken to her. She looked a lot like Amber. Same blonde hair, same baby nose. She wore a wide smile, so forced it looked painful.

Michelle put a cold hand on my back as she led me through the house. It was clear Amber's family had money. The house had plush carpets and warm lighting. From the outside, it looked like every other home on the block. New, going for old. Colonial style. But because they were all grouped together on that one street, the houses had the effect of shrinking each other. From the driveway, Amber's home hadn't appeared particularly grand. It was about the same size as the one next to it. And the one on the other side, too. But once inside, I realized the illusion. They were all large and excessive.

"Amber!" Michelle called, knocking a knuckle against a closed bedroom door upstairs.

Jess answered, wearing only a purple push-up bra and a tight miniskirt.

"Winnie!" She grabbed my arm, pulled me inside. Jess shut the door rudely behind me. I imagined Michelle standing out there all alone, her huge smile twitching.

"Want some?" Amber asked, eyebrows raised. She was pouring shots of white rum into teacups.

"Sure." I sat down on the bed next to Jess.

Amber passed me a teacup. The two girls downed their shots in one go, so I did the same. The rum tasted like sweet, burning death on my throat and tongue. I hated it. But that seemed appropriate.

Amber's room was predictable. Like the rest of the house, it showed off the family's wealth. Dove-grey curtains with an expensive sheen, coordinated lampshades. A floor-to-ceiling mirror that made you look skinny. Her crisp, white bedspread was covered in clothing options for the dance.

"What are you wearing?" one of them asked me.

My mind scurried. I hadn't thought to bring a special outfit to Amber's house. I wore my regular stuff. T-shirt, jeans, tennis shoes. I now realized that was all wrong. The outfit was the whole point of getting ready together. Picking it out, trying it on, deciding between. I came up with a lie quickly. "I couldn't find anything." I shrugged.

"Were you planning to go in costume?" Amber asked.

The Halloween dance. Right. "I've never really liked dressing up," I said.

Jess nodded. "Me either. Amber makes me."

"I love it." Amber flashed a smile reminiscent of her mother.

They were going as twin cats. "Kitties," they said. Their "costumes" consisted of all black, barely there clothing and ears attached to headbands.

Amber encouraged me to "at least try on a skirt." I pretended to evaluate her collection, but they all looked similarly unappealing. Small and tight, like they would restrict movement.

"Oh my god." Jess grabbed my arm, gaping at me. She was always touching, always fixing Amber's hair, or placing a hand on my arm or leg while she spoke. It reminded me of Ruth, but more aggressive. Almost desperate. "*This* one. It's perfect for you. Your butt will look great."

Amber nodded, splashing more rum into her cup. "You've got a great butt. I'd *kill* for your legs."

I stifled a laugh, imagining Tom saying something similar to Jake. "Dude, your arms look ripped. I *have* to start going to the gym."

"Try it on!" Jess urged.

I knew what was required of me. I had seen enough films. Strip down in front of them. Unbutton your pants, Winnie. Put on the skirt.

I don't know why it bothered me so much. Maybe because this was all so new, so lacking in intimacy. There was no real friendship in that room. But I did as I was told. I unbuttoned. I tried on. They didn't watch but they didn't *not* watch either. Amber was sitting on the bed looking at her phone. Jess was primping in the mirror at Amber's vanity. But I noticed they both kept glancing over at me occasionally, indifferent, their faces unmoving. I had never seen Tom naked, and I hadn't seen Jake naked since we were little kids, when Mona used to give us baths together.

Just like a bathing suit, I told myself. *A bra and underwear are no different.*

But it was different. It felt very vulnerable, stripping down in front of two clothed girls I didn't like, acting out the script of "getting ready." Giving in to what was expected of me. Especially in that strange bedroom on a street in Wolfville I had forgotten the name of. Hidden in the trees.

"Like I said," Amber exclaimed once I had the skirt on, "those legs."

I stood in front of her mirror. I looked small, uncertain. A pale face. Disappearing eyes. You start to lose perspective when you hang around the bronzed and the linered. Faces so exaggerated, they make yours look barren.

I hated the skirt. It was short and close-fitting and I felt cold as soon as I put it on. But I would wear it anyway. That would really mess with him.

⁊⁘⁘⁊

By the time we were ready to go, the girls were drunk. I felt a little tipsy, but I had been careful to drink less than them. I needed a clear mind; it was my only real friend at this point.

When Michelle knocked on the bedroom door and told us it was time to go, Amber pulled out a jar of peanut butter and three spoons.

"What?" I didn't understand.

"For our *breath*," Amber whispered, stray spit flying in my face. "So we don't *smell* and get caught for drinking."

So that's how they did it. The boys wouldn't have thought of that.

We ate the peanut butter in silence and then we were out the door, into a large SUV. Michelle was driving. Amber turned up the radio and sang along to a song I didn't recognize, and I realized how out of touch I was. Popular culture felt foreign to me. I sat in the back seat with Jess, staring out the window at the surrounding dark.

Michelle was taking the back road instead of driving through town. Up and across the ridge, with Gaspereau on one side of the hill, Wolfville on the other. It was the fastest way to the school.

I wondered if Jess had ever been out there, in that dark. Had she ever run through an empty field after midnight, trusting blind steps and the surging momentum of speed? Had Amber ever watched the sun rise up over one end of the valley and set down under the other? Did they play in the woods? Did they know anything about grapes, or the birds that nested in our vineyards?

⚜

We heard the dance before we saw it. Heavy bass, leaking into the parking lot of the school. I was the only one who thanked Michelle for the drive. Amber and Jess were already running inside, arms linked, cat ears lopsided.

"Come on!" one of them called, and I ran to catch up, pulling the skirt down over my thighs.

Jess linked her arm in mine and then we were three. We went from a too-bright coat room to the darkened cafeteria. Ghosts and ghouls hung from the ceiling. Our classmates squished together, moving their bodies to the beat.

Just like at the bling party, the dancing was less like dancing and more like dry sex. Hips rubbing hips, chests close. Faces pressed into necks, into other faces. Sweaty and perverse. How did the teacher-chaperones just stand there, watching?

Amber and Jess pulled me into the crowd. Our arms were still linked. Like magic, they found boys to grind against. I blinked and there were Jeremy and Chris. I knew I had to do something. I was just standing there, surrounded by bodies. But I hadn't thought this far ahead. I wasn't willing to dance like that and wasn't sure I even knew how.

I need water, I mouthed to Amber. She nodded absently.

I contended with the crowd, side-stepping couples making out. I was watching two girls stick out their butts while they performed some obscene version of the twist when I heard my name.

The boys had just arrived. Tom, Jake, and Sam. I didn't see Caleb. They looked sober, or sobered. Maybe at seeing me. Or maybe they were smart enough not to risk drinking this time.

"Winnie?" Tom said again.

"Hey."

"What are you doing here?"

I shrugged. "Am I not allowed to be here?"

Tom shook his head no, but it was unclear at what.

Jake was staring at my exposed legs. Sam shook his head too, but not unhappily.

"Gotta go," I said, pointing at the mass of writhing limbs, "I'm with people."

I allowed the crowd to devour me, moving toward its centre and then out the other side. I was smiling, imagining their confusion as I walked away. Would they tell Caleb I was here?

"Winnie!"

"Hey, Dylan."

He was sitting on the edge of the crowd, watching. I had hoped he would be here. Along with Amber and Jess, he was a useful tool. Someone I could use to get to Caleb.

"We meet again," he said, grinning.

"Do you want to dance?"

Dylan looked surprised but he nodded and stood up. "I don't dance like that, though," he said. "I'm old school."

He grabbed my hand and pulled me towards him. The force of his pull made me spin, turning me into his chest. He pushed softly and I spun back out. I laughed. *This* was dancing!

"Where did you learn how do to that?" I asked.

"My sister," he put one arm around my back, the other holding my hand upright in the proper dance partner position. "She's made me dance with her since I was little."

I followed his lead, stepping and turning and swaying my hips. Our dancing didn't match the modern music, but it was fun. I almost forgot there was a purpose to all of this. That I was dancing with Dylan for a specific reason.

When the song ended, we broke apart, sweaty and exhilarated. I spotted Caleb, staring at us across the room. His face was hard, eyes unblinking. I smiled and turned back to Dylan. I grabbed his hand to keep dancing.

⚜

A week or so after the dance, it was the last football game of the season. Our team was supposed to win, and then would have gone on to the provincial semifinals. But the players performed terribly and lost miserably. Some embarrassing score I can't remember.

It was another cloudy, teasing day, the promise of rain that never came. The wind lashed our hair in all directions. I sat in the stands next to Mona and Fred and pretended to pay attention to the game. I cheered when the others around me cheered and booed when they booed. Amber and Jess waved, excited to see me, but I pretended I didn't see them.

I kept my eyes fixed on Dylan, ignoring the other players. Whenever he looked my way, I smiled and waved. I knew I looked like an idiot, like someone else, but I didn't care. There were bigger things at stake than my reputation. Lucky for me, he always waved back. Twice, Caleb's head whipped around, seeking the source of Dylan's distraction.

When they finally lost, the team wandered off the field, chin to chest, holding their helmets. Their knees were grass-stained, their spirits deflated.

"Too bad," Mona sighed, while we waited for the boys to change out of their uniforms. "But I knew it would end this way. I saw it the day Jake joined up. Almost told him but then I thought, let him have some fun. Next year, they'll win."

Fred and I nodded along as we had learned to do whenever Mona foretold the future.

After a final team meeting and a shower, they emerged. We all hung around, waiting with the friends and families of the other team. Our team had played on home turf; at least the drive home wouldn't be long.

I spotted Tom first. He wandered over to us, then stood in silence next to Mona, who patted him on the back. Next came Sam. Then Jake. They all looked wilted and top-heavy. I couldn't understand it. I didn't know what it meant to risk all that time and energy only to be disappointed, to disappoint.

Caleb came last. He didn't look depressed like the others. He looked like the storm cloud we needed so badly. Dark and turbulent within.

"Ready?" he asked, an edge to his voice.

Mona had said she would make dinner for us after the game either way, win or lose. I was invited too.

"Hold on," I said. I spotted Dylan leaving the school gym. He didn't look sad either, more relieved. I wondered if he was happy the pressure of being captain was all over. The need to attend parties and dances, to participate in teenage life alongside his teammates. I ran over to him.

"Great game," I lied.

He grinned with his mouth closed, a shrug. Freckles dotted his cheeks and nose. "Thanks."

I chanced a glance sideways. They were all looking, including Caleb. This was my opportunity. I leaned forward. "You were great out there," I said in a voice I didn't recognize. My mother's voice? Right in his ear. Then I kissed him on the cheek. When I pulled away, Dylan looked happy. His smile opened up.

"I've gotta go," I said. "See you later?"

He nodded. I didn't look back as I ran towards the others.

Dinner was ham and scalloped potatoes. Mona's "fancy" meal. I could smell it as soon as we walked up to the house. Nutmeg lingering in the background.

"Made it this afternoon, before the game. Knew you would be hungry," Mona said, taking off her jacket.

And they were. I watched the boys eat three portions with alarm. Where did it all go? Caleb and Jake were tall and muscular. Tom was getting there. But little Sam. I didn't much like ham, so I took a small piece, cut away at it, and tried to swallow without tasting. The salt was overpowering, sharp on the tongue. The potatoes, all cream and richness, helped.

The dinner conversation was a careful dissection of the game, led by Caleb. Where they went wrong, how it could have gone differently. He seemed to have memorized the game as a series of distinct moments, all of which could have been improved if only Chris had thrown to Donnie, if Sam had run right instead of left. As he explained Dylan's fatal mistake—how he had fumbled the ball halfway through the game, how he sent them off course from then on, ruining everything—Caleb stared straight at me. No blinking while he spoke. I chewed slowly, with my lips pressed together. I didn't break his gaze.

The other boys were silent. They did a lot of nodding, and I wanted to scream: *Who cares?* Mona listened, but with a knowing smirk that said: *There are powers greater than you, boys.* When the plates had been cleared and Caleb was still talking, Fred slammed his fist down hard on the table.

"Enough," he barked.

Caleb shut up, but his face hardened. I noticed him glaring at Fred as the conversation moved on. I could imagine Caleb thought very little of Fred—uneducated, unsophisticated—but he was also unaccustomed to being shut down so definitively. Shocked into submission, perhaps.

We didn't stay long after dinner. The discord that had been building between me and the boys was exaggerated by their disappointment. I offered clichés: "It's just a game! You had fun, right?" and "You were either going to win or lose, fifty-fifty. You knew that going in." But my uncharacteristic cheer didn't help. We stood at the end of Jake's driveway with nothing to say and more than ever, I felt, with nothing in common. They were part of a team and I was separate.

Tom's father, Peter, arrived to pick him up and drive Sam home too. Caleb and I could walk. It wasn't far.

"Hey, Winnie!" Peter said, like he hadn't seen me in years.

I waved into the dim light of the car, his face obscured.

They drove off and Jake said a glum goodbye, heading back into the house. Caleb and I started home. Our paths would overlap for a few minutes and I hoped I knew what was coming.

"So, Dylan, hey?" he asked immediately.

I shrugged, looking ahead. The road was black, empty.

"What do you see in him?" He sounded incredulous, a raw honesty in his voice I had never heard before. Frustrated and probing.

I considered. "He's very nice," I said, after a moment. "Much nicer than anyone else at school."

Caleb laughed cruelly. "Nice isn't anything."

"No?"

"Nice is boring. Nice is benign. You're none of those things."

I shrugged again, trying to appear unmoved.

"Are you two seeing each other outside of school?"

"Why do you care?" I asked.

"Because," he said, "you're better than him. You're better than all of these people."

"Yeah?" I tried to sound skeptical. "How so?"

Caleb took a deep breath, staring ahead. "You're like me, Winifred. We're different. I saw it in you early on. You're not influenced by the same nonsense as everyone else. You and I, we don't care what people think and we don't let other people stand in our way because we know, deep down, other people don't matter."

Other people don't matter. Sometimes I felt that way. Sometimes I looked at other people and felt nothing for them, no sympathy or warmth. But I *did* care about some people. About Ruth and Mac. About the boys. I even cared about Allison. I hated what they did to her.

"If other people don't matter," I said, "why are you on the football team? Why are you hanging out with Amber and Jeremy and all the rest of them?"

"Because," Caleb said, "it serves a purpose. There's value in befriending certain people. Social value. That's where you've always been wrong. You thought you were exercising power by exiling yourself from the crowd but if you really want to stay in control, you have to get to know people intimately, even the shitty people. I don't care about those kids but they're useful to me. I arrived here a stranger, but I made myself known as soon as possible so I get to be in charge." He paused. "I'm speaking frankly but I believe I can with you, Winifred. I know you get it."

I let what he was saying sink in. Control—the need for it—really was his most glaring flaw. Was I really like him? I had strategically involved myself with the kids I was indifferent to just to achieve a strategic purpose, but surely mine was more honourable. I didn't want control for its own sake. I wanted to put an end to Caleb's tyranny over my friends, to bring them back to me, to stop them from hurting anyone else.

He was right. We were both different from most people, but I wasn't just like him.

I was better.

We stood at the end of his road. I looked off into the fields at the tall, yellow grasses undulating in the moonlight.

"Maybe you're right," I said. "Maybe I've been running from my true self all this time." I reached out a hand and touched his forearm. "Show me. Meet me, tomorrow night."

He hesitated, considering. "Okay," he said finally, nodding. "Where?"

I pretended to think of a place on the spot. "God's Palm?"

He nodded. It was a date. Our first.

⚜

By some strange miracle, I slept in the next morning, the day of the fire. It was a Saturday. I awoke from a thick sleep to a hot, stuffy room. The window closed, sunlight beaming in. I threw off my covers. I was sweating through my T-shirt and my head felt heavy. I looked at the clock. I had slept for nearly eleven hours. I wondered if that was my body's way of sheltering me from doubt, keeping me on the path I had chosen.

When I came downstairs, both Ruth and Mac were gone. Probably at the farmers' market. That was good too. Facing Mac was inevitable, but it would be excruciating. I was happy to delay our encounter.

I ate breakfast, showered, and dressed.

I then left the house on foot, turning off the River Road into the woods that stretched behind Jake's farm. I needed to remain unseen and the farm was always a hive of activity.

The woods offered a meandering path to the back of Jake's property, the long way around. When I reached the perimeter, I stayed hidden in the bushes, taking stock of who was working and where. Fred was several yards away, repairing a fence. Jake wandered out to the chicken barn, carrying a plastic pail. The farmhands were busy throughout the property: one leading a horse, another raking leaves. Watching them all, I felt the familiar throb of my pulse, growing louder in my ears, just as it had every time we had broken in to someone's home.

When everyone seemed sufficiently occupied, not looking in my direction, I crept from the woods to the apple barn, where we had first drunk the stolen wine with Caleb, where he and I had danced together. I had a memory of gas cans, red with rounded edges, stored in the corner of the barn, the stuff our lawn mower drank. I opened the sliding barn door as quietly as possible. It screeched a little, causing me to stop and listen (was anyone coming? had anyone heard?) but no sounds followed.

The gas cans were there waiting for me, right where I remembered them. But they were heavier than I thought. I couldn't imagine carrying one all the way to God's Palm. I wondered if I even needed it. It had been so dry for so long. Wouldn't the flames just catch and go wild? But I couldn't risk it. If the fire didn't take, it would all be for nothing.

I would have to go slow, back through the woods. I would have to leave the gas near the winery, hidden in the trees, until nightfall.

I crept from the barn back to the dense forest. My progress was slow, and it was still too warm out for October. I began to sweat, stopping every few minutes, arms aching, hiking up my sleeves. There were moments while I lugged the gas can through the woods that I thought about stopping. I kept thinking of Mac, all he had built. Was saving three boys from becoming horrible men really worth destroying his life's work? But then I remembered Allison, their grubby hands on her chest, and I trudged on. I couldn't let the boys become like all the others.

When I got close enough to God's Palm, I set the gas down with a thud. I was exhausted. I had been walking for nearly three hours. Gaspereau was small but I had taken the long way, through unused woods along the South Mountain, to avoid running into anyone. I couldn't risk being seen.

I stood in the trees on the far side of the vineyard. I could see Mac's winery off in the distance. The sunlight sparkled on the metal rooftop and I scanned the green fields, the vines twisting in the breeze.

AFTER

꧁✿꧂

Mac and Ruth decide to go out to dinner. It was Tom's idea. "Why don't you get out of the house for a bit?" he suggests. "We'll stay here with Winnie."

They head to the pub in Wolfville. There will be live music. A pile of French fries, cold beer. I guess life does go on.

The trick-or-treaters are sparse and intermittent. They show up in cars and shiver on the front step, teeth chattering and face paint smudged because of all the rain. I am delighted by their ignorance. Maybe they know about the fire, but they don't know the details. Maybe they know about Mac, but they don't connect him to me. They say "trick or treat!" like they do every year, like a song, and look up at me expectantly. We throw extra candy in each pillowcase. There is more than enough to go around. Their parents wait in the car, safe from the rain.

Sam is still quiet but less quiet than before. We watch a horror movie on TV and pass the candy bowl between us. Wrappers of tiny chocolate bars litter the floor like petals.

The doorbell stops ringing and then it rings once more. "I'll get it," Tom says. I'm sleepy on the couch.

I'm certain of who it is when I hear nothing. Silence betrays him; Tom must be speechless at his arrival on my doorstep. I sit up on the couch to listen. Jake and Sam tilt their heads, alert as dogs.

"Where have you guys been all day?" That smooth, entitled voice. "I've been calling."

Their footsteps get louder down the hallway. When they appear in the living room, Caleb wipes his hair from his face, wet from the rain. He sits down in an empty armchair.

"What?" Caleb asks, because we're all staring at him.

Tom and I exchange a look. Our plan was to fade into the background, but that's hard to do with Caleb sitting in my living room.

Before I can think of what to say, Jake speaks up.

"You've got some nerve," he says, surprising us all. "Showing up here."

Caleb is confused but he is also smart. He looks at each of us and then back at me. "Right. Winnie. I was sorry to hear. How is Mac doing?"

Sam laughs at the question. A mean, fake laugh.

"Dude." Caleb frowns. "What?"

Jake tries to say something more but can't. I can feel him shaking beside me on the couch.

"You went too far this time," Tom announces calmly. "Just too far. We understand there's probably no way to prove you did it. Fine. You're too smart for us. But that doesn't mean we have to stand for it. We want you gone. Out of here. We'll leave you be, won't cause a fuss. Just please, go."

Caleb is smiling, and if he really had set the fire, that smile would be chilling.

"You think I did this?" he asks, pointing at himself. "You think I burnt down the vineyard?"

"Who else?" Jake spits.

Caleb shakes his head, incredulous. Then his eyes land on me. He looks into me like he did the first day we saw him. Standing in his driveway. Arm up, hand open. He looks into me like he has countless times before. His grey eyes gleam and I know he understands. Recognition. Realization. I win.

"Right, then," he says finally, standing up. How long has he held me with those eyes? "I guess I'll see you guys around."

And just like that, he leaves. The door shuts quietly behind him.

BEFORE

❦

I arrived back home just as it was getting dark. I had a few hours to wait until Caleb and I had agreed to meet. I figured I would camp out in my bedroom until it was time to go. I wasn't sure what else to do. I desperately hoped Mac and Ruth were out so I wouldn't have to face them, but when I opened the front door I heard voices at the back of the house, in the kitchen. Ruth and Mac laughing, the satisfying pop of a cork eased out of a bottle.

"Winnie?" Ruth called. "That you?"

I hesitated in the front hallway. I didn't want to see either of them. What if they read guilt on my face, or the anxious anticipation of what was to come? But not checking in would seem more suspicious. I steadied myself with a deep breath, trying for a blank face.

"Hey," I called back, walking towards them.

The kitchen seemed overly bright, severe after the dark outside. I squinted while my eyes adjusted, leaning against the doorway.

"Where have you been?" Ruth asked, opening the fridge and pulling out a head of broccoli, a bunch of carrots.

It was an innocent question, perfectly normal, but it made my stomach twist. Mac was sitting at the kitchen table, a glass of wine in front of him. He looked happy, a relaxed smile.

"Nowhere, really," I said. "Went for a walk."

"Dinner will be an hour or so," said Ruth, starting to chop the carrots. "Can you help with the potatoes?"

I hesitated and then nodded, grabbing the vegetable peeler from the drawer and the bag of potatoes from the counter. I sat down across from Mac and started peeling, a bit dazed. The potato skins fell off in long, damp strips, forming a heap in front of me. I glanced up at Mac. He was watching me work.

For a moment, I felt like I was dreaming.

"Aren't you going to ask why Mac looks so damn pleased with himself?" Ruth asked.

I swallowed. "What's up?"

"It's finally time," he grinned, taking a sip of wine. "The harvest starts tomorrow! I've had a group of pickers on call for about a week and they're ready to go. We're starting bright and early, Winnie, if you want to join. I know you're interested in how it all works."

I swallowed again, my throat dry. Tomorrow? Why did it have to be tomorrow? The fact that he wanted to begin the harvest the next day made what I was about to do so much worse.

"Maybe." I nodded. "I mean, sure. Why not?"

Mac beamed. "I think you'll find it fascinating. It's hard work, mind you, but the energy in the vineyard, all those people picking grapes, it's intoxicating. I really think you'll enjoy it."

I smiled because it would have been odd not to.

"Can't wait," I said.

Dinner was painful. Mac wouldn't shut up about the harvest and I was trapped listening to it, trying to remember to look happy for him. I picked away at the food—roast chicken with rosemary and garlic—and wondered why I hadn't made an excuse not to join them. I could have said I wasn't hungry. I could have said I was eating at Tara's. Anything but this.

But surprisingly, eating dinner with Mac didn't deter me. I wondered if this was because, as Caleb had said, I was "different." He was wrong when he said other people didn't matter. The boys mattered. I wouldn't let them turn and become something else. I told myself it was a simple equation: one beautiful, vibrant winery for the souls of three boys. Boys who would become men, and go on to meet countless women. I'm not proud of hurting people, but I'm proud of what came after. And I still blame Caleb. It was his fault I needed to do this. He was bad for the boys. For everyone.

After dinner, I announced I was going to Tara's.

"What time will you be home?" Mac asked. I knew he was thinking of the next morning. If I was up late it would be hard for me to rise early for the harvest.

"Not too late," I mumbled, tying up my sneakers.

I pedalled fast, shivering though it wasn't cold, the night wind catching in my hair. When I arrived, God's Palm smelled earthy and alive after another day absorbing the late, unseasonal warmth. Fallen leaves scurried in the wind and the grapes looked overfull, as if about to burst. The field was ready, swollen with ripe fruit.

I took a brief moment, watching the vines in the moonlight. I thought of Mac. I thought of Tom, Jake, and Sam. I thought of Caleb. Then I got to work.

I retrieved the gas from the woods and splashed it where I could. Over the grapes, the leaves, the wooden posts that mark the rows. I walked down the line, lighting a few leaves at the end of each row with matches. It was shocking how fast the flames took. Or maybe I was so focused on the task, I didn't notice the flames advancing. But all of a sudden, I looked up and the whole field was on fire. The dancing blaze was shockingly bright. It leapt upwards against the dark night and stretched in all directions as it devoured the vineyard.

I ran back from the flames. The heat was a wall, intense and impenetrable. But it was the sound that surprised me. The roar of a lion, building to the groan of thunder. It seemed to fill the whole valley, the entire sky.

I left before Caleb showed up. I had timed it perfectly. I lit the fire just before we were due to meet.

I biked fast, and then hid in the dark woods off the River Road. I couldn't go home. I was supposed to be at Tara's. It was the perfect place. Tara and Les didn't listen to the radio. No one would call them, tell them the news. I could arrive home, seemingly oblivious. *What? A fire? How?*

I knelt down for a long time, my knees aching. I wondered if Caleb was there yet, or if he would purposefully show up late, make me wait for him a little longer.

I imagined him seeing the flames. Would he panic? Fear I was in there somewhere, in need of saving? Alive, but writhing. Dead? Would he turn around right away or stay and peer into the light, trying to find me? Would he think what I made was beautiful?

※※※

Hours later. Mac and Ruth weren't home when I got back. They had received the call and hurled themselves at the disaster. The urge to do something when there was nothing to be done. The fire was too vast, unmanageable.

Up in my bedroom, I stripped down, threw on a T-shirt, and lay under my bed covers, trying to remember how to breathe. I was suddenly very aware of each inhale, each exhale. Measured, deliberate. If I stopped trying, would I keep breathing? I closed my eyes. I tried to sleep.

Ruth came home just after two in the morning. I had drifted; I had continued breathing. I heard footsteps on the stairs. Ruth opened my door. A pane of yellow light framed her figure. She looked like a shadow.

"Winnie?" she said, voice husky. It was an attempt at a whisper, but it sounded like a scrape. We came from different planes: sleeping and waking, emptiness and full-bodied terror.

"Mom?"

She sat on the edge of my bed, then lay across me. Her arms held my shoulders, a kind of hug.

"What happened?" I asked from beneath her.

AFTER

꽃봉오리

G od's Palm opens up again, but it isn't the same. The vines don't grow with the same vitality. The land seems trauma- tized, oppressed by the violence of heat and searing light.

After the fire, I learn that burning is not unusual in farming. Fred tells me how he used to burn the wheat fields after harvest. An easy way to clear the stubble left behind, causing no harm to the land.

But grapes are different than wheat and my fire causes harm, scarring our perfect palm, causing irreparable damage. Despite all this, Mac rebuilds the winery. For months, he obsesses over blueprints laid out on our kitchen table, developing a new, nervous habit: pulling compulsively on the hairs of a beard he's just grown. The redesign takes a whole year to draw up and even more time to bring to life.

When the first wine is made, years later, it is passable but not like it once was. Not as special. I start to wonder if it's the field or the people who have changed. Which trauma stands in the way?

AFTER

꽃꽃꽃

The boys and I try to return to what we once were. It's easy to sit at our old lunch table at school and fill the weekends with each other's company because it's what we had always done, before Caleb. We know the routine, reflexive and familiar.

But it no longer comforts. It's as though we've forgotten how to be our former selves. I start to understand this on the very first day back at school after the fire. Jake picks me up like he used to. It's still raining. It hasn't stopped since we stood in God's Palm, looking out at all the ruin. Because of the wet, the four of us—Jake, Tom, Sam, and I—need to squeeze into the truck. Automatically, I move to sit on Tom's lap, as I would have done any other time before. But as soon as I do, the air in the truck feels tight and constricted. Tom is extra quiet and Jake is looking away. Sam swallows loudly.

"What?" I say, directing my annoyance at Sam.

"Nothing." He shrugs.

"We're gonna be late," I say, prompting Jake to get going.

The windows of the truck grow steamy as we drive, and Tom's lap seems to burn underneath me.

꽃꽃꽃

The following weekend, all of us flopped on couches in Sam's basement, stuck inside again because of the rain, I listen to Sam and

Tom discuss old music like they used to. Jake is his usual quiet self. I try to fall back in love with their nerdy banter—innocent, energetic—but I am haunted by what I saw them do that night with Allison. I may have saved them from doing further damage but I still know what they are capable of, what they did when given the opportunity.

The more time we spend together, the more I find myself wanting our time together to end. Many days, when we're hanging out, I look at the clock and think about leaving. I see them differently. We are all tainted now.

I look at their faces and wonder: did they change, or did I?

AFTER

I often wonder what Caleb thinks of all that has happened. He seems to accept that I've won somehow—with the fire, with taking back the boys—and doesn't seem interested in a rematch. Maybe he thinks he helped me get to this point. That he mentored or pushed me to do what I did, and so he didn't lose, but rather succeeded in some grander scheme.

I admire the boys' ability to ignore him. Football is over but they join other sports teams, which Caleb is inevitably a part of. But he remains dead to the boys. They are loyal to me.

I never hear them speak another word to him. I barely see them look his way. Caleb continues to negotiate the social hierarchy of our school, positioning himself at the top, but unlike everyone else, the boys ignore the force of his pull.

I learn that I am not as strong as them, not as loyal. I often catch myself gazing at Caleb. And despite everything, I feel myself flush.

AFTER

We all go on to different things after high school. Sam attends the university in town, playing soccer for the varsity team, a sport he showed a surprising aptitude for in twelfth grade. Tom goes to the liberal arts college in Halifax, which we had once planned to attend together, and Jake begins his long, predictable life on the farm.

Leaving them all behind, I go farther by myself than I ever have before. I move to Montreal, with its stinking summers and raw winters and its seeming vastness that starts to shrink the longer I stay. I study English, but unenthusiastically. I read like I've always done, but my professors push me to read in other, more analytical ways that remind me too much of Caleb.

I don't like the city, but maybe that's not fair. Maybe I wouldn't like any city. There are too many people and the only place I can be alone is in my own apartment. I crave green, open space more than neatly defined city parks. I start to fantasize about escape plans. Other things I could be doing.

The boys and I don't talk much my first term away from home. Tom and I keep in touch better than the others, but the longer we're apart, the longer the silences between our phone calls become.

On Christmas break, we reunite. Home for the holidays. I don't appreciate the saying until I live it. Mac and Ruth pick me up, a teary gathering at the airport. There's a stubborn grey sky and snowflakes that toss back and forth before they fall. My favourite foods, warm at home. My bed.

The boys and I rush to each other but there is no centre. When we meet up again, I find nothing more than what we once had, and it feels like less. A part of me hoped that by finishing high school and going away, we might have changed in interesting ways, allowing us to come back together as mature, challenging versions of ourselves. But we're the same people we were after the fire and I now find them boring. No longer enough.

We catch up, we laugh without heart. Ruth serves us Christmas cookies and I turn inward. I think about the boy in Montreal I sleep with semi-regularly. I think about the professor I wish that boy was. I wonder if Tom has someone to watch movies in bed with, to walk to the meal hall hand-in-hand with. I wonder if Sam does bad things to girls at parties. He seems colder than I remember. Less loopy and goofy. And I want more for Jake than his farm life can give him. I want more for them all, really.

AFTER

༄༅༅༅

don't stick with it. I leave Montreal two years into my degree, explaining to Ruth and Mac that it's just not for me, not right now. "I want to go to Europe," I say, a cliché. "I want more than this."

Mac uses his connections to get me a job at a winery in Italy, outside of a small, picturesque village called Greve. Tuscany, sun-drenched and glorious. "They have work for you if you want it," Mac says, and I nod into the phone, my eyes unfocused.

The winery gives me a small bedroom above the tasting room. The smell of wood and a lumpy mattress. My coworkers speak little English, but that's why they want me. I can talk to the tourists. I can show people around.

I do a bit of everything. I sweep the floor and pick the grapes at harvest. I call out pleasantries to bus tours, groups of old people wearing numbers like they're in preschool, squinting in the sun. I press labels onto bottles and learn about winemaking from Alessandro, the owner. He whispers to me in Italian and I smile, responding in English. Somehow, we manage, understanding each other enough to communicate the essentials. He is more than twice my age and while he lays with me on my uneven bed, face between my legs, I realize I am more like Ruth than I'd like to admit.

I send photos of Greve to Ruth, a letter about my life here, and she calls and says, "That looks like home." I don't remember Mona's prediction that I would live in a place that looked like the valley until one night I wake up and hear the river that carves Greve in half rushing by. For a moment, I forget. For a moment, I am home.

I build a life. There are people whom I spend time with, go into town with, feast with on holidays, but no one I answer to. No one I call a friend, and I learn I really do prefer it this way. I spend most evenings alone. I drink wine and read more books than I ever have before, devouring stories about complicated women, eager to find myself represented on the page, without success. I think about why that might be. I read of women grieving, struggling, failing, falling—always in and from and through relationships— and though I prefer the company of these characters to that of real people, I'm left wondering why there are so few stories about women who willingly choose solitude.

I walk through vineyards and remember a time when I ran.

My hunger for more from life, a craving awakened by Caleb, grows deeper. I experiment with delaying gratification, mercilessly flirting with men at the bar in town—locals, visitors—but leaving just before the exchange reaches fruition. I flee and stumble home, yearning to be touched, to feel. I lay in bed, restless, and learn to love that state.

Eventually, I receive a promotion, and another after that. By the time I am twenty-six, I manage Alessandro's winery, our awkward romance long dead, but his respect for me affirmed. I do everything, much like I did when I was the lowliest employee, but now it is by choice. I take great pleasure in the work and wonder why I ever thought I needed to go to university to be happy.

Over the phone, Mac tells me I should come home. Do the same work for his winery, which is struggling. Pangs of guilt make me consider, but only just. I sometimes wonder if the fire was worth it. Did keeping the boys away from Caleb justify my actions? In high school, your friends are your whole world. Protecting them feels like an act of life-saving. But then you grow up, you move on. The people who were once everything become memories. Were the boys worth all that effort and pain? Far away from the valley, I'm safe from having to face these questions.

AFTER

✍

I am in New York on vacation when I see Caleb again, twelve years after the fire. Through the winery, I get to know wealthy wine importers. A few of them become close acquaintances, visiting the winery a couple of times a year, tasting and choosing wines to bring to other parts of the world. One of them offers his empty New York apartment for me to use over Christmas break and I accept the invitation immediately. I've never been to Manhattan until now.

I walk the city streets and shiver, wearing a thin wool coat intended for Italian winters. I wander into museums and restaurants and burrow into my scarf, smiling. I breathe in the snowflakes as they fall.

One night, I duck into a small wine bar in the West Village. Evergreen boughs dotted with holiday lights line the windows. It's old and a bit grimy, in a way I like. I sit at the large wraparound bar and am shocked to see a valley wine on the menu. Not one of Mac's, but a trendy white from a new vineyard. The German grape Scheurebe. I order a glass and ask to see the bottle.

I am looking at the label when someone sits down beside me, two seats away. I smell her perfume before I pull my eyes from the bottle and look to see who's there.

Blonde hair. A thin grey coat. Cold like me, not dressed for this weather.

"Do they have food?" she asks her male companion. She sounds judgmental, disappointed with the surroundings.

"Everyone is eating," he responds. "So, yes."

I know it's him without having to look. The sound of his voice. Abrupt, condescending. What are the chances of seeing him here, in this big city? It's laughable, ridiculous. But then again, there was always something impossible about Caleb.

I hesitate, heart pounding. Should I say hello, make myself known? But the freedom just to listen. To observe who he is now, who he's with. Too good. I feel jitters in my stomach. I am light-headed and dizzy with the unknown.

The blonde decides for me. "I have to go to the bathroom," she says. "Should be interesting, in a place like this."

He doesn't respond and she clacks to the washroom in tall, heeled boots. I sip my wine slowly, looking ahead, willing him to see me.

"Winnie?" My name is a question.

I glance over, fake confusion on my face. "Is that you?" I ask.

He laughs and moves to his companion's seat, letting her grey coat fall to the wet, salty floor. "What on earth are you doing here?"

"I'm drinking wine," I say calmly. "And having dinner. What are you doing here?"

He gazes at me. "The same, I hope."

He has barely aged. He's wearing his hair shorter now, so it's less curly, but his smooth olive skin still seems lit from within.

"Are you here on vacation?" I ask. I hate small talk and I'm sure he does too, but I don't know what else to say.

"Yes," he says, nodding. "You?"

"Mm-hmm."

"Winnie," he says again. He stares into me like he used to. "I have to tell you, I still think about you."

I blink.

"About what you did. It still amazes me how you got your way. I was proud of you. I still am."

I hesitate, unsure how to react. I've never before talked about what I did. Saying it out loud—admitting I started the fire—feels dangerous, even now.

When I say nothing, he asks, "How did it feel?"

I consider, pulling my gaze from his. I take a sip of wine, then shrug.

"You were wrong about me," I say. "I don't get off on control like you. We're not the same and the fire taught me that." I pause. I've had a lot of time to think about this, but I've never expressed it out loud. "Getting the boys back was survival, not pleasure. I still lost them, but at least I saved them from you."

Caleb's smile fades. I recognize a look I haven't seen in years. What I've just said doesn't align with his limited understanding of the world. He wore that look when he realized Tara and I were becoming friends, when I started flirting with Dylan. When he saw me at the dance, slipping from his grasp.

"It's okay," I reach a hand out, rest my fingertips on his arm. "You might have been wrong about me in some ways, but it was you who first showed me that I don't always need to have the things I want. In fact, there's a beauty in not having them."

I remove my fingers and take another sip of wine, more of a gulp this time. Caleb looks dumbstruck, still digesting my words.

"Caleb?" We both turn. I hate her voice. Snobby, accusatory. Not like his or mine. A different register.

"This is Winnie," he says, like he's talked about me before.

"Hello," she says without warmth, assessing me. She looks from his face to my own and then down at the floor. "Caleb, my coat!"

Caleb doesn't look away from me. "It is so good to see you," he says.

I nod. "You too."

What comes next? How will we eat dinner next to each other, together but separate? The blonde saves us.

"I don't like this place," she announces, attempting to wipe dirt from her coat. "It's too dark. I doubt they even do gluten-free."

Caleb concedes, nodding absently. He still looks unsettled by what I've said, brow furrowed, mouth slightly open. "All right." He sighs, standing up. "Let's find somewhere else."

He nods at me and just like that, they are gone. Just like that, I'm alone again.

I order another glass of the valley wine, and another after that. Swallowing until the candles on the bar extinguish themselves. Craving more.

ACKNOWLEDGEMENTS

've been fortunate to befriend a number of incredible boys throughout my life, all of whom inspired this book. In particular, I'm grateful to Nevin Cussen and all the other Gaspereau boys. You made growing up in the valley so much fun.

Thank you to my editor, Sarah Faber. Your guidance and insight were invaluable to telling this story and your keen editorial eye has forever changed how I write and read. Thank you also to Whitney Moran and everyone at Vagrant for turning this story into a book, and to my agent, Stephanie Sinclair, for taking a chance on me.

A few former teachers also deserve acknowledgement. I'm grateful to Bonnie MacPhee for being the first person to tell me my writing should be published and for making so much space for creative writing in her grade four classroom. Also to Tim Charles and David Sheppard, who nurtured my love of words, and who celebrated literature in high school when many others did not.

Thank you to Lindsay Pearl, Lauren Maxwell, Zaren Healy White, Julie Cameron, Laura Tumulty, Charlotte Sachs, Kait Pinder and Ivana Botic for your friendship; to Naben Ruthnum for the encouragement and the introduction; and to Alexandre Bergeron for talking through the earliest notions of this story at a kitchen table in Montreal.

Endless gratitude goes out to my family, including my four extraordinary grandparents. Dad and Matthew, your love and support mean the world to me. George, in addition to being infinitely generous in all ways, you taught me how to live a life committed to art and beauty. For that, and you, I'm so very grateful. Mom, you've encouraged, inspired, and celebrated me every day since my first. Thank you for being my best friend.

And finally, thank you to Geoffrey: for all the early mornings; for being the first reader; for listening; for loving; for calling me a novelist long before I was ready to call myself one; and for amplifying every day in a way only you can.

Geoffrey Whitehall

Deborah Hemming lives and writes in Wolfville, Nova Scotia. She holds an MA in English from McGill University, a BA in English from the University of King's College, and an MLIS from Dalhousie University. *Throw Down Your Shadows* is her first novel.